I0761710

THE FIGHTING FOOL

Also by Dane Coolidge and available from Center Point Large Print:

The Desert Trail

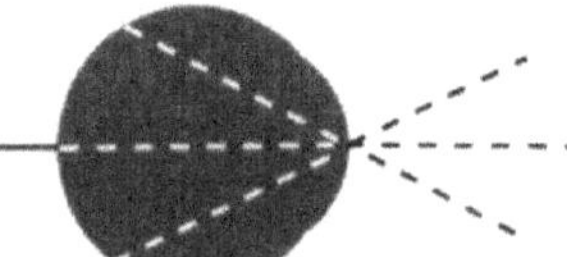

This Large Print Book carries the Seal of Approval of N.A.V.H.

THE FIGHTING FOOL

A Tale of the Western Frontier

DANE COOLIDGE

CENTER POINT LARGE PRINT
THORNDIKE, MAINE

This Center Point Large Print edition
is published in the year 2023 by arrangement with
Golden West Inc.

Copyright © 1918 by E. P. Dutton & Company.

All rights reserved.

Originally published in the US by
E. P. Dutton & Company.

The text of this Large Print edition is unabridged.
In other aspects, this book may vary
from the original edition.
Printed in the United States of America
on permanent paper sourced using
environmentally responsible foresting methods.
Set in 16-point Times New Roman type.

ISBN 978-1-63808-902-5 (hardcover)
ISBN 978-1-63808-906-3 (paperback)

The Library of Congress has cataloged this record
under Library of Congress Control Number: 2023940531

CONTENTS

CHAPTER I

THE CALLING OF SYCAMORE BROWN

It wasn't the Fourth of July in Hackamore—and no one was getting killed, either—but the prairie-dogs out along the edge of the town, who were gun-shy, had already taken to their holes and several prominent citizens had done the same. Farther out on the flats the dogs were sitting up on their mounds in families, jerking their tails and chirruping; within the city the houses were closed; and up and down the main street a band of twenty or thirty cowboys rode and rollicked, casting their ropes at everything that moved and shooting off their pistols. It was the wild and woolly G Bar outfit, in on a drunk; and like a flock of ducks that rise for flight they circled back and forth, wearing themselves out with meaningless maneuvers until such time as their leaders should feel the call and lead them back to the ranch.

At the head of the bunch rode G Bar Hopkins, as reckless a border Texan as ever branded a freighter's ox-team or swam wet horses across the Rio Grande. G Bar was a good hand with cattle and caught lots of mavericks for the boss, but he had one limitation, common to his kind—

he hated the sight of a Mexican worse than a hydrophobia skunk. Not that a Mex. was not all right, in his place; but that place, according to G Bar, was up on a wood-wagon or swamping around some corral—assuredly not on the saloon corner with a big badge labeled Town Marshal. G Bar and his punchers had spent many a pay-check in Hackamore, spent it gladly and never asked for change; and if in their cups they had happened to go too far they had always been arrested by an officer who was a Texan and a gentleman—a man to whom any cowboy might give up his gun with good grace. But now what had this prairie-dog village done but elect a Mexican, Town Marshal? A Mexican! And it a cow-town, dependent upon the good will of Lone Star punchers! This thought rankled deep in G Bar Hopkins' breast and would not down with drink—he could not leave the town until he had registered his protest. So he rioted up and down the street, whooping and shooting and making a show, and at last he pulled up before Garcia's store where the recreant marshal was supposed to be hid, and gave voice to his proud defiance.

"Come out of thar, you saddle-colored ossifer!" he shouted, as his clan wheeled in at his back. "Come out and arrest us, you chili-con-carne Greaser! We done heerd you was elected and we want to see you act! You're scairt, hey?" He turned to his gang and laughed hectoringly.

"Bill, you low-down, Teehanno cow-thief," he yelled, "I'll dare you to go in thar and git 'im!"

"I'll go you!" shouted three cowboys named Bill; and the rest, not to be kept back by the mere accident of a name, responded to the general call for cow-thieves. The result was a willful, malicious and felonious invasion of private property, in which two or three dozen silk shirts and handkerchiefs were taken from the stock of E. Garcia y Cia and ordered charged to the account of Juan Bustamente, the same being the Mexican Marshal, who had important business elsewhere; and the peace and dignity of the Territory of Arizona was, in fact, by these acts, all shot to pieces.

In a community that numbered a lawyer or two among its population this dereliction might have ended in bench warrants and scurrying deputies, but the only jack-lawyer in town was holding down the office of Judge and the citizens of Hackamore were mad clear through. The minute the G Bar boys galloped out across the plain they swarmed out of their houses like ants from a trampled nest, some dragging ropes and all bearing arms and at sight of the devastation the cry went up for revenge—revenge and a cowboy hanging.

This was not the first time that lawlessness had whirled through Hackamore. The new marshal, who had been elected through some oversight on the part of the gentlemen who counted the Mexican vote, had been on the dodge ever since his induction into office, and now the G Bar cowboys were getting rampant. It was evident even to Mr. McMonagle of the Cow Ranch Saloon that something would have to be done, and while E. Garcia, who by a liberal dispensation of mescal had elected his brother-in-law marshal, pulled down bolt after bolt of calico and showed the bullet-holes to sympathetic citizens, the Vigilance Committee went into executive session on the spot.

"These G Bar boys *are* getting a little rough," conceded McMonagle, who had sold them most of their liquor. "That Hopkins is a wild one."

"A wild one!" repeated Garcia, raising his elbows and eyebrows. "I guess *so*—look at *dat!* Forty yards in thees bolte, gentlemens—at twenty centes a yard—and luke at dat hole clear t'rough!"

"Oh, what do we care about your squaw-colored calico," broke out an indignant citizen. "Why didn't you call in that brother-in-law of yours and have them boys arrested?"

"Arrested!" shrieked Garcia, throwing up his hands, "arrested! Them Texanos? Eeef he—"

"Well, if he can't hold down the office, let 'im git out!" broke in the citizen again, and his words roused a chorus of approval.

"Sure," thundered J. F. Benson, the principal

American merchant, "and be quick about it, too! What are we paying him for, anyway?"

"I move we abolish the office," chimed in the indignant citizen, whose pet dog had been roped and "drug," "and clean up this town ourselves! Them G Bar boys is worse than Apache Injuns—it's gittin' so a man ain't safe to walk the streets!"

"Nor a woman, neither!" added another. "My wife was coming out the gate and—"

"They busted three winders for me!" interpolated a third, and a babel of clamoring voices showed the damage to be universal.

"But this here breaking into stores is what gets me," rumbled Benson, speaking loud for the crowd to hear. "First thing we know, boys, we'll be nothing but a wide place in the road. We won't have no town—it'll be all tore up or burned down by these here Texas cowboys. Now you all know me—I'm a law-abiding citizen—but Judge, I think we ought to abolish this job of constable and town marshal and tend to Hopkins ourselves. What do you think about it?"

It was a momentous question and, while the gentleman addressed as Judge did not know it, the peace of half of Arizona was waiting on his words. Old Judge Purdy was a weak, cadaverous little man with sunken black eyes and wiry whiskers which he stroked when he studied the law. There was mighty little law in his few dusty books—and little of that he knew—but respect for authority had struck in through the calfskin bindings and he made the wrong guess for Arizona. Also for Sycamore Brown, the fighting fool.

"Well—ahem—gentlemen," he began. "Of course, while I deprecate the lawless acts which have prevailed, and—ahem—well, it seems to me that the machinery of our law is not at fault so much as—well——"

"That's it!" broke in McMonagle, the saloon-keeper, who had seen his profits in the jack-pot, "that's the idee! Get a gun-man on the job and let him do the work! These cowboys spend their money free, gentlemen, as you all know; and not only at my place, but with you all. They're good-hearted boys—we don't want to do nothin' hasty—just a good town marshal to tame them down a little and you wouldn't know the bunch!"

"Well, somebody's got to take their guns away from 'em," announced J. F. Benson, "and enforce this ordinance about riding through the streets! Do you know a man that can do it—because if you do, he can have the job!"

"What's the matter with Buckskin Bill?" queried McMonagle eagerly.

"He's worse than any of 'em when he's drunk."

"Well—Sim McDougall, then."

"No good—he's a cowboy himself—he wouldn't stand up to 'em for a minute. No, sir," continued Benson, beginning his oration, "this is a job for the whole town—we take the law into our own hands, gentlemen, and—"

"Lum Martin!" shouted McMonagle, waving his finger in front of Benson's face, "that's the man—Lum Martin! He's ridin' shotgun for Wells Fargo—or was until last week—and he's over in my saloon right now, playin' solitaire!"

"He killed a man over in El Paso last year," interposed E. Garcia hastily.

"It was only a Mexican!" retorted McMonagle ruthlessly. "What do you say, Jim?"

"That Lum Martin is a dumb kind of a feller," observed Benson, squinting his eyes up shrewdly. "We want to look out who we get for this place—or we may wish we had the wild bunch back on our hands. That's why I say we ought to tend to this ourselves and—"

"But Lum's all right," protested the saloon-keeper, "ain't he guarded treasure for Wells Fargo? What do you want, then? Now you listen to me, Jim Benson! I know cowboys—I been one myself for years—and if you rise up and lynch G Bar Hopkins or make some such ranikaboo play they ain't a puncher in the Cimarron Valley that will come here for so much as a drink—no, by Joe, not if he was snake-bit! But if Hopkins should happen to come into town and git into a racket with the marshal—well, you see yourself there won't be no hard feeling and—"

"Well—bring Lum down here then," ordered

Benson, whose political authority had never been questioned in Hackamore yet, "there's a majority of the town council present! Bring 'im down and we'll see what he has to say!"

So it came that Lum Martin, express messenger, border deputy and gun-fighter was summoned before the council, and he listened till they had all finished before he said a word. He was a tall, hulking man, close-eyed and silent, and those who knew him best said that his dark skin was from a strain of Indian blood. As each man began to speak he glanced up at him, and the rest of the time he looked at the ground; but when they all sat waiting for his answer he wet his lips and seemed to want for words.

"What's the matter, Lum?" urged McMonagle, "ain't the pay enough? You ain't scairt, are ye?"

The piercing black eyes leapt up and met his for a moment, and then Lum Martin spoke.

"I might have to kill some of them boys," he said, and a nervous thrill passed over the crowd.

But J. F. Benson was game.

"Oh, that's all right!" he said. "That's what you're hired for—only don't go and pick a row. But we'll stand by you, all right!"

The quick eyes of the fighting man sought out his again—it took the place of words—and then they fell to the ground. Something else was on his mind. Impatiently they sat and waited for him as he plotted out his task, and at last he looked up again.

"Well?" demanded McMonagle expectantly.

"I got to have a lookout," he said. "Some outside man. I'll go you if you'll give me Syc Brown."

Sycamore was far to the west, watching the sun go down over the desert and peaceful Papaguería, but with those words his destiny was changed—the wires summoned him, and he came, to be the outfightingest fool in Arizona.

CHAPTER II

THE WAR WITH TEXAS

It was a cold windy morning in March when Sycamore Brown rode up over the high Dragoon divide and looked down into the broad valley of the Cimarron. Behind him and far to the west lay the limitless desert of Papaguería, a land of heat and sand and hidden water, green with the flamboyant tops of creosote bushes and forested by full-bodied giant-cactus, but unpeopled by the drought—Papaguería, the home of Indians and Mexicans and big families by the name of Brown. Before him in this land from whence the cold wind came there was nothing much but bunch-grass and soap-weeds—and prairie-dogs, creeping about on the flats; but the light of a great adventure was in his eyes and he rode down into it joyously. No longer would they need to call him Sycamore Brown to differentiate him from his clan—the malefactors of Hackamore would spread his name in a circle and his front name would be just plain Mister.

A cheerful grin mantled Sycamore's sun-burned face as he dwelt upon these dreams and every time a prairie-dog sat up and barked at him he pulled his gun and shot. There was something startling and sinister about that whip-like movement, the flash of the gleaming weapon and the *pop, pop* of the shots; but it was a game often practised by idle riders in Arizona at that time. The first great wave of the Texan invasion had thrown the southeast into a turmoil and in the struggle of the old settlers to hold the range it was often left to old Judge Colt to decide which man was right.

At Dragoon summit, where the prairie-dogs had reached their farthest west, the sons of wind-swept Texas had halted too—and all to the west of that was old-time Arizona. There the native cowboys still rode single-cinch saddles as their fathers and the early Spaniards had done before them. Their spurs were the spurs of the conquistadores, heavy-roweled and clanking with chains; their bits the same barbarous combination of curb and spade and wheels; their *chaparrejos* were leathern trousers, with strings and conchos, and their ropes *reatas* of plaited rawhide, held free in the left hand until the steer was noosed and then wrapped around the horn in a Mexican turn or *dalavuelta.*

In such a school had Sycamore Brown learned his calling, riding a center-fire saddle and taking his "dally" at every throw, but now he was in the land of the Texanos, the wild horsemen of Texas, who hung two "girts" to their saddles and tied their short grass ropes to the pommel.

More than once he had thrown it into some wandering Texan about his rigging and he knew his welcome would be a rough one in return, but trouble was what he was looking for and he had never seen the Teehanno yet that looked real bad to him. With his leg across tireless Round Valley and his wooden-handled Colt in his shaps he would take his chances with the best of them and take them on as fast as they came. Fights and brawls had had their full part in his life, but until he had met Lum Martin and learned the part of a shotgun messenger Sycamore had never dreamed of fighting for pay—with him it was a pleasure in itself, a wild delirium, fiercer than the joy of getting drunk, and when he got Lum's telegram with the prospect of another shotgun job he had quit without drawing his pay and rode until it was dark. On this, the second day, his ecstasy had subsided and he was riding easier; but when in the shimmering distance he made out the mirage of Hackamore he leaned forward and shook Round Valley into a lope.

Always before him stretched the railroad that binds the two oceans together and makes the thirsty desert safe; but as he rode down, down towards the gleam of water and the bed of the dry alkali lake, quivering patches of white rose up before him, with crazy mirage trees waving above them—the whitewashed walls of adobe houses, with windmills towering beyond—and that was Hackamore. At intervals great clouds of dust would whirl in upon him from the southeast, blinding him with their sand and fury; and again long lazy whirlwinds would trail down from mountain passes to the west and wander aimlessly out across the plain—but there was one cloud of dust to the south that never dwindled and as it fell in behind him Sycamore saw that it rose from a group of horsemen, galloping furiously towards the town. Soon he could make out their hats and ponies and his keen eye told him that they were Texas cowboys. They came up behind him rapidly, slowed down, and then rode by in the high, rough trot that cow punchers affect for show, rising on their long legs in the stirrups and spreading their elbows until they looked like a flock of sandhill cranes, just stretching their wings in flight.

"Look at them spurs," said one in passing.

"And that rigging," added another with biting scorn.

Then a tall hawk-eyed man who wore a high-crowned hat, a pair of shaps like a blacksmith's apron and two bone-handled pistols in his belt pulled up short before the stranger and looked him in the eye.

"Hello thar, Dally," he cried, "whar'd you steal that hawse?"

"Huh?" enquired Sycamore, looking him over in return.

"Whar'd you steal that hawse, I said!" repeated the tall Texan, and if he was jesting he masked it all too well. Only the boisterous comments of his companions as they scrutinized his mount conveyed to Sycamore the general intention to make a show out of him, and instantly his pride was roused to match them, gibe for gibe.

"I stole him back in Texas," he answered, "like the rest of you!"

A grim smile crept over his rugged features as he launched this barbed jest, and it evidently touched a sore spot with the Texans for their faces came suddenly straight.

"What's that," demanded the hawk-nosed leader, pulling the glove from his pistol hand, "what's that you say?"

"I say I stole him back in Texas," answered Sycamore stoutly, "like the rest of you gentlemen."

He edged his horse out of the road as he spoke, putting them all to the right of him, and he also stripped the glove from his hand. This was a strong play to make and it evidently served the purpose for the talk switched back suddenly to derisive personalities.

"Yes, like hell you did!" responded the Texan, smiling scornfully at the thought, "you never been within a thousand miles of Texas, you box-headed, center-fire stiff. What're *you* doin', over here in a white man's country—d'ye reckon yuh can git a job with that outfit? Lawzy, lawzy, jest look at that catgut rope! Looks to me like you done robbed some pore widow-woman of her clothes-line and run away to be a cowboy!"

A chorus of hectoring laughter rose at this sally and, finding himself at a loss for a ready answer, Sycamore reached suddenly for his six-shooter.

"Don't you worry none about my *rope,*" he snarled, and with the same whip-like motion that he had used to surprise the prairie-dogs he jerked out his gun and covered them as they wheeled to face him.

"Come on, you smart-aleck, rim-fire Texicans, you!" he shouted. "You can't run it over me none, I don't care how many you are! Come on!" he yelled, as they motioned and muttered among themselves. "Come on, if you're huntin' for trouble! I'll take you all on at once!"

"Aw, you talk too much!" retorted their leader scornfully. "We got no time to monkey with a little squirt like you, nohow! Come on, fellers, let 'im go to hell! We got a *man* on our hands!"

He whirled his horse as he spoke and as a cloud of dust enveloped them they tipped their broad hats to meet the blast and galloped on towards town.

"Huh!" grunted Sycamore, putting up his gun, and though he had been talking with G Bar Hopkins and his gang, his opinion of the fighting qualities of Texas cowboys went down to stay. A man can never be too careful, however, especially when he is off his range, and when upon riding into town he saw their horses standing in front of the Cow Ranch Saloon Sycamore passed it by without stopping for a drink.

Even to Sycamore Brown's frontier eyes, which were educated to regard any house with a pitch roof and a front porch as palatial, the city where he was to get his start did not meet with favor. From a distance it looked too much like a freight wreck, strewn along the railroad track, and a closer view did not entirely obliterate the impression. There were wide gaps and holes between the houses, an absence of gardens and trees, and a rear view gave the idea that the burg had sprung up during a strong wind. In this the residents were not altogether at fault, as it takes a strong windmill to hold its own in those parts—but the principal cause of all this devastation was G Bar Hopkins. What the wind could not tip over, two cowboys and a rope could, and there is no doubt that Hackamore needed a new town marshal.

There was only one man in Hackamore that knew the stranger—and he was not the kind to show it—but everybody looked Sycamore over furtively as he jogged by on his dust-covered horse. The dally man was not very much to look at—just young and sandy and eager, with a bristling red mustache and a forward thrust of the head—but he carried himself like a fighting cock and the citizens knew that pose. At the corner by the hotel he met his prospective superior and grinned impersonally but Martin gave him a forbidding glance and Brown continued to the Lone Star Corral. There he turned Round Valley over to a roustabout, with orders to rub him down and stuff him full of hay, and returned to meet old Lum.

No feeling of resentment or concern came over him at the cold reception he had received. Lum Martin was a silent man, full of subterranean thoughts and worries—the only way to get along with him was to take orders and not talk too much. If there was any talking to do, Lum would do it—otherwise he wanted to chew tobacco and look at the ground. For three months they had convoyed treasure together from the Gold King mine and Sycamore had pleased him well. From a rattleheaded cowboy, always singing songs and making jokes he had changed under Lum's tuition to a quiet guard, watchful at all times and intent upon small things—old tracks in the road, the flight of birds, faint clouds of dust against the sky. That was a shotgun messenger's job—never to go to sleep and never to show his hand—and if Lum didn't want to recognize him in public there was some good reason therefor. So Sycamore walked back along the plank sidewalk to meet him privately, and incidentally he took in the town.

Two big stores, a hotel and a Chinese restaurant, four saloons and a dance-hall behind—these with the shipping pens and water tanks made up the greater part of Hackamore. An uneven plank walk, very deceiving to drunken men after dark, extended the full length of the street, which faced the railroad track; and cross-walks led back through the sand to the family-men's residences behind. Sycamore took it all in in passing—also a rear view of Lum Martin, disappearing significantly into an alley. Thither he followed, clanking his spurs as he walked, and Martin scowled, for the enemy was in town and he was nervous.

"Well," he said, fixing him with his eye, "you come, huh? Did you see that bunch down at the Cow Ranch?"

"Sure," responded Sycamore, "G Bar outfit."

"Well, them's the fellers—they've certainly been raisin' merry hell in this town. Had a Mexican marshal and now they won't mind no kind. The citizens got together and was goin' to shoot a few of 'em, but that would hurt business, so they made me marshal. Do you get the idee?"

"Sure," answered Sycamore, "but where do I come in?"

"I want you for a lookout—your job is deputy marshal. My orders is to disarm every man that comes to town and enforce this ordinance against ridin' through the streets. That means trouble, you understand, and I expect you to stand up to it. Now how about it? You draw seventy-five a month."

"It's a go!" cried Sycamore with enthusiasm. "Is that little bunch down in the saloon all you got to handle?"

"No," said Martin, his voice going harsh as he spoke, "it's only seven of 'em—but G Bar Hopkins is there, and he's the leader."

"Is he a tall, ganglin' proposition with a hook nose and eyes like holes in a blanket?" enquired Sycamore eagerly. "Then I know the dastard—I had a round-up with him and his bunch this mornin' and stood the whole outfit off with a six-shooter. Huh, he don't look bad to me!"

"You don't know him," observed Martin, and fell into one of his silences.

"What's that you say he said?" he snapped, as Sycamore was giving the details of his encounter.

"He said," repeated Sycamore, with grievous emphasis, " 'we can't stop to monkey with a little squirt like you—we got a man on our hands!' I'd like to show 'im!"

"Aha!" muttered Martin, turning over his cud of tobacco and spitting thoughtfully, "them fellers come in here to kill me, then. Well, that's all I want to know—you come along with me and I'll git you sworn in."

Ten minutes later Sycamore Brown emerged from Judge Purdy's office a full-fledged deputy, with a nickel star pinned to his left suspender where he could flash it at a moment's notice. Lum Martin lingered for a few hasty words with the judge and then they went down to the big store where J. F. Benson was to be found.

"Benson," said the marshal, when they had retired to his private office, "G Bar Hopkins and six of his punchers are down at the Cow Ranch and I git it straight from Mr. Brown here that they come in to do me up. Now the question is: what do you want done about it?"

"Mr. Martin," began J. F. Benson, speaking very slowly and impressively, as became the boss of the town, "the citizens of this town have engaged you to enforce the law. I don't want to make any suggestions to you whatever, *but,* in case you get into any trouble in the performance of your duty, J. F. Benson will stay with you till the hair slips."

"That's all I wanted to know," said Martin, and without further words he rose up to do his duty.

They went down the street together, the marshal and his deputy, but as they passed a convenient alley Lum Martin turned aside and looked at his guns. One was a heavy Colt .45 and hung low at his right side; the other was a light, long-barrelled pistol, thrust inside the waistband of his trousers and ready for his left hand. These he drew out, one after the other, and after twirling the cylinders and testing the action he filled the hammer chambers, ordinarily left empty, with a couple of cartridges from his belt.

"Them fellers come into town to kill me," he said, casting one of his sudden glances at his deputy, "and I'm goin' to shoot it out with 'em, right now. Either they give up their guns or we down 'em, I don't care which. That G Bar Hopkins is left-handed—you want to look out for him."

"All right," said Sycamore, overhauling his old Colts, "but say, Lum, that bunch don't look bad to me—I bet yuh I can clean the whole outfit!"

"Nope," responded Lum, "them boys is dangerous—they've killed men back in Texas. G Bar has downed three that I know of."

"All the same," continued Sycamore, "I bet yuh a new hat I can do it. Now you stay just outside and let me go in first and I bet yuh I git the drop on 'em. That G Bar Hopkins feller insulted me this mornin' and I want to git my revenge."

For one tense moment Lum Martin gazed at his deputy and then he laughed harshly, half to himself.

"Well, you *are* a fighting fool," he said, "but go to it!"

"You jest watch me," answered Sycamore, shaking his gun loose in the holster and without more words he walked briskly over to the Cow Ranch Saloon.

The Cow Ranch stood on a corner, with a side door opening out on the cross street. A wide acquaintance with border saloons told the new deputy marshal that this door would probably put him in close to the bar and, shutting his eyes for a moment to get the sunlight out of them, he cocked his pistol and stepped inside.

The entire G Bar outfit was lined up against the bar with their glasses before them, when they saw his image in the mirror. They turned, but quick as a flash Sycamore twitched out his ready pistol and had them covered.

"I'm the new deputy marshal," he announced, holding his gun by his hip. "Now you fellers onbuckle your belts and drop 'em on the floor—and the first man that bats an eye I'll kill 'im."

There was a ring of sincerity in his words that convinced them against their will, and one by one the belts fell to the floor. Only one man held out, his gun still at his side. It was G Bar Hopkins.

"I never give up my gun yet," he said, "and I never will."

"You'll give up your gun," answered Sycamore, "or I'll kill you."

For a minute they stood glaring at each other, the Texan scowling and malignant, Sycamore frowning and resolute—then G Bar unlatched his belt buckle and his heavy guns fell to the floor.

“Now back away from there,” ordered the deputy, and as the gang slouched reluctantly over towards the wall he advanced and stood straddle of their weapons.

“Next time you boys come to town you better leave your guns with the bar-keep,” he said, as he hung the heavy belts over his arm. “All right, Lum!”

The town marshal of Hackamore stepped in through the side door as he spoke and looked the G Bar outfit over quietly. There was still a bad glint to his eye and his jaws were set tight—so tight he could hardly hear himself speak.

“You boys can come round to my office before you go,” he said at last, “and git yore guns. You know the laws here—a man has to leave his gun with the bar-keep within half an hour after he hits town—and no fast ridin’ through the streets. Come on, Syc!”

Sycamore followed, and half an hour later the G Bar boys rode up to the marshal’s office and asked for their guns. There was an ominous calm about their manner that spoke louder than any threats, but Sycamore delivered up their belts to them unhesitatingly and Martin stood by without a word. Not until they turned their horses to go did the G Bars show their hand—then G Bar Hopkins looked over his shoulder and said:

“All right, Mr. Town Marshal—we’ll be back!”

CHAPTER III

AND THE PASSING OF G BAR HOPKINS

A week passed, dull and uneventful, and then the G Bars came back. There were thirty of them and they traveled in a cloud of dust. War was painted on every visage but Lum Martin did not weaken—he went down to the Cow Ranch alone and saw that they put up their arms—then he came away and left them to get drunk. Only one untoward event had happened to shake his iron nerve. An old acquaintance among them, Joe Sykes by name, had stumbled up against him as he was going out and cursed him in the jovial, smiling way which is allowed to pass between friends on the frontier.

"Lum," he said, "you big, left-handed man-killer, I'm goin' to shoot you. Yes, sir, I'm goin' to shoot you before the sun goes down—they'll be a dead dog around here pretty soon."

To this he had replied lightly, putting the matter off with a jest, but as he waited for the trouble to break Martin began to get uneasy.

"Syc," he said at last, turning to his faithful lieutenant, "go down and see what them fellers are doin'—and say, there's a little feller down there by the name of Joe Sykes that talks too much—find out if he's got a gun on 'im."

"All right," answered Sycamore Brown and, thrusting his pistol well down inside his waistband where no drunken roisterer could grab it and turn it upon him, he sauntered off down the street. It was already well along into the afternoon and the G Bar horses, still saddled as they had come in, stood in dreary groups along the Cow Ranch horse-racks waiting for their masters. From within came the noise of loud talking and boisterous laughter and Sycamore paused a minute outside the swinging doors before he entered.

"Yes, sir," a voice was saying, "I cut the low card and I'm goin' to kill him—I'm goin' to shoot him before the sun goes down. Gimme another drink, Bill—or Charley—come on, fellers, let's have another one." It was the voice of Joe Sykes, the man who talked too much.

Sycamore had noticed him earlier in the day—a small, grizzled man with a wild, excited look in his eye—and though he drank continually the liquor did not seem to affect him. Even yet he was perfectly sober, but the wild look was still in his eyes, and he talked incessantly about killing, killing. Sycamore followed along behind him as the crowd trooped noisily up to the bar—and he noticed it the more because every other man in the outfit was half drunk. G Bar Hopkins himself was boisterous and unsteady on his feet; but his eye had lost none of its quickness, for the moment Sycamore stepped through the door he saw him. At the bar Hopkins drank with Joe Sykes and they lingered there together, engaged in an earnest conversation, while the others went back to their games. As the deputy marshal came up they watched him closely, and Sykes put one hand under his arm where a slight bulge suggested a gun in a harness.

"Hello there, Dally," said Sykes, smiling insolently as he signaled for a bottle, "come up and have a drink before I kill you."

"No thanks," responded Sycamore distantly, "I'm not drinking to-day."

"Come on," urged G Bar with feigned solicitude, "have a drink with white folks!"

"Nope," answered Sycamore, "it's my treat if it's anybody's—you fellers better have a drink with a gentleman!"

"Huh," sneered G Bar, "you're gittin' swelled up some, fer a Mexican! Whar's that Injun Marshal you're a-workin' for? Does he think he can run it over this whole G Bar outfit?"

"That's what," replied Sycamore. "How are they comin', McMonagle?"

The saloon-keeper, who was perspiring behind his bar, mumbled sulkily and went on with his work. To him it seemed very poor taste on the part of the deputy marshal to pull off this war-talk in front of his five-hundred-dollar mirror—and that with thirty G Bar pistols behind the bar—so after an awkward pause he set out two drinks for the cowboys and Sycamore took the hint to depart.

"He said he was goin' to shoot me, did he?" enquired Lum Martin, as his lookout made his report. "Huh, we'll see about that!" He sat looking at the ground for a minute—then he rose up and put on his coat. "Come on," he said, cloaking his pistols beneath it, "that feller's got a gun."

They entered the side door together and without a glance for any one Lum Martin walked straight over to Sykes, who rose up to meet him, startled.

"You come out into the backyard, Joe," he said, fixing him with his eye, "I want to talk with you." And before the G Bar boys realized what was happening he had led Joe Sykes to the door. There for a moment they paused together, both conscious of the conflict to come—both distrustful of the other's intent. Then Lum Martin took the lead, never looking back. He passed out, walking with a masterful stride. Joe Sykes followed like a man in a daze—and before the door swung back a muffled shot was heard; a shot, and the thud of a fall. Then the door opened again and Lum Martin appeared on the threshold, thrusting his pistol into its holster.

"You'll find your friend Sykes out in the backyard," he said, as the G Bar men halted in their rush. "I just killed him." He looked them over a moment coldly, glanced at Sycamore

Brown, and then stepped out the door. Sycamore followed, but he was silent, stunned by the swiftness of the tragedy. Yes, and by more than the swiftness—he felt that Joe Sykes had been killed, as he had said he would kill Lum Martin, like a Mexican dog, a dog that is taken out and shot. It was that which held him silent, for he had always fought on the square, and for all his gun-plays and broiling he had no man's blood on his hands. A sudden doubt as to the chivalry of his chief swept over him, and he felt the revulsion which assails a soldier when he witnesses an execution beneath the flag. But for his pride he would have quit and turned in his badge, but the war was on now and he could not abandon his leader.

Lum Martin stood alone against the crowd and, right or wrong, Sycamore knew that his place was at his side. Even as he followed along behind him he heard a rush of feet in the Cow Ranch and the G Bar men belched out into the street, cursing as they ran for their horses. Already they had regained their gun belts and were strapping them on again, and the hasty tightening of cinches showed that they would come a-riding. At the doorway of the little shack that served the marshal for an office Lum Martin turned and looked down the street—then he laid aside the coat which had concealed his pistols and stood quietly waiting for the charge. A thrill went over Sycamore as he beheld him and, throwing aside all scruples as to the past, he shoved his six-shooter well up in front and ranged himself alongside his chief.

But war to the knife was not what the G Bar punchers wanted, strong as was their lust for revenge. They had been gazing upon their dead, and it had killed the drink in their breasts. Even the best of them were daunted by Lum Martin's ruthless action and their rage, tamed by more prudent thoughts, turned away from that grim figure by the marshal's office to wreak itself upon the town. It was Lum Martin indeed who had killed their friend, but Hackamore had hired the killer and paid him to do the deed. So they reasoned, and rightly, and turned upon the town. First it was up a side street, shooting and roping at lapdogs as they dashed by the dance-hall; then, as they became emboldened, they swung back down a sandy passage and swept the whole main street.

All day the citizens of Hackamore had lain low, waiting for the battle to begin, and very few of them were caught out. E. Garcia y Cia had even closed their iron fire-shutters, and for once they escaped unscathed; but J. F. Benson was not so fortunate, nor were others along that street. But as the procession whirled past Lum Martin he only stood there waiting, and they in turn were content to pass. Once more they swept up the street, whooping and spurring madly, and even then he did not shoot. But by now the mad blood was coursing freely in their veins and as they rode back again they taunted him openly and called him a coward. Still he stood there, his black eyes burning, letting them do their worst.

"He's afraid!" shouted G Bar Hopkins, reining in his bronk, which had taken to pitching. "Whoa, you fightin' bastard—stan' up hyar, now—come on, boys, let's make him fight!"

With a shrill yell he put spurs to his half-wild pony and went charging up the street, and at every shot from his gun the bronco leaped and plunged.

"You're afraid, Lum Martin!" he cried, reining up before him. "You're scairt, you murderin' whelp—I dare you to arrest me! I dare you!"

He drew a spare gun from his saddle flap and emptied it into the air defiantly, but Lum Martin only stood facing them, with his lip skinned back like a wolf's. At the shots G Bar Hopkins' horse rose up beneath him, but he jerked him back on his haunches and leaned down to sheath his weapon.

"You're afraid!" he yelled, and whirled his horse to go; but in that very moment Lum Martin's murderous left hand leapt to the scabbard and he shot him three times in the back. It was a thing too quick to see, like a trick of legerdemain, and few of the G Bar men heard the shots as they turned to follow their leader. Only his bronco mount sensed the change and as G Bar flinched and reeled he threw down his head and bucked. But even in his death anguish G Bar was game. For fifty yards he rode as he had always ridden, head back and swaying in the saddle; then as his knee-grip loosened and the blood burst from his lips he pitched forward, and before he hit the ground he was dead. So passed G Bar Hopkins, and as they rode slowly out of town each puncher turned back in his saddle and cursed the name of Martin.

CHAPTER IV

A MAN WITH A PAST

Days passed, and there was a reward up for Lum Martin. Though he was still town marshal of Hackamore, and a deputy sheriff to boot, he kept in the shadows like a criminal and went warily upon his way. Even as he had killed Joe Sykes and G Bar Hopkins, so his enemies were trying to wipe him out, by guile and a resort to swift treachery. Many was the evil story that was spread against him, and men who had known him fell silent as he passed. Not that G Bar and Sykes had not died with guns in their hands, but they had been taken at an advantage and killed before they could shoot, and so the feud was declared. Strange men dropped into Hackamore and watched for Martin after dark; and in the end he hired a Texan to join them and find out all their plans.

Often at night they would meet in secret—Lum Martin, Jack Haines and Sycamore Brown—and as the Texan spoke more freely it was clear that he was a man with a past. That his past was not at all to his credit and that his true name was not Jack Haines the stranger did not deny—he seemed, in fact, to glory in the acts which prudence forbade him to discuss—and at each meeting Sycamore Brown felt more and more abashed before him, like a boy in the presence of men. Jack Haines was a tall, slender man, very dark, with long black, snaky mustaches and a sinister squint to his eyes, and all his plans and counsels bespoke a man who was lawless as well as bold. He went among their enemies fearlessly, and as plot after plot was frustrated and a dead man was found on the flats, the men who had sworn to kill Lum Martin weakened and slipped away and peace fell upon the town.

But peace is a deceptive thing—and Hackamore had suffered much. On the day that Lum Martin and his deputies left, the G Bar outfit and their friends might come back, as they had threatened, and wipe their fair city off the map. So reasoned the citizens of Hackamore and, as prosperity had come upon them suddenly in the shape of a mining boom in the hills, they decided to retain all three of their peace officers and practise municipal economies elsewhere. But the weight of this burden was soon lifted in part, for the fame of Lum Martin and his assistant had spread throughout Arizona, and both Lum and Sycamore were soon on the payroll of Gunsight County as deputy sheriffs, with headquarters as usual at Hackamore. Jack Haines, being of a more retiring disposition and extremely adverse to public gatherings, was given a position as night watchman, and so the peace of Hackamore seemed safeguarded for all time.

But it has often been observed that the only guarantee of order in a community is a law-abiding spirit among its citizens—and in this Hackamore was lacking in at least three instances. Shortly after the town had been pacified Sycamore Brown got into a row with a faro dealer and left the Cow Ranch a wreck; Jack Haines, in a jealous rage, beat up a woman at the dance-hall; and Lum Martin, though his sins were not known for certain, was suspected of breaking the decalogue. Discontented murmurings began to rise, the victims moved to cut down the budget, and in return the three officials denounced them as ingrates.

"Huh!" commented Sycamore Brown, who was the talkative one of the three, "it's all right for you folks to talk, but I noticed when the G Bars come to town and Lum and me took 'em off your hands you was glad enough to pay our salaries and hunt yore holes like prairie-dogs. You pay a man two dollars and a half a day to risk his life and then, when things quiet down a little, you want to can him right away, or win all his wages back at faro." This to Mike McMonagle, who hated him worse than a till-tapper and was already trying to get him fired.

"At faro!" cried McMonagle, getting red in the face and preparing to pound the bar, "who are you to talk of pinching when you broke four chairs and a table to get back a four-bit bet?"

"Your dealer tried to rob me!" retorted Sycamore, hotly. "I had the queen coppered to lose, and turned my head, and he up and raked in my stake. He never played no queen—win, lose or splits—and his own lookout told him so, but he thought he'd get fresh and keep my money anyhow. But I moneyed him! I guess I know a crooked deal when I see it, and if I can't collect my bet from the dealer I'll take it out of his hide!"

"Yes," sneered McMonagle, "that's what I'm kicking about. You knowed very well you wouldn't be arrested, and so you come into a nice, quiet saloon where as you know I'm trying to keep everything decent and orderly, and raise a big hooraw and rough-house over nawthin'. Why didn't ye complain to me, if ye wasn't satisfied, instead of breakin' the table? But that's it—you think because you're an officer ye can run the town! But I'll tell ye right now, you're mistakened!"

So spoke McMonagle with ten big drinks under his belt, and the courage of his emotions, but other citizens were more circumspect and wary; and Lum Martin did, as a matter of fact, run the town. At first he ran it right and all went well, but as bad men and evildoers learned to give him a wide berth Lum began to get lonely. More and more he was seen in the company of Jack

Haines, the man with a past, and one day in a fit of confidence he whispered Jack's real name to Sycamore and told him he was on the dodge for train-robbery. Jack Richardson! It was a name known far and wide on the Texas frontier—the only member of Sam Bass's gang who had escaped the posse at Round Rock—the man who had even whipped the Texas Rangers in his long flight to the Rio Grande and liberty.

When he had whispered that glamorous name Lum Martin slipped away and left Sycamore to himself, and only at the end of a long line of wonderments did Brown wonder why Lum didn't give Jack up. For, after all, Lum was an officer of the law. But on the border the law is a relative thing, and men have not learned to fall down in worship of any statute. The rows of books are nothing to them—it is the sheriff and his deputies who represent what little majesty the law has, and even those officials are known to be distinctly human and fallible. The real hero of the frontier, even as he is the hero of the city streets, is the outlaw; the man who defies all the minions of vested authority, who robs and kills and then, by boldness and cunning and the strength of his good right hand, sets all the powers at naught. Jesse James, Cole Younger and Sam Bass—those are the men whose names are known to song and story, and Sycamore had often sung their fame. Lolling in his saddle on the long night guard he would sing the tale of each, but chiefly he sang "Sam Bass."

"Sam Bass was born in Indiana, that was
  his native home,
And at the age of seventeen young Sam
  began to roam;
He first came out to Texas a cowboy for to
  be;
A better-hearted fellow you'd scarcely ever
  see!"

The swift and easy way in which poor Sam got shot full of holes and planted "six foot under clay" conveyed no sinister impression to Sycamore—he was young yet and his mind dwelt by preference upon the robbing of trains, "passenger, mail and express cars, too," and that happy verse about how:

"Sam used to coin the money but you bet he
  spent it free.
He always drank good whiskey wherever
  he might be."

Sycamore could understand that.

And now he actually had been sitting at the same card table with Richardson, the man mentioned in the song as chief of Sam's "bold and daring lads." At that very moment Sycamore owed him half of his next month's salary as the result of an injudicious bluff at poker—the idea of a kid like him trying to run a bluff on Jack Richardson! No, there was no tense moral struggle in Sycamore's swelling breast as he wondered why Lum didn't give Jack up. Six months of loafing around a tough border town had not served to tone up his moral fiber at all; but it had always been his religion that Lum Martin was right, and he wouldn't give Jack up himself.

That evening Lum Martin invited Sycamore to come out to his house to sit in on the usual game. In the perilous days when the G Bar boys were on his trail Martin had moved to a lone adobe house far out on the alkali flat, and there he had continued to abide when the danger of ambush was past. It was a square structure, built solidly of twelve-inch mud bricks. There were no windows to invite the treacherous, and Lum tended the door himself. It was a good safe house to live in and particularly so at night since not even an Apache Indian could creep up to it across the flat, and no one passed that way. The fact is people were afraid of Lum Martin and they left him strictly alone. Even Sycamore Brown, light-hearted roisterer though he was, had begun to feel the chill of social ostracism and since his fight at the Cow Ranch he had thrown in with Lum and Jack Haines.

Sometimes they played poker together in the card room of one of the saloons but when the town was quiet, with no cowboys in from below, Lum and Jack formed the habit of retiring to the 'dobe—and now Sycamore was called in, too.

It was a great event in his young life when these two men first took him in. For the yellow down had hardly stiffened to a bristle on his lip, and they had seen the great world. There was hardly a town in the west where Lum had not lived or stopped, and he had guarded the treasure from many a city and mine. On stages or driving at midnight he had brought in great ingots of gold; and for years he had been messenger and outside man for the railroad express, guarding the express car with a sawed-off shotgun or slipping out on mysterious quests. Even as far as Old Mexico his name was known, and when the mood was on him he would tell of hold-ups and sudden adventures, but in general he sat in silence, chewing tobacco and looking at the ground.

Jack Haines, too, was a man of deep silences, but with a fierce manner of speaking out his mind, and when any crisis called for action, he seemed to dominate them all. Now that the fighting was over he had become morose and restless and his black eyes wandered about as if seeking some man who would dare oppose him. Of late he had taken to wearing loud clothes and lording it over the cringing creatures of the night world; but his nature seemed to crave some greater excitement, commensurate with his wild past, to which he reverted constantly in spite of his attempts at concealment. But now that the secret of his name was out he told of nothing but hold-ups and robberies, of flights and pursuits and wild orgies in towns where his identity was not known—all this to two deputy sheriffs, both sworn to enforce the law. He seemed to take it for granted that no treachery would enmesh him and after the tale was ended he walked back to the town with Sycamore, talking so confidentially that the deputy was pleased against his will. So it was that a new outlook was opened before his eyes, and every evening he went back to the house to hear the strange tale again.

How it came about Sycamore Brown never rightly knew, but one night as they sat by the dim light Lum Martin began to talk about express shipments.

"There's a big shipment of gold goes through here every Friday," he said, "sacks of specie from the Denver mint. Sometimes when I was messenger the through safe wouldn't hold it all and they'd put part of it in the local. You was a fool, Jack, to be robbing them little Jim Crow trains in Texas—Number Nine carries more gold and bills than Sam Bass ever dreamed of."

There was silence for a moment and then Jack Haines spoke up sharply.

"Well, what's the matter if we hold it up, then?" he challenged, and though Sycamore did not notice it they both waited for him to speak. But conflicting thoughts were racing through his brain and he did not make any reply. The question was addressed to Lum, and Lum ought to know what to say. So he held his peace and Lum made some laughing rejoinder, but the next night they brought it up again.

"Where would you hold up old Number Nine, Jack?" enquired Lum Martin casually, as Jack Haines reverted to the gold shipment. "This here is a mighty open country—I bet I could trail you up and bring you back in a blanket."

"You might trail me," retorted Haines with spirit, "but you'd never bring me back—blanket or no blanket. I'd be across the Line and into Mexico before you could see my dust."

"Sure," returned Lum grimly, "but how would you get the gold? Where would you hold her up at?"

The outlaw sat studying a minute, and then he laughed.

"You're tryin' to cap me into tellin' you my plans," he said, "so when I do the job and make my git-away you can ketch me and make a rep.!"

"Oh, I don't know," replied Lum Martin, "my services as an officer don't seem to be much appreciated in these parts—I might throw in with you."

He spoke so easily that Sycamore was deceived at first, and then he sat up and began to listen eagerly. All of a sudden the hidden intent of their talk became evident to him. If he had known how carefully they had planned it he would have been less ready to show his hand, but caution with him was a thing entirely reserved for his enemies.

"Well, you wouldn't lose nothin' by it," answered Haines, still speaking in the half-bantering tone they had maintained from the start, "how would you like to come in with us, Syc, and see a little high life?"

"It'd suit me all right," grinned Sycamore, convinced at last that they were joking, "only I ain't got nerve enough."

"Whoo! Listen to the boy!" exclaimed Haines with an unction well calculated to flatter his pride. "He's the finest kid in the country—I bet he'd go further than Lum!"

"Oh, he's got nerve enough," agreed Martin. "That ain't what's worryin' him—it's how to spend all the money!"

The joke went no further that night, but in the days that followed Jack Haines took Sycamore under his wing and prepared his mind for great things. Then on another night as they sat around the dim and mysterious lamp and took drinks by turns from a quart bottle they came back to the subject again.

"That Mike McMonagle makes me tired!" declared Haines with bitter emphasis. "Him and the whole bunch of those yahoos up there—talkin' about layin' us off because they's nothin' goin' on! I'd jest like to go out some night and start something and then pursue the perpetrators—we'd have 'em sittin' up around their holes like prairie-dogs, eh, Lum? What's the matter with holdin' up old Number Nine some night and give 'em something to talk about?"

"I'll tell you what I'll do," volunteered Sycamore with enthusiasm. "I'll come into town like a drunk cowboy some night and shoot out all the lights. Then you and Lum can chase me and we'll have a drink together."

"We can do that as it is," suggested Haines, passing him the bottle, "but what's the matter with makin' something out of it? We're the only officers this side of Gun Sight, and that's more'n forty miles, across country. Gimme a chance at that express car when they open her up at Mohawk Junction and I'll clean her in half an hour and be back here again before daylight. Then we can organize a posse and lead them off to the mountains and when the excitement is over we can go back and dig up the gold.

"No, by Joe, I mean it! Didn't I tell you I was a hold-up? Well, let's scare these yahoos up and git some of that express company gold!"

"Count me in," responded Sycamore, swaying

bravely in his drunken valor, “I never laid down on a job yet!”

And so, without further reference to the moralities of the case or the penalties that follow such crimes, Sycamore Brown shook hands with them both, the ex-train-robber and the recreant town marshal, and swore to stay with them till hell froze over and the devil learned how to skate.

CHAPTER V

A PLOT ON NUMBER NINE

Considered in the light of later events it is very probable that Sycamore Brown never gave the moral aspect of his defection a second thought. The world is full of men who would rob trains if they had the nerve, just as it is of people who would swear if "Oh, dear!" meant the same as "Oh, damn!"—which, as a matter of fact, it does. A cowboy without nerve is a contradiction of terms, since every act of his life calls for resolution and courage, and Sycamore happened to have so much that it got away with his judgment.

In their assault upon Number Nine—a scheme which they had cherished for months—Lum Martin and Jack Haines needed a boy to do the dirty work and take the unnecessary chances and Sycamore filled the part to perfection. If anyone had to be killed, Sycamore could be relied upon to kill him; and if by any chance their plans should happen to go wrong Sycamore Brown was fore-ordained to be found there holding the sack. Very craftily they had moved in upon him, taking advantage of his impetuous youth, and now that he had joined they were quick to send him running, the better to keep him in hand.

First of all they would need some dynamite—for the through safe was locked except at junctions—and the messenger might not open the car. So Sycamore was sent to the mountains, where the gold excitement was still on, and by skirmishing around in the night time he got the powder, a stick at a time, from different shafts, so that it would never be missed. With equal caution he prowled for the caps and fuse, covering his activities with a John Doe warrant for an imaginary horse-thief. Next he was sent out for canvas—to make bags to hold the plunder—but in this his search was vain. Now in the plan laid down by Jack Haines canvas bags played an important part. The gold was to be divided into equal packs and hung across their saddles for the flight—and only new canvas would do. Gold coin is heavy and old cloth might rip and spill. To buy the new material at a store would be suicidal, since the detectives would be sent into the country to look up just such clues—and yet canvas they must have.

So far it had been Jack Haines who had led in the plotting, but now that they were thwarted Lum Martin came forward with an idea.

"Jack," he said, "your scheme is a good one, but I'll tell you one place where you're wrong. You're spendin' too much time figgerin' out how to get them sacks."

"Well, why not?" enquired Haines with heat.

He was a hot-headed man, jealous of his right to leadership and quick to take offense. “Why not, then? Ain’t we got to have bags?”

“Not unless we git the gold,” answered Lum with a cautious smile. “Now, f’r instance, it’s been nigh onto a year since I was messenger on the express. Mebbe they don’t ship that gold on Fridays no more—and mebbe they don’t open the through safe at Mohawk no more. They’s lots of things we don’t know that might leave us belly-up.”

“Well, what you goin’ to do about it?” demanded Haines, imperiously. “Don’t sit there lookin’ wise now—talk up!”

“The thing to do,” responded Lum calmly, “is for me to ride that train through on Friday and see how they handle the stuff. Then I can buy the canvas for you in Los Angeles and bring it back in my grip.”

Past experience with men of his profession had given Haines a dour view of life. He squinted his eyes down suspiciously and tried to figure out some double cross in this simple solution of their ills.

“Who do you want to see in Los Angeles?” he drawled sarcastically.

“Nobody,” replied Lum succinctly, and his manner of chewing tobacco told Sycamore that he was sore.

Again Haines pondered upon the project, and

he could not deny that it was good. He could not deny it, and yet it pained him to admit it. So far he had been the leader, but for once Lum had showed up the best. A doubt rose up in his poisoned mind—perhaps Lum Martin was deeper than he knew. Perhaps—but there are a thousand such fears that come to those who steal. Spoilers and self-seekers themselves, the one thing they seek most vehemently in life is a partner who will be honest and true. Of Sycamore Brown there could be no doubt—but Lum Martin was deep—deep!

Yet in the end Lum went to Los Angeles, and he brought back Jack's canvas in his grip. As they worked over the bags in the 'dobe that night Jack Haines returned again to his plan, but when he had finished and was silent Lum came out against him once more, and this time with more sinister intent.

"You got a good scheme, Jack," he said again, "but they's one place where you're wrong—Mohawk Junction is too big a town."

"Well, what do we care?" retorted Haines. "The train gets in there after midnight—we frisk the express and get away before the folks are wise. I've done the trick before."

"Sure, but supposen that express messenger should happen to get his gun—or refuse to open the door. No time to do any dynamitin'—and you're sixty miles from home."

"Beat him to it," grumbled Haines, scowling menacingly, "git the drop on him and *make* 'im open up!"

"Sand Tanks up here is better," continued Lum with ponderous certitude, "there's nobody there but the operator and it's only eleven miles from home."

"But the through safe is closed!" objected Jack Haines.

"Shoot it open," said Lum.

"It's too *damned* close to home!" protested Haines petulantly.

"Nope," responded Martin, "that's the best part of it!"

"Say, lookee here!" cried the ex-train-robber, rising up suddenly in a rage, "who's doin' this, anyhow?"

"Well—*I* am!" answered the marshal, with brutal directness, "that is, if I do it at all. It's all right for you to go ahead and take fool chances—you're nothin' but a train-robber on the dodge nohow, and likely to get took up any time. But I'm a town marshal, I want you to know, and deputy sheriff to boot—and I've got something to lose."

"Oh!" sneered the bandit, a bitter smile distorting his face, "so I'm only a common train-robber, hey—and you're a dep-u-ty sher-riff! Mebbe you was figurin' on takin' me up yourself and gettin' a cut on that reward? Because if you was, Lum Martin, or if I ever for a minute ketch you snitchin', I'll kill you, by God, if it's my last act!"

It was dark in the low-ceiled room, except for the smoky lamp, and the man who had fought rangers with Sam Bass paced back and forth in the murk, but Lum Martin sat stolidly in his place and his nerveless gaze never flinched.

"You're a hard man to git along with, too," he stated, "and that's another reason why I'm goin' to quit."

"Are ye goin' to *quit?*" screamed Haines, his voice breaking in dismay.

"Unless I have my way, I am," answered Martin.

"Yes, but Lum," begged Haines, "look what a chance you're missin'! The whole through safe—full of gold! We're officers—nobody'll suspect us—we can lead the posse away!"

"All well and good," responded Lum. "But if you're goin' to git excited—if you're goin' to make these talks about killin' me, and all that—then I don't want a thing to do with you. I'm done."

For a moment the man who had been so defiant and self-sufficient stood gaping at him, all his plans fallen to the ground, and in that moment he realized that he needed Lum Martin far more than Lum Martin needed him. More than that, he saw himself conquered, outmastered by the nerve of the man, and as the realization of his position swept over him he weakened and lowered his head. “You’re right,” he said, and left off pacing. “You’re right, Lum, and I’m sorry I spoke. But if you want to go ahead on this hold-up I’ll do anything you say. Here! Will you shake on it?”

“Don’t need to shake hands!” grunted Martin, turning sulkily away. “I’m not goin’ into this because I like you. It’s a business proposition—with me—and if I can’t make a big stake I don’t run. Now I got a plan, and you can listen to it, and if you want to go in you can. But I don’t want no more of this war-talk. And if you think you’re as good a man as I am you want to git over it—because you ain’t. No matter what I tell you to do now, I don’t want no come-back—do what you’re told to and you git yore share of the loot. Otherwise you don’t git nothin’. Now listen!”

The new chief glanced from one to the other—from Jack Haines, now crushed and subdued, to Sycamore, who looked on in silence—and then he laid forth his plan.

“Number Nine stops at Sand Tanks for water,” he said, “and that’s our first station west, across the lakes. Now I want you two boys to pull off yore horses’ shoes and ride over there bareback—and when you’ve robbed the train I want you to come back across the dry lake-bed, and give me the treasure, and then turn them horses loose. I’ll hide the boodle while you’re walkin’ into town—

and right there you prove yore alibi. Them flats is covered with wild mustang tracks and no one can foller yore trail—yore horses is turned loose and they's no way to prove where you've been. Then I summon you for my posse and we ride back along with the rest. What's the matter with that, now?"

He gazed about him triumphantly and Sycamore Brown leaped to his feet.

"Lum," he cried, "you got a head like a tack! It's a cinch, Jack; we can't lose nohow! Come on, let's finish up them sacks."

They returned to their sewing with renewed vigor, but Jack Haines was strangely silent. Though he said nothing, he had discovered the joker already—they were both working for Lum. Who was it that was to rob the train? Who took the big chances on getting shot? And once again—who was it that took the treasure while they walked back to town! But a single glance at the stern face, the tight, thin lips and the dominating eye, told him that it would do him no good to object. Lum Martin was master of all their destinies and unless they played the game his way it would never be played at all. So he sighed—and bided his time—for even the lion must sleep.

CHAPTER VI

THE HOLD-UP

It was a beautiful evening in September when Sycamore Brown set forth to be a hold-up and like many a lonely cowboy he had no one to talk it over with but his horse. Just after dark he went out to the gate of the pasture where Round Valley was kept, and whistled. It did not require a hatful of grain to bring Round Valley to the bars—he had that same loyalty that we love in dogs, and came when his master called. He was a good horse, better than most, for he came from the old Mexican strain called *palomino*—cream-colored, with silver mane and tail—which, if current report is true, are descended from Arabian chargers, brought to Spain by the conquering Moors. The conquistadores brought them across the sea to Mexico, and nowhere in the West are they excelled, either for speed or bottom or for faithfulness to a kind master. Sycamore had raised Round Valley from a colt and trained him to understand his voice—so now he rubbed his nose and talked to him about bags of gold before he slipped on the rope.

But the lure of the great adventure was before him and he mounted eagerly, riding bareback as gracefully as an Indian, with his knees clamped close to the ribs. At the adobe house he joined his partner—they exchanged the last words with Lum, slung the sacks on their horses for saddles and then drifted out into the night. The train was not due till eleven-thirty and they had time for their ride and to spare. Sand Tanks lay off to the west, a single light in the dim distance, and as they passed down through the dry bed of the lake where the ground lay naked and bare, their horses' hoofs rang out on the packed bottom as if they were actually back on the asphalt, spending their money in gay New York. It was a ghostly place, that broad, white alkali flat, and the glisten of the slick crust in the moonlight made it look as if it was frozen, like the land of their dreams. But all that great flat was dead and deserted, for no one ever passed that way. The wagon-road followed the railway, securely fenced off with barbed wire, and all the travel went round that way, whether the lake was empty or full. Now it was dry—dry and desolate—and only stray bands of wild horses, going down to the lower water to drink, saw the conspirators as they passed.

They both rode silent, for voices carry far in the windless night, and there was nothing much to say. Since Jack Haines had had his quarrel with Lum, Sycamore did not think so much of him. He struck him now as being something of a blow-hard; rough and lawless, to be sure, but weak on management and likely to ball things up. It was for this reason more than any other that he had volunteered to hold up the express car while Haines brought back the engine crew. Of course there were more chances of getting into trouble on the express car—for they carried an extra shotgun messenger on Fridays and he was hired and instructed to shoot—but rather than be compelled to blow the car open later Sycamore had undertaken to get the drop on the messenger and make him come out of his hole. That was better than to let Jack bungle it, anyway. As for Jack, he had part of a charge of buckshot in one shoulder, and that was reason enough for him. And besides, he was no dynamite expert, while Sycamore had worked in the mines. So they rode along together, mutually despising and mistrusting each other, until they had gone a full mile past Sand Tanks and come to the place that they sought. Here they tied their horses to a mesquite tree a hundred yards or more from the track and, taking with them the giant powder and moneybags, went over to view the scene. The country is all alike around Sand Tanks, a low, level sand-flat, studded evenly with salt bushes and scrubby trees; but at this point there stood a white mile post and a pile of railroad ties that would help them know it at night. Beneath the ties they concealed the bags and dynamite, and a canteen of water to mix mud to confine the powder; and after a long look at their identification marks they set out slowly down the track.

The station at Sand Tanks is small and lonely—nothing but a double-roofed house, the tank and a disused cattle pen. Not even a passing hobo wandered by to break the long monotony of their wait. Number Nine was late, as usual, and when her headlight finally pierced the eastern gloom, both Haines and Sycamore were glad of it, if it meant they were both going to get shot. Waiting is a thing that kills men's nerve, be they train-robbers or soldiers under fire; but once they are in the open with their guns in their hands and the hot sweat running down, then they are brave again. Up the track they came now, from their hiding-place by the shipping pens, and Haines stepped behind the water-tank to surprise the engineer while Sycamore crept up to the station to lie in wait for the express car.

Yes, it was a lonely place, this Sand Tanks—nobody there but the telegraph operator, and he was shut up inside. Sycamore crouched in the shadow of the building, a dark silk handkerchief drawn tight over the bridge of his nose for a mask, and as the train pulled in he loosened a pistol at his belt and breathed hard, for courage. He was stripped to his shirt and trousers—two pairs, after the custom of all cowboys—and in the belt of these he had two pistols, held in place by the ejector flange, one ready for each hand. On his head he had a Texas sombrero, pulled far down over his eyes to conceal his face; and on his heels Texas spurs, to hurry him over the plains. No dally-man's outfit for him on this emprise—there would be a description out for him later, and he was willing to let the G Bars claim all the glory.

And now the agent ran out and set the light. Then he hurried back inside—and the great train rumbled in, shaking the earth. A lantern dropped down to the ground as the conductor got off for his running orders. The air-brakes were thrown on explosively—the train stopped—and with a wary eye on the conductor's back Sycamore slipped out and stepped up close to the train. To the casual eye he was a hobo, for that is their way of doing when they are trying to dodge the "shacks," but at that moment Sycamore was afraid of no man—not even the shotgun messenger. He looked up ahead and saw Jack Haines swing up on the engine—then, as he waited below it the broad door of the express car rolled open and the messenger stuck out his head. He was smoking, very peacefully, and his eyes opened up wide as he stared out into the night. Here was the chance that Sycamore had waited for, for it was the shotgun man himself and he was caught without his gun.

Rising up slowly out of the gloom Sycamore

whipped out his heavy pistol and pointed it full at his chest.

"Jump down out of there," he ordered quietly, "and be quick about it," he added, "or I'll blow your head off!"

There was no doubt about his intentions, but for a moment the messenger wavered, his thoughts on his sawed-off shotgun. A messenger is hired for his nerve, and it pained the man to do it, but he had to jump or die. The gun was too far away and the pistol point too compelling.

"Now call yore pardner out," continued Sycamore, "and call him so he'll come or I'll shoot a hole in you!" He stepped behind the shotgun man as he spoke, still menacing him with his pistol, and at the call the express clerk, still wearing his eye-shade, came running to the door. But either he caught the note of trouble or, in looking out, glimpsed Sycamore with his black mask, for the instant he showed himself he leapt back again and ducked down behind a safe. Here was a bad fix, and the chances were good that it would get worse, but Sycamore had seen the man's face and knew that he would not fight; so, ducking quickly down behind his prisoner, he leveled his pistol at the doorway and made a grand-stand play.

"Don't you move away from there, you big stiff," he said to the shotgun messenger. "I'm goin' to kill that feller, if he shoots at me—but if he comes out it'll be all right." There was tense silence for a minute—and then the clerk came out.

"Don't shoot!" he called, "I'll come!"

"Well, hurry up, then," answered Sycamore, and as the man held up his hands and jumped Brown swore fervently under his breath, for it took a great load off his mind. If that clerk had wanted to be bull-headed he could have made him a lot of trouble. As it was he paid particular attention to the shotgun man, who was a tall, square-jawed proposition and ready to jump him any minute.

Meanwhile the train stood still and nobody knew it was being robbed. The conductor had gone inside the station, the passengers were all asleep, and the clerk in the mail-car ahead never so much as looked out. So for a few minutes they waited, Sycamore and the shotgun man eyeing each other furtively, and then there was crunch of gravel from up in front and Jack Haines appeared, driving the engine-driver and firemen before him.

"Keep yore guns on these men," he directed, taking command on the instant, "while I frisk them for the gats." He searched each of the prisoners in succession and then herded them off to one side.

"Now uncouple that express car," he said, turning to the engine-driver and fireman, "and we'll take a run up the track. And remember now—no monkey business!"

He stood at their backs as they worked and followed them off into the darkness. Then the engine puffed, the coaches began to roll and, as the express car trundled by, Sycamore sheathed his guns with a triumphant gesture and swung up on the rear end of his treasure ship. Just at that moment the conductor, not knowing what was the matter, came rushing out of the station, waving his lantern frantically; and Sycamore, having nothing at hand to answer with, responded with a high shrill yell. They could talk as much as they wanted to about punching cattle, or being deputy-everything at a hundred a month; but plain, ordinary train-robbery was good enough for him!

But now to get at the gold—the gold which filled the through safe to the doors and sometimes overflowed to the local. The moment the train stopped at the rendezvous Sycamore was off and running for the tie-pile. First he fetched four or five ties to make a step beneath the high door—then, as Jack Haines filed by with the engine crew and the mail clerks and went back to guard the approach, Sycamore passed the dynamite up ahead of himself and leapt lightly into the car. There on the further side stood two safes, one locked and the other half open; and as he looked into the local safe his heart almost stopped, for it was crammed with bags of money. Money,

money! The car seemed to be filled with it—and the bags were heavy, awfully heavy. He reached for his knife and cut into one but as he grabbed out a handful of coins his rapture began to subside. It was money, all right, but silver money, and Mexican money at that. Ten thousand dollars in Mexican silver, a load that would break a mule's back and was hardly worth carrying away—that is, if a posse was after you.

With a scornful grunt Sycamore heaved the heavy bags aside and went further into the safe. There were packages of all descriptions—mostly heavy and small—and these he grabbed out in eager handfuls and shoveled into his sack. So much, then, for the local! He finished with it quickly and turned his attention to the through safe, which offered a more fitting return. It was a large and ponderous affair built to withstand dynamite, fire and wrecks, and fitted out with a time lock which was set to open at Mohawk. But Sycamore's time was too valuable to wait upon any such a mechanism and, all things having been prepared in advance, he laid four sticks of giant powder on top of it, all carefully tied together and equipped with caps and fuse. Then with his canteen of water he mixed up some mud on the ground and, slinging it in a canvas, climbed up and plastered it over the charge.

A minute later the fuse was sputtering—he ran out across the prairie—and then a great light flashed out against the night, the earth heaved, and a loud explosion rent the air. A few seconds later and splinters of wood began to fall, but when he ran up to the car and swung his lantern inside the great safe stood firm and solid as adamant, and a hole in the roof of the car showed the course the explosion had taken. Against that massive body of chilled steel the dynamite had been as nothing—its force was lost and dissipated and thrown off against the roof.

But all was not lost yet. Sycamore still had six sticks of dynamite in his powder cache and, hurrying out to where it was buried, he wrapped it in a sack and carried it back to the car. Once more he piled it on the safe and connected the caps and fuse—and then he looked about for something heavy enough to confine it. He kicked one of the sacks of Mexican *pesos*. Yes, they were heavy, fully sixty pounds to the sack, and since there was gold within the safe the silver would be no more than an ante, to sweeten this fabulous jack-pot. So he reasoned, and quickly, for the time was passing; and lifting them one by one he piled five or six of the sacks on top of the giant powder. Once more the fuse hissed and sputtered, and this time he ran far away; but even then the explosion was deafening and the Mexican *pesos*, blown sideways through the car, whistled by him like shots from a cannon. Then a hail of them began to fall, Mexican dollars from high up in the air, but Sycamore did not wait for it to slacken. He had shot off his last stick of dynamite; yes, he had played his last card to win, and in the intoxication of his great expectations he rushed back through the rain of money, unheeding its heavy strokes.

Once more he swung up his lantern, and the whole roof of the car had vanished. A great hole had been blown in the back as well and there before it, crushed and dismantled, stood the through safe, its top broken, its massive gate ajar. With a cry of delight Sycamore Brown ran back to get his pack-sacks; then with both pairs of them slung over his arm he swarmed up into the car and stuffed them full with the treasure. Bags, bundles, papers, flat packages that looked like sheafs of bills, everything that he could find in the scattered wreckage he grabbed up and shoved into his bags, and only when they hung heavy and he heard his partner's hail did he finally quit his scrambling and think about getting away. For that glorious half hour he had rolled in riches, spurning common silver dollars like iron washers, and it lit a fire of avarice in his heart that it took years of punishment to quench. But now he shouldered the bags—for they were hung together in pairs—and went staggering down the railroad track to where Haines was flagging him with a lantern.

"Now you fellers sit down on the track," he

heard Jack say, “and stay there, and the first man that starts for the station will git a bullet in his back.”

Then he came running up through the darkness and made a grab for the gold.

“Come in!” he cried, shouldering a pair of the sacks as he ran. “For God’s sake, what you been doin’—you been monkeyin’ around here for an hour!”

CHAPTER VII

THE STALL

It is one thing to steal a big bag of money, and another to get away with it; but Lum Martin had a plan of flight laid out that would baffle an Indian trailer, although it was intended only for express company detectives. Due south of Sand Tanks lay the headquarters of the G Bar outfit; and beyond that the Mexican line. South also, as well as east, lay the bed of the wet-weather lake, now baked so hard and solid that an unshod horse would not dent it by so much as a footprint. There was mounting and riding in hot haste when Sycamore Brown and Haines reached their horses with the money-bags—and they rode due south as they had been directed until they reached the dry bed of the lake. Then they whirled and rode east again, never drawing rein till they saw the lights of Hackamore.

There are some towns of the size of Hackamore where the folks ring the curfew bell at eight and go to bed with the chickens, but a certain part of the business of Hackamore flourished better at night and even at two A. M. it was not uncommon to see the lights. On the morning when Jack Haines and Sycamore Brown came riding in with their booty the streets were bobbing with lanterns and the bright lights of the Cow Ranch Saloon shone upon an excited group of citizens summoned hastily from their slumbers. Not that Sycamore and Jack Haines rode near enough to be seen, but as they came in across the flats they could see the dark forms darting to and fro like insects around a lamp. They rode more cautiously then, heading straight for the lone adobe house, and soon they made out the bowed form of Lum, sneaking stealthily out to meet them. In one hand he held an armful of clothes and in the other he bore their hats, which they had left at home for the occasion.

"You're late, boys," he whispered, grabbing the high Texas sombreros off their heads and jamming on their old ones. "Now change yore clothes and boots—hurry up, now—and give me yore other ones—and chase yoreselves over to the saloon. Here, gimme them bags—I'll turn yore horses loose—and you keep them boys busy over there while I go and hide this plunder!"

Without letting them answer a word he threw each of them his change of clothes and boots, stripped the winded horses of their rope hackamores and, slapping them on the rump, sent them trotting off into the darkness. Then he shouldered the heavy bags, grabbed up their discarded clothes and, peering hastily about to see that no tell-tale garment had been left, went scuttling off towards the adobe. It was a cyclone finish that he had planned for them, and so perfectly were they hypnotized that neither of them even looked up to see which way he went, although they had a third interest apiece in the money he was about to hide. It was the alibi they were thinking about—but the devil only knows what Lum had in his mind.

It was a wild-eyed and talkative bunch of men that they encountered when, with all the appearances of a hasty arising, Jack Haines and Sycamore butted into the Cow Ranch Saloon and asked what was all the excitement. A chorus of different answers conveyed the general idea that Number Nine had been held up at Sand Tanks, the passengers beaten and robbed and the express and mail cars blown up with dynamite. Some claimed that they were entirely destroyed and that the train crew had all been killed; but the telegraph operator, who had come running with a message for Lum Martin, corrected this by the statement that Nine had already been reported out from Sand Tanks.

"Where's Lum Martin?" he cried, waving the sheet of yellow paper above his head, "here's a message from the sheriff!"

"I dunno," said one, "he was here a minute ago!"

"He's gone to hunt horses," spoke up another.

"Well, who'll take this to him?" appealed the

operator, "I've got to get back to my wire. Oh, *you?*" And he thrust it into Sycamore Brown's hands and flew.

"What does it say?" the crowd clamored. "Read it!"

"Train robbed at Sand Tanks," read Sycamore. "Summon posse and be on grounds by daylight. Wire which way they went and follow. Dillon, Sheriff."

"Well," remarked Sycamore, as the noise died down, "I guess I can attend to this as good as Lum. Who wants to volunteer for this posse?"

There was a rush to sign up—and that killed some time—and a great deal of explaining and protestations from those who refused, which took more. Then there was a general scattering for guns and pistols and wild attempts to catch bronco horses out of big pastures in the dark, and when Lum Martin finally rode in, leading two horses for his deputies, he was in plenty of time to lead the posse. In fact, he was so far ahead in general preparedness that no one could have suspected him of other business than that which was immediately at hand. In some miraculous way Jack Haines and Sycamore were also armed and equipped to the minute, and when the posse comitatus finally went dashing off down the track to Sand Tanks the two hold-ups and their general manager were well up in the lead.

It was daylight when they arrived at the lonely

station and by the time they got to the scene of the robbery the sun was over the mountains. They rode up the track, inside the barbed wire fences that served to keep out the stock, and were proceeding at a canter when suddenly one of the leaders stopped short and flung himself from his horse.

"Look at that!" he cried, holding up a battered dollar; and then there was another rush, and another man dropped off his horse. They had encountered the furthest fringe of that great hail of *pesos* which had followed Sycamore Brown's last shot, and as they worked up towards the storm-center the posse became demoralized. It was like a band of boys at a money-scramble and Lum Martin and his stern-eyed brother officers glanced back at them with well-simulated disapproval as they dashed forward to the scene of the wreck.

"By Gawd, Syc," muttered Lum, gazing about at the splintered upper-works of the express-car, "you shore shot things up some. But you did well, boy," he added hurriedly, "you did well. Now ride around and tromple out all the tracks you can and we'll lead 'em off to the north."

As deputy sheriffs the posse that came out from Hackamore had promised well, but as sleuths they were far from being a success. Several of them were ex-Indian fighters and old trailers, but in spite of their past training the lure of the

Mexican dollars was too much for them and in the general rush that followed the tracks were badly trampled. Even after Lum Martin had called a halt and made every man empty his loot at his feet the tracking did not improve; for the posse, instead of looking the ground over with an eye single to the detection of criminals, succumbed once more to the gleam of the scattered *pesos* and, under the pretext of trailing the hold-ups, spread out across the desert and picked up money on the sly. There was no one then to deny him when Lum Martin hastily announced his conclusions, and with their boots and pockets full of Mexican dollars the posse rode back to the station and followed him off to the north.

Had Mr. Slocum, the head detective for the express company—who was now on his way to the scene—been present and had he lined up the bunch and looked them in the eye to detect the thief, his old-sleuth methods would have led him astray; for every man in the outfit looked false as Judas, and all but three of them had their pockets full of money. And to show to what depths a shower of Mexican dollars will sink a free and law-abiding people, the members of that posse began to drop away by ones and twos—and the minute Lum Martin was out of sight they headed their ponies for the storm-belt. By twelve o'clock, when Mr. Slocum and his assistants did arrive, the ground was stamped flat for a great distance and there was hardly a *peso* to be found.

Chief of detectives Slocum arrived on a special that came panting in from the west and the first thing he did was to make every looter shell out his Mexican money, down to the last dollar. Then he cleared the ground entirely, allowing no outsiders to come near, and began to search for evidence. With him in the special car were the two express messengers who had been robbed, the engineer, and a squad of railroad detectives. There were other men also, men dressed roughly enough to pass for hobos, who dropped off the car unobtrusively and mixed with the retreating crowd to snoop for news. Then Dillon, the sheriff, and his posse rode in from Gun Sight; and when Lum Martin and his faithful deputies finally returned from their trip to the north they found something big going on. Nobody knew for sure, but it was rumored that from forty to eighty thousand dollars had been lost and Slocum was working frantically to get a clue.

The engineer who had been held up had showed him just where the robbers went through the fence and had sworn to it that they rode off to the south, so when Martin rode in from the north he was called upon to explain.

"What's the matter with you, Lum?" inquired Dillon, the sheriff, "what'd you go chasin' off up there for? We found a trail here leadin' off to the south!"

“Well, that’s it, then,” agreed Lum, shifting wearily in his saddle. “I’ll tell you, Dillon,” he went on, as Slocum drew near and fixed him with his hunter’s eyes. “That posse I got at Hackamore was nothin’ but a gang of bums and I ain’t goin’ to pay ’em a cent. The minute we got here they began scramblin’ for money, ’n trompled all the tracks down, ’n rather ’n see ’em spoil the whole thing for you and Slocum I called ’em off and hit out for the mountains. How’d do, Mr. Slocum!”

He nodded familiarly to the head detective, whom he had known in his messenger days, and Slocum wiped the sweat from his brow and stared at him again. He was a small, eager man, with a shock of grizzled hair that stood straight up from his broad forehead and a pair of eyes that stood wide open, like an owl’s. Though he was of no more than average height he was muscled like a tiger-cat, and every line in his leonine face bespoke the man of power. His hard-boiled shirt was melted down by the sweat of his exertions and his derby hat was no protection against the sun, but even though his attire was incongruous Lum knew him for a dangerous antagonist. More than once he had gone on such jaunts as this himself, to help out on the trailing, and every detail of his plan had been worked out with old Sam in mind. They had met now, the arch-conspirator and the master sleuth, and Lum glanced at him once and looked away, just as he had always done.

"Lum," said the detective coming over to him, "you're the man I'm looking for."

He beckoned him off to one side where they would not be overheard and laid the whole matter before him.

"Now here," he concluded, "I've got a description of those two fellows, and that's about all I have got. Just look this over and see if you can guess who they are."

He thrust a careful description of the robbers into his hands and waited impatiently while he pored over it; but Lum's education, though he carefully concealed the fact, had been completed in seven days and the paper did not give him much information.

"Um, what kind of hats does this say they had?" he inquired, pretending to squint at the handwriting.

"High hats!" snapped Slocum, "high crowned, with broad brims, turned up along the edge!"

"Well," answered Lum, handing back the paper with an air of finality, "if that's the case they was Texas cowboys, because them fellers wear nothin' else. What kind of spurs was they?"

"The man that got on the engine had a pair of long-shanked ones, with a rowel in the shape of a star—"

"That's them!" broke in Lum. "Them fellers

was cowboys and I miss my guess a mile if I can't trail 'em to the G Bar headquarters, down there at the foot of the lake. Them G Bar boys have been raisin' hell around here for years and it's a wonder they hain't took to train-robbin' before this. Come on, let's foller them tracks!"

They followed and when the barefoot pony-tracks were lost on the hard floor of the lake the posse kept on to the south, where the G Bar boys suffered a crowning affront at the hands of town marshal Martin. With the sheriff of the county at his back and Sam Slocum well up in front Lum Martin searched the G Bar bunk-house from fire-place to war-bags, prying into their intimate affairs with such an assumption of virtue that it left the outfit in tears. There was no occasion for a cut at the cards to see who should kill Martin now. Once before when the G Bars were after his scalp they had resorted to a cut, so rumor said, and Joe Sykes had drawn the deuce and died—but now a call for volunteers would have been answered by the whole G Bar outfit. Not only had their Texas records been called to public notice and their private love-letters been read, but their reputation had suffered a cruel blow, and if a train could not be robbed twenty miles away without their bunk-house being rustled for the loot it was time that somebody got killed. Or so the G Bar boys said, and while they never quite got Mr. Martin in the days to come, they certainly tried until men could truthfully put on their tombstones those proud lines which end: "Angels could do no more!"

But in the meanwhile, well-pleased and laughing at their stratagem, Lum Martin and his partners rode back to Hackamore, leaving the G Bar funeral in the hands of old Sam Slocum.

CHAPTER VIII

AND A STEER

Three days after the great hold-up and while the country was still seething with the excitement of the mad pursuit, Lum Martin yielded to the importunities of his partners in crime and let them come out to the house. Not since they held up the train had they so much as seen their plunder; and up to date the men who had left the posse to pick up Mexican dollars had more to show for their trouble. Jack Haines was getting surly over the repeated delays, and Sycamore couldn't sleep nights for dreaming of piles of gold. But not of gold alone—for most of the money was in paper—sheafs and sheafs—he had seen it when he grabbed it out, but had never broken the packages. Would they be ten-dollar bills, or hundreds? Somebody had even told him that there were thousand-dollar bills!

They slipped out to the adobe separately—in the heat of the day, when nobody was around—and Lum received them nervously, pacing up and down like a prisoner and going back to look out the door.

"Well, where's the swag?" demanded Haines, as soon as he arrived.

"Shhh!" hissed Martin, glancing about as if he expected the walls to give up armed men, "don't talk so loud, for Gawd's sake—this town is alive with detectives!"

"Well, gimme my share of the boodle then," rejoined Haines, "so I can have something to travel on in case I should have to skip!"

"Lawzee, Jack," protested Lum, "don't you never think of driftin'—those detectives would follow you a million miles if you'd skip out of town. No, sir! The thing to do is to lay low and go about yore business—don't say a word—don't look like you knowed anythin'—and whatever else you do, *don't spend no money!* That's the way they ketch all these hold-ups—they ketch 'em when they spend their money!"

"Well, what'd we git the money for?" enquired Haines, swelling up a little and swaggering. "I guess me and Syc has got something to say about this—let's have a look at it, anyhow!"

"Sure, Lum," chimed in Sycamore, "let's git it out and divide it, anyhow. I want to know how much we got."

"Well, by Gawd, boys," protested Martin, still pacing to and fro, "I hate to go anywheres near it. These fellers are likely to get something on us, any minute, and if they do they'll rake this country with a fine-toothed comb until they find our cache. I know that old Sam Slocum, and I tell you he's a dangerous man to monkey with.

Now let's jest wait a while—don't be in sech a hurry—"

"No, I'm damned if I will!" broke in Jack Haines. "I've worked for that money and I'm goin' to have it!"

"Let's see how much we got, Lum, anyhow!" urged Sycamore. "I was in such a hurry I never had no time to look at it!"

A sigh that was almost a wail broke from Martin as he gazed from one to the other.

"If you boys knowed half as much as I do about this detective business," he complained, "you wouldn't go nigh that cache for a year. Old Sam is workin' on them G Bar boys now—he's lookin' up their Texas records and findin' all sorts of things—and he don't suspect us nohow. But the minute one of us goes to spendin' more than his salary—look out! He'll have detectives on our track in a minute." He paced up and down again, sighing and shaking his head lugubriously. "Now listen to reason, boys," he said. "What do we need the money for now, anyway? We all got good salaries, and we're gettin' pickin's on the side—jest let this boodle lay awhile until Sam Slocum goes. Then we'll divvy up and slip out of the country and go off and live like kings!"

"Well, let's look at it, anyhow!" insisted Sycamore eagerly. "We don't need to spend none, but let's see how much we got!"

Jack Haines said nothing at this but stood off to

one side, craftily watching the chief to see how he would answer his favorite. This tendency on the part of Lum to hold back their money looked very bad to him, especially as he had foreseen it from the start, and he was glad to see Sycamore awakening. So he stood silent, waiting for the reply upon which would hinge his future actions. Perhaps Lum Martin discerned the secret of his pose—for he was quick to read the evil in men's hearts—for he checked the stern refusal which leapt to his lips and turned to pace the floor.

"If I give you boys this money," he said at last, "you got to promise not to spend none."

"All right," responded Sycamore. "Where is it?"

But Haines said nothing.

Once more Lum Martin paced the floor.

"I hate to divide that money up," he said, talking half to himself, "it's jest three times as likely to git found."

"Well, let's look at it!" cried Sycamore, impatiently. "I don't want to take it away, I just want to see how much we got!"

"Yes," observed Haines quietly, "here too!"

For a last time the arch-conspirator dropped his head in thought. The two of them were against him—he must set them against each other—and then he could win back Sycamore. He glanced out the door again, closed it, and walked swiftly across the darkened room. They would quarrel if he threw out some money. For a moment he knelt in the corner behind some boxes, rose up hurriedly, and came back with a small canvas bag.

"Here!" he said, and with a dexterous flip he let fall a shower of gold upon the floor. Instantly the two men flung themselves upon their knees and scrambled for it, clutching at the fat tens and twenties first and raking the dust for the fives, while Lum Martin gazed down upon them with a saturnine smile. He too had this lust for gold, but it did not lead him to clutch at it. He could look ahead and calculate.

"Now put it all together," he continued as they stuffed it into their pockets, "and we'll have an even divide."

"Uhrr!" protested Haines, who had seized the major share of it, "I thought you was givin' us a money grab!"

"No such thing," returned Sycamore; "he threw it for us to look at. Say, where's them bundles of bills, Lum? Them's the boys that interest me!"

"Well, I'm goin' to keep these, anyhow!" asserted Haines doggedly.

"You *are* not!" answered Sycamore with spirit. "This ain't no hoggin'-match, it's a straight whack-up. So jest shell out, Mr. Haines—I reckon I got something to say about this too!"

"Oh, who are you, you big, swelled-up kid?" sneered Haines, reluctantly giving up the money.

"You think you're hell, don't you? Since you busted that car up with dynamite!"

"Well, that's more'n you c'd do!" retorted Sycamore, and Lum Martin sat back and watched them quarrel. He had to give up something, anyhow, and while they were quarreling about the gold they were asking no questions about the rest. So he let them wrangle until they were tired, and then he dealt out the money. Piling it up before him according to the denominations, he took a stack at a time and dealt the coins out like playing cards—one, two, three—until each had an equal share.

"That's right, ain't it?" he enquired, counting his own back into the sack.

"Sure!" answered Sycamore carelessly, "and here's that seventy dollars you loaned me." He counted the gold off his stack and was putting the rest away when Haines spoke up.

"How about the fifty you owe me?" he suggested.

"You'll git it!" replied Sycamore shortly.

"All right," said Haines, holding out his hand.

"When I git good and ready," finished up Sycamore.

"I'll git it now!" answered Haines hotly.

"You've got it, you damn thief!" cried Sycamore, suddenly threatening him with an accusing finger. "I seen you slip them twenties into yore pants!"

"You lie!" snapped Haines, and as each man went for his gun Lum Martin drew like lightning and covered them both.

"That'll do," he observed quietly. "Now you boys see how long you'd last if it wasn't for me here to run things. A gun-play, mebby, and somebody hurt—the folks come runnin', and find you full of twenties. Then we'd all go to the pen for life and Sam Slocum would be happy. Now listen! If you boys don't quit yore foolin' and do what I say I'm goin' to blow on you and run you in for train-robbin'! *I* never robbed no train!"

"Huh!" grunted Haines disdainfully.

"No, and Sam Slocum will believe me, too!"

"Not if he knowed you like I do!" responded Haines, but after a minute's silence he thought better of his grouch. "What d'ye want us to do?" he asked.

"No more'n you'd do for yoreselves," answered Lum feelingly. "Be reasonable—that's all! Don't quarrel—don't flash yore money—don't make no breaks! And whatever else you do, boys, stand together! Because if one of us falls down, we're all down. We're down and done for and they'll railroad us to the pen. I don't want you to fergit that." He paused and looked at them a minute, and then his thoughts came back to the fight. "Now, Jack," he said, "if you've got any money held out I want you to give it up!"

“Ain’t got no money!” replied Jack shortly.

“All right, then. Now Syc, you pay him that fifty you owe him, and I want you boys to quit fightin’.”

They quit, and Syc paid over the fifty dollars; but when they met again over in town they glanced at each other in surly silence and passed on by. Sycamore buried what remained to him of his money—it was less than three hundred dollars—by a fence post in Round Valley’s pasture and tried his best to be good, but Jack Haines went on a strike. Money had no value to him unless he could spend it and, intoxicated by the clink of the big twenties, he embarked on a wild carousal which strewed the town with gold. Three days later detectives dropped into town—as hobos, as miners, as cowboys out for a time—and sooner or later they all edged in on the night watchman and insisted upon buying the drinks.

The secret was out, for every one of those gold pieces was of a certain mintage and stamped with a certain date. Gold coins are rare in Arizona and the records of the express company and the Denver mint left no doubt as to the facts—but there is a big difference between facts and legal evidence and no man could prove that Jack Haines had stolen his gold. There were other coins of that same date and mintage in circulation, and a man is presumed to be innocent in this enlightened age until he can be proved good and guilty. That is what the detectives were there for—to get evidence on Haines—but from the time the first false friend arrived and tried to get him to talk Jack Haines became suddenly and aggressively sober. He realized, when it was too late, that he had made a slip; and from that day to the end of the chapter he never gave out a hint. Strangers who accosted him met with sudden and stinging rebuffs, often with a curt warning to leave the town; and more than one of Slocum's men saw the inside of the local jail. Lum Martin noted their advent and suspected the cause, and the "move on" ordinance of Hackamore was enforced to the very letter.

It was a fight now, a struggle between the detective forces of a great and powerful corporation and three grim officers of the law—and at a word from their chief the two deputies would do anything short of murder. All social relationships were cut off; even the local "kids" with whom Sycamore had been wont to exchange jests were told to go their way, and it settled down to a question of endurance. All eyes were upon Sycamore as he passed—the bantering, jovial welcome which every man had given him was forgotten and he walked by without a word. But when he met a G Bar man, as now and then he did, a secret, sneaking twinkle would show in the cowboy's eye, and then he would turn suddenly grave. The G Bars had suffered much, but now they were waiting, waiting!

That was one thing that Sycamore was not good at—waiting. Anything that called for action was right in his line but this loafing around under surveillance, this keeping a careful pose and never submitting to any friendly impulse, was beginning to get monotonous. Sam Slocum came to town and talked the matter over with him impersonally, with a chance word here and there about the advantages and exemptions attending upon turning state's evidence; but Sycamore answered him guardedly, taking it for granted he was talking about somebody else. For Sycamore had never spent a dollar of his stolen money and there was no man who could prove that he had stolen it—no man, that is, except Jack Haines.

They were crowding Jack pretty hard now, and his record was against him. What if he should weaken and confess! Then it would be Sycamore Brown who would serve the long prison sentence while Jack and Lum dug up the treasure. These and similar thoughts passed through his mind as he dawdled about the town, loafing in front of saloons and walking up and down the streets; but he put them resolutely away from him, for they had all sworn to stand pat to the end.

It was while he was in this uneasy mood, his young blood clamoring for action, and his mind clouded by doubts, that he happened to wander down to the depot one day to meet the train from the west. More than a year had passed now since he had come to the short-grass country but his mind kept turning back to the old range—the *sahuaros*, the sandy desert, the Mexicans and Indians, and all the old boys around town. Even as he was conning them over the train came in and a gay young man with a cigar in his face dropped down from the rear of the smoker. He was dressed in the latest style and had on a derby hat, but somehow his walk seemed familiar. Though he had no friends who wore hard-boiled hats Sycamore looked at him again, and at the same moment the stranger recognized him.

"Why, hullo, old socks!" he shouted, struggling with a heavy sample case as he rushed over to shake him by the hand. "I thought you was punching cows back on the Gila!"

He wrung his hand effusively and as Sycamore looked it gradually dawned upon him who the man was—Roy Hackett, a boy who had been shotgun messenger with him when they were bringing out treasure from the old Paymaster Mine at Chula Vista.

"Well, hello—Roy," he said, backing off and sizing up his loud attire. "Well, who'd a thunk it—where'd you git that hat?"

"Chicago!" answered Hackett briskly. "On the road now—selling clothes to order. Have to rag up, you know. Say, where's the best hotel in town?"

"Right over there," replied Sycamore, pointing to Hackamore's one caravansary. "And the worst, too!" he added, "but for cripes' sake, Roy, where'd you git them pants?"

"Made in Chicago, old boy—The Bon Ton Tailors. Come around to my room and I'll measure you for a pair, free of cost, for old times' sake. I'm traveling for 'em, you know. No more cow-punching for me, brother—I make more money on the road in a week than I made on the ranch in a year. Gee, I'm glad to see you again, Syc, how are they coming, anyway?"

"Oh, so so," answered Sycamore, "I'm deputy sheriff here now. But say, I got to git me a pair of green goggles if I'm goin' to look at that suit much—how long you goin' to be in town?"

"Over night—that's all. May stay another day if I can get orders enough to justify. By George, Sycamore, you're just the man I'm looking for—gimme a knock-down to your friends and say a good word for me and I'll rig you out like a king. Come on over to the hotel with me and we'll talk it over—and I'll show you the latest spring styles!"

They hurried off together and in the excitement of looking over the styles and samples Sycamore entirely forgot what was on his mind. Here at last was a chance to spend some of his hidden money and have it go out of town, and after a jolly supper together he left his old companion and slipped out to the hole by the fence. After all, it is the joy of spending the money that counts—the knowledge that you have laid it away gives pleasure only to a miser. And to meet an old friend like Roy Hackett! Why, he and Roy had took the town of Chula Vista several times, when they were off duty at the mine. He was a great kid, old Roy, always laughing and talking—but he had his nerve with him, too! So thought the simple-hearted Sycamore as he rooted out part of his treasure—and in a manner of speaking he was right, for in the interval of his absence the nervy kid Roy was holding a hurried conference with Sam Slocum.

The stage was all set when he returned, and Roy was just as laughable and talkative as ever, but as he measured Sycamore for his new suit he became silent and prepossessed.

"All right, old man," he said at last, "there's the measurements—and I'm sure it'd be a good fit—but by God, Sycamore, I kind of hate to take your money!"

"Oh, that's all right," laughed Sycamore. "I got plenty more. Here!" He chucked him fifty dollars as if to make light of the sudden display of anxiety, but Hackett still looked at him solemnly with anguish in his eye.

"Syc," he said, "I've always been a good friend

of yours, haven't I? I wouldn't give you a steer if it wasn't right, now would I? Well, while you was gone I was out looking around and I heard something that give me a scare. I don't know what you've been up to, Syc, but if half of what this feller said was true you won't be here when I get back—so you better keep your money!"

He sighed regretfully and handed the fifty dollars back, but Sycamore paid no attention to it—he had suddenly caught the idea.

"What did the feller say?" he asked, and though he spoke calmly and quietly there was a wild hunted look in his eye—for if it ever came to a pinch he had made up his mind never to be taken alive, not if he knew in time.

"Well, I'm a stranger here and couldn't make much out of it, but he said you and another feller had robbed the train—and a feller named Lum Martin had arrested your pardner—and he was going to confess. Jack, he called him, and he said the judge was up there waiting for him now!"

"Jack who?" demanded Sycamore, his eyes dilating with fear.

"James—or Hayes—or something like that," answered Hackett, "but I couldn't just—"

"Jack Haines!" corrected Sycamore, "a dirty, low-flung hound!" Then loosening the pistol beneath his belt he started for the door. "But the lyin' whelp will have to be pretty quick to beat me," he cried impulsively. "If he's there already

I'll shoot it out with him, and if he ain't—I'll tell myself!"

He hurried up the street, with Hackett following; and sure enough, when he came to the Justice's office there was a light inside and Judge Purdy sat waiting at his desk. Behind him stood Sam Slocum, the detective, his big eyes looking out into the night.

"Where's Jack Haines?" demanded Sycamore, striding in before them.

"He's not here," replied the old judge, primly.

"Well, I understand him and Lum Martin are comin' here to swear me into the pen—is that correct?"

"Ah—ahem," quavered the judge, "I—I really cannot say!"

That settled the matter with Sycamore. The old judge, trembling and evasive; the detective, looking past him and saying nothing—here were the men he was looking for and Haines had not yet arrived.

"Mr. Slocum," he said, turning upon that man of iron, "I want to make a confession to you—about that train robbery. Will you promise not to prosecute me if I tell you all I know? All right, then! You're witnesses to that, Judge and Roy—now git me a piece of paper and I'll put it down in writin'."

"Better let me write it," said Slocum, sitting down and grabbing up a pen, "it'll be quicker.

Go ahead now—you can sign it afterwards."

He balanced his pen and looked up, his eyes still vaguely interested in the black night without, and Sycamore began to talk.

"One night last August Lum Martin took me out to his house," he began, and as he hurried on, oblivious of the limitations of a writer, Sam Slocum's pen fairly raced across the pages to catch the precious words. He told it all, circumstantially, and Slocum did not interrupt him, though he was in a fever to get to the end. Roy Hackett closed the door behind him and stood breathless; the old judge made careful, laborious notes, stopping at every fourth or fifth word to dip his pen; and still the tale ran on. The plot, the quarrel, the plans for the hold-up and escape—and then the fateful night.

"And so we took the empty bags," Sycamore was saying, "and Jack and me got on our horses bare-back, him with one of these here strap bridles and me with a regular rope hackamore, and—"

"What in hell!" exclaimed a sudden voice outside—an angry voice.

There was thud of feet on the sidewalk as two men leapt up from the street; then the door burst open and Lum Martin and Jack Haines rushed in, wild-eyed and panting with rage.

"Syc, you damn fool!" cried Martin, "what yuh doin'?"

“Shut up!” thundered Slocum, leaping suddenly to his feet and confronting them. “Don’t you interfere here, Lum Martin, or—All right, boys!” he sung out, thrusting a hand inside his coat, and the next moment a side door was thrown open and the muzzles of two sawed-off shotguns shoved in. The chief himself held a six-shooter; Roy Hackett was behind with two more; and in the sudden calm that followed Sam Slocum’s voice rode out harsh and rasping.

“Lum Martin—Jack Haines—I want you boys for train robbery!”

“Well—I’ll—be—damned!” muttered Martin, and together they held up their hands.

CHAPTER IX

THE FIGHTING FOOL REPENTS

Sycamore Brown was a fool. The look on Lum's face, the staring shotguns, and his own heavy heart, all told him so. He had listened to a friend who was not a friend and now Lum Martin was in the toils. There was no occasion for Jack Haines to curse him—he knew what he was, better than any cursing could tell. To save his own hide in a panic he had sold out his partners to the sleuths—his name would be a byword now, whatever he might do. A wild rage, a fierce longing to strike out and defend himself, swept over him at the very moment and regardless of shotguns and pistols he turned and felled Hackett at a blow.

"Well, shoot me then, you coward!" he cried, as Hackett sprang vengefully to his feet. "Go on and shoot me, you express company sneaks—"

"Aw, shut up!" scoffed Jack Haines, scowling over his shoulder as they led him away, "you're nothin' but a stool-pigeon yoreself!"

"You're a damned fool, Syc," said Martin as he turned to go, and he said it in such a way that Sycamore never forgot it. A fool indeed he was, but no stool-pigeon; and from that day forth whatever else he did, he was always true to Lum Martin.

They put Lum in his own jail that night for safe keeping, and early in the morning with a guard they took him over to Gun Sight. It was not the first time in Gun Sight County that a deputy sheriff had broke into jail, but when the sheriff booked him and "frisked" him for his valuables he stripped him of his star. There was an election coming in the fall and Dillon could see his finish if he kept such men as Martin and Jack Haines on his staff. Already they had discredited his administration, for the Los Angeles and El Paso papers were big with scare-heads which linked his name with theirs. The style of the write-ups was bad, too—with "Train Robbed by Sheriff" for the headline and only the small type to explain that the sheriff was a deputy. Then the Alkali Ike cartoonists got busy and there were pictures of train robbers with badges on their breasts. It is the kind of advertising that Arizona gets too much of, and the citizens of Gun Sight were scandalized and indignant.

So the sheriff put Lum Martin into the county jail where he would not offend them by his presence, and every time one of the aforesaid scandalized citizens butted in to gloat at the miscreant the prisoners' kangaroo court laid hands on him and fined him at least a dollar. This was a bold proceeding, truly; but the prisoners were bold, bad men who took advantage of every opportunity. Some there were who protested against this outrage—the idea of prisoners seizing a visitor's hat and holding it till he paid a dollar—but there was one party which gave up without a murmur. The G Bar outfit rode over en masse and took a good, long look.

But while the G Bars and others were laughing their heads off and declaring that it was all over but the shooting Sam Slocum and his lynx-eyed associates were in a lather of exasperation. Immediately after the arrest of Lum Martin they had searched his mysterious adobe house from the mud roof to the dirt floor and thence on down till they got tired and the only thing they had found was a dollar watch, buried in a tomato can. As to just why a man should bury his watch in a tomato can echo answers not, but certainly there is nothing criminal about it and even an expensive lawyer would have trouble in persuading a jury that this bit of jewelry was loot. But that was all, absolutely all, they got for their trouble. They went over the flat with a fine-tooth comb and dug up every post in the corral but their labors were in vain.

And to cap the climax Sycamore Brown, their one and only witness, repudiated his alleged confession and absolutely refused to talk. More than that, he defied them to arrest him or prove that he had done aught that was wrong. If he had been weak or easy in the beginning he was roughshod and insolent now and met all attempts to placate him with a snort and a toss of the head.

"Ump-um," he grunted, when Sam Slocum offered him inducements. "I learned my lesson from Roy Hackett, blast his heart. I ain't got no friends now—nobody but Lum Martin—and I wouldn't testify against him if you filled my hat full of twenties!"

At first old Sam only laughed at this, for he had heard such talk before, but as the time wore on and his search turned out bootless he found that it was so. Sycamore was only a boy, but his pride had been touched. He had betrayed his friend and sent him to prison, but he would never send him to the pen.

Even so then, reasoned Slocum, perhaps he could use the boy yet. From what he had learned already he was satisfied that Lum Martin, and Lum Martin alone, knew where the treasure was buried; and the treasure was what he was after. It was a great treasure, minimize it as they would, for besides the money and jewelry that would be of value to the robbers, there were bundles and bundles of papers that meant fortunes to the owners. And the owners were clamoring for them—there were indemnities due on them—his own position was in jeopardy if he failed to produce the goods. So he came back once more to Sycamore; this time to appeal to the very passion which, so far, had balked him.

Sycamore was ashamed that he had betrayed his chief, he reasoned. He would do anything to retrieve his mistake. Very good. Now Lum Martin was a man who could never be influenced—he would carry his secret to the grave. But Sycamore had been worked once and he doubtless could be worked again. This was no time to balk at trifles or consider the abstractions of the law—it was better to turn Lum loose, if necessary, if only he would show Sycamore the cache.

"Mr. Brown," said Slocum, after thinking this over, "I'll make you another proposition. You go over to Gun Sight and square yourself with Martin and find out where that stuff is hid. Then you tell Lum that if he will come through with the boodle the case will be thrown out of court and I'll turn the two of you loose. Now that's fair, ain't it? Jack Haines is the man that hatched all this deviltry. All right, let him pay for it then—what we want is the boodle."

"*I* ain't got no boodle!" answered Sycamore rolling his eyes warily.

"No, I know you ain't," responded Slocum with a wise smile. "But Lum has. Now he can take his choice between giving up that plunder or going to the pen for life. A jury of these cowboys would soak him for stealing that old dollar watch—and that ain't all we got against him—by no means.

Now here's the point—old Lum is obstinate. If I go to him with this proposition he'll refuse. But if you go over there and talk with him, why perhaps you can work it—and if you do you'll more than make up for getting him into jail."

"He ain't got no use for me now," murmured Sycamore despondently. "They's no use of *my* goin' around."

"Oh, I don't know," countered Slocum. "Now what's the matter with this for a play? I'll arrest you and put you into jail with him—you'll be in the same cell together. And then you can ask him where that treasure is buried. It ain't much—I'll take my oath there wasn't two thousand dollars' worth of gold and bills in the whole safe. The rest was just papers—stocks, bonds and securities—worth a whole lot to the men that shipped them but nothing at all to you. Now I don't believe that Lum knows that—he took them bags in a hurry and buried 'em somewhere and thinks they're full of bills, and that's what's making us all this trouble.

"Now here's the proposition, Sycamore, and I just want you to take it quietly and see if I ain't right. Either Lum Martin intends to tell you where that treasure is, or he don't. If he don't, that's just another way of saying that he intends to beat you out of it—the thing has been done before, my boy, many's the time. And if he does intend to tell you it's to your interest to find out right away; now isn't it? As it is now, you stand to lose either way; because if you want to be a crook you've been buncoed out of your swag, and if you want to be straight and help your friend out of jail you've got nothing to square yourself with—nor him. Now what do you say—I'll put you in jail with Lum—you find out where the stuff is buried and tell me and I'll turn you both loose the same day. That's fair enough, isn't it?"

"Ump—don't like it," grunted Sycamore, "sounds too damn slippery and crooked."

"Well, what do you want?" demanded the chief indignantly. "What're you going to do—bum around town till I get tired of talking to you and send you back to jail? Make me a proposition of your own then if you think you're so awful nice!"

"Well," responded Sycamore, with a sudden flash of spirit, "I can tell you one thing right now—I'll never take up no proposition that comes from a company detective! If you think you've got the evidence to convict me they ain't nothin' I'd like better than to go to jail and have it over with—then after I was acquitted I could tell you all where to go. But as long as you keep these low-browed sleuths followin' round behind me I won't do nothin'—that's all."

"And suppose I call 'em off?" suggested Slocum.

"Well, in that case I'd like to go over and see Lum and see what he has to say."

"All right," responded Slocum heartily. "I'll go you."

"And you understand," warned Sycamore, "I don't guarantee you nothin'. I ride out of this here town a free man, with my own horse and my guns and my deputy's star, or I don't go out at all. And I don't promise no man nothin'. May break the damn jail down, for all I know, and turn old Lum into the hills—but the first time I see one of them skulkin' detectives of yourn, and I reckon I know 'em all by sight now, I'll either take a shot at the dastard or turn around and come straight back home. Now there's the proposition and you can either take it or leave it."

"I'll take it," said Slocum promptly. "When do you want to start?"

"Can't git away too soon to suit me," answered Sycamore, rising up to stretch his slack limbs. "How about right now?"

The chief nodded, for he was a man of great decision and he thought he read Sycamore Brown like a book. And so he could, for there was no guile in Sycamore's heart; but on the way out to get his horse a brand new idea came over him, and so powerfully did it appeal to his simple mind that he went straightway and dug up the rest of his money. This was *lèse majesté*, no less—and it was also taking a big chance—but Sycamore was a man who was strong for hunches, and the impulse of the moment was good enough for him.

Catching up his horse he rode back to his humble lodgings, fetched out his saddle-gun and two pistols, and ambled off without looking either to the right or to the left. No longer was he a hang-dog culprit, a suspect, subject to the beck and call of sleuths; his carbine was under his leg again, and in his heart he was an outlaw.

CHAPTER X

A JAIL DELIVERY

Far out over the plain galloped white-maned Round Valley, rejoicing in his strength and the long road that lay before them; and that night they camped in the open, Sycamore rolled in his saddle-blanket and Round Valley feeding on his picket. At dawn they were on the move again, picking their way through mountain passes, and when at last they gained the rugged valley where Gun Sight lay in the shadow of its lofty pinnacles the sun was well up in the sky. It was a great city yet, this town in the heart of the jagged, granite-spired sierras, though its first glory had departed. On the hillside above it, everything was modern—hoists, mills, corrugated iron buildings and smoking stacks; but below lay the same old city that had been built by the flamboyant discoverers and dedicated to the pleasures of life.

This was the spot to which the wild adventurers of that wildest and most adventurous land had rushed with a unanimity so startling and overwhelming that they had driven the Apaches from their very stronghold; and here, fighting against every adverse force in nature, they had mined and milled and separated until their gold could be measured by wagon-loads. Within a year Gun Sight had become a thronging metropolis and now in its serener days it still gave forth its riches, though the waters had crept in and flooded the lower levels. It was quiet now, so the old men said, but to Sycamore it seemed big and populous and he rode in by a side street, unostentatiously, for he harbored that in his heart which called for silence and stealth.

But had he not told it already? Yes, he had given fair warning, and to old Sam Slocum himself! And now he had come to make his word good—to break the jail open and turn Lum Martin loose. Men said he was a stool-pigeon who had sold his friends to the law—he would show them now that he was a man of honor, and a fighter second to none. For he would either save his friend and fly with him across the Line or he would die in the attempt and go down with guns in his hands. But now he hid his pistols cunningly, slipping them inside his waistband and covering the butts with his vest, and when he rode up to the court house he tied Round Valley where he would not be noticed, at the same time scanning the string of horses at the hitching-rack for a likely mount for Lum. Then, as the mill whistles shrilled the hour of noon he stepped out boldly and went straight to the sheriff's office,

"Here's a note from Slocum," he said, as that

official surveyed him coldly, and dropped the missive before him.

"Umm—ahumm," grunted Dillon, as he read it through. "So you want to see Lum Martin, do you? Umm, 'see him in private,' eh? Well, I'll tell Charley about it—come on!"

He rose and led the way down the corridor to the jail, which occupied the rear half of the court house on the ground floor. Unlike most Arizona jails it was shut off from the public absolutely, a steel grating and a solid iron door serving the double purpose of excluding visitors and confining the noise of the prisoners. Dillon pressed the electric button for the jailer and waited sullenly. If he could have followed his own instincts in the matter he would have seized Sycamore by the scruff of the neck and thrust him behind the bars too; but when at last the solid inner door was swung open he merely passed in Slocum's note, nodded dumbly to the jailer and went out to get his dinner.

Once more in his turn the jailer read the letter through and grunted at the contents. Anything that Chief of Detectives Slocum asked would be granted, of course, and that without question, but along with his chief and the rest of the deputies Charley Randall held a grudge against Sycamore which he felt under no obligations to conceal.

" 'Bout my dinner time," he observed, as he unlocked the outer door, "so cut it short."

"All right," answered Sycamore, stepping in and peering about in the gloom. He watched the locking of the doors and noted the particular pocket in which the jailer kept his keys. Then he followed along behind him as he led the way to the cells, passing down a darkened passage, around a corner, and stopping at the cell-room door.

"Lum Martin!" called out the jailer, striking with his big key against the bars, and as Lum shambled up he passed him through the gate without a word.

Inside the bars the prisoners were resting at their ease, some stretched lazily upon the floor, others sitting in groups and smoking, others perched on top of the steel cages and reading or playing cards. It looked more like the reading room in a cheap lodging house than the jail of the most lawless county in Arizona, but many of these men had friends on the outside and it was no part of the policy of Thomas Dillon to maltreat and harass his charges. Indeed, so freely were they indulged that the prisoners' kangaroo court was practically in charge, and trusties were often allowed in the corridors, to apprehend unsuspecting visitors and shake them down for their dollar. But in return for this the prisoners confined their depredations within the bounds of reason and strictly enforced the rules of decency and communal order.

It was one of their rules that no prisoner should approach within listening distance of any other who was talking with a visitor and, though many a furtive glance was cast in Sycamore's direction, no one came near to overhear their conversation. The jailer also retired up the corridor, in order to leave them alone, and the moment his back was turned Sycamore winked at his partner significantly and touched a bulge at his belt. Then, to divert suspicion, he talked upon different topics for several minutes while the fierce light glowed and grew in Martin's eyes.

"Lum," he said at last, still speaking in his ordinary voice, "Sam Slocum has got it in for you. He's going to send you up for life unless you come through with that treasure. Now I got you into this, Lum, and I'm goin' to git you out of it if you jest say the word. I got two pistols here, and when Charley comes back to lock you up I'll throw down on him, take away his keys, open up the doors and turn you loose. You can git yore pick of the horses at the hitchin'-rack and we'll pull our freight for Mexico. What do you say?"

For a minute Lum Martin's deep-set eyes gleamed and glinted as he thought out the possibilities, but in the end he shook his head.

"What's the matter?" enquired Sycamore, grieved that his rash plan was not approved.

"Old Sam can't get me on what evidence he's

got," answered Martin. "I ain't agoin' to take no chances—they might ketch me and give me the limit for jail-breakin', or horse-stealin', or somethin'. Nope, he can't convict me on his evidence, and once I'm acquitted I'm safe—a man can't be tried twice for the same offense."

"No, but listen," protested Sycamore. "Sam Slocum knows that you've got that boodle hid, and that Jack and me don't know where it is. He told me so, and he told me to tell you that you could have yore choice between givin' up that cache and goin' to the pen for life. He means it, Lum! That feller will bury a can of Mexican dollars in yore house, if he has to, and then dig 'em up for evidence. He's offered me every inducement he can think of to testify ag'inst you—and if he can't git me he'll git somebody else. Now I'm tellin' you what I know, and I been with him a month. But say, Lum," he continued, leaning closer and speaking eagerly, "I'll tell you what I'll do. I got you into this—now you tell me where that boodle is buried—Slocum says it ain't nothin' but papers nohow—and I'll go and dig it up and tell him it was me that did it. Then he'll turn you loose and—"

"Not much!" rasped Martin, shaking his head knowingly, and regarding Sycamore with a malevolent eye. "You can't work that on me, Mr. Stool-pigeon!"

"Work what?" cried Sycamore, aghast at this

sudden change. "You don't think I'm tryin' to do you, do you, Lum?"

"No, I *know* it! You done me dirt once, by Gawd; but you won't git to do it again!"

"All right, then," answered Sycamore smiling bitterly. "I jest come with this offer to square myself for what I did—if you don't want to take it I won't bother you again."

He turned to go, but Martin clutched at him, a new terror in his heart. What if Sycamore should go back and tell? What if he should testify against him now, out of spite, and send him to the pen? That would be the last of his treasure, and the last of his hold on life.

"Here! Wait a minute!" he hissed. "What's yore blasted hurry? Are you on the square with this, or is it another steer?"

"You know whether I'm square or not," grumbled Sycamore scornfully. "Old Sam told me you was tryin' to beat me out of that money and I begin to think he was right. I don't owe you nothin', Lum Martin—I come over here to help you, but now you can go to hell!"

He tried to jerk away, but Martin held on to him resolutely and at the same time there came into his voice a sudden note of pleading.

"Now here, Syc," he entreated, "don't go off and leave me in the hole. It's awful, shut up here for days and days, and I want you to help me out. I didn't mean nothin' a while ago—"

"Say!" broke in the voice of the jailer. "Ain't you boys pretty near through? I want to go out to dinner?"

"Jest a minute, Charley," answered Martin, hastily. "Now here," he went on, speaking earnestly to Sycamore, "we got to be quick about this. When Charley comes down with the keys you hold him up, I'll frisk him, and we'll turn the whole jailful loose and skip out while they're ketchin' 'em—savvy?

"All right, Charley!" he called over his shoulder, and stood back with a wise look while Sycamore felt for his guns.

The jailer was a thin, nervous man, bleached pastey white by his confinement but no less resolute for that. Only the dead drop would make him give up, and if he had a gun he might fight anyway, so Sycamore fell behind and watched him warily. Very glumly he took out his bunch of keys, selected one, and opened the outer lock-box. He was just unlocking the inner combination when Sycamore whisked out his long, hidden pistol and shoved it against his back.

"Throw up yore hands, you dastard," he ordered, "and do it quick or I'll shoot you full of holes!"

"You damn coward!" sneered the jailer, looking back at him over his shoulder; but at the same time he held up his hands.

"What d'ye think y'r goin' to do?" he demanded, turning suddenly and facing him.

"Never you mind," returned Sycamore significantly, "but jest keep them hands up high. Frisk him for a gun, Lum; he's gettin' fixed to shoot!"

"Ain't got no gun," declared the jailer, as Martin felt him over, and so indeed it proved.

"Keys are what we want," commented Lum, and relieved him of his key-ring instead. "Now you jest stand right there, Mr. Randall, while I go and unlock that door."

He shook out the bunch and began to fumble among them for the keys to the outer doors.

"Here, give me them keys," broke in Sycamore impatiently. "I know which ones they are. You take this gun"—he drew his spare gun left-handed—"and watch Charley—and give them boys a talk!"

A sudden tumult and excitement had broken out inside the bars, some of the men demanding to be released while others threatened vengeance if the jailer was harmed or hurt.

"Here, you boys key down a little!" ordered Lum, flipping his pistol muzzle in their direction. "What d'ye want to do—give the whole snap away?"

"Well, let us out, then," clamored the leaders, "or we'll holler out the winders!"

"Wait till he gits back with the keys," answered

Martin roughly. “Git a move on, Syc, and open them front doors!”

Sycamore rushed down the dark corridor and threw himself upon the solid iron door, but hardly had he fitted the key to the lock when he heard a scramble, a warning shout, and then the resounding *whang* of Lum’s pistol. There was an instant’s silence, and then the voice of the jailer spoke up.

“Don’t shoot,” he cried, “I’m down!”

“Well, stay thar, then!” cursed Martin, and at the sound of his voice Sycamore turned back to his job on the doors. The moment they were open he came running back to help, but Randall was doubled up in the corridor nursing a bloody wound in his leg.

“Never mind him!” shouted Martin, as Sycamore stopped to look. “Let his damn stool-pigeons take care of ’im—here, gimme them keys!”

He reached out and grabbed the bunch and, before Sycamore could do more than drag the wounded man aside, the first of the escaping prisoners came rushing around the corner and went scuttling out like rats.

Close behind the leaders came Lum Martin, still bearing his revolver and the keys. Then the voice of Charley Randall rose up, calling to the men to help him and not to leave, and as the crowd hung back, irresolute, Lum clutched Sycamore Brown by the shoulder and dragged him to the door.

"Hurry up to them horses!" he cried, "before somebody else gits 'em. But don't run when you git outside—and ride slow till we git out of sight!"

They hurried out the court-house door, tucking their guns under their waistbands and looking about warily, but the street was silent and deserted. The first rush of men had passed out and disappeared and no more came out from behind—Charley Randall was holding the short-termers with the fear of a swift return. Only a row of sleepy cow-ponies, standing along the hitching-rack, met their eye—and they made for them with a rush.

"Take that blue-roan," said Sycamore, hustling off to get Round Valley, and a moment later they were both in the saddle and loping quietly out of town.

But now a sudden popping of pistols broke out behind them—six-shooters being emptied into the air as fast as the owners could shoot—and every man in Gun Sight ran out to fight the fire. Often in the still of night that same *pop, pop, pop,* had burst forth and whole streets had been wreathed in flames—for Gun Sight had burned down twice. So the entire population surged into town, while Lum and Sycamore rode out—and when the alarm had spread and men came galloping on their trail they were several miles in the lead and well on their way to the Line.

"How'd you come to shoot Charley?" enquired Sycamore, as they rode out the mouth of the pass and headed across the plains for the Line.

"Huh?" grunted Lum, waking sullenly from his long silence.

"I say, how'd you come to shoot Charley Randall? Did he make a break to git you?"

"No," grumbled Martin, "he made a break for his guns!"

"He's a fightin' dastard!" observed Sycamore, hoping to extract a few details, but the master mind was silent—old Lum did not reply.

So for twenty miles they rode, each deep in his own thoughts, until they were safe in Mexico. No one pursued them across the open and there was no one at the Line to turn them back. Arizona is a big country and a man is hard to catch. They passed through the barbed-wire drift-fence that the cattlemen had built between the monuments and stopped to breathe their horses and close the gap, and still Martin was glum and silent.

"By Joe!" exclaimed Sycamore striking his knee as if taken by surprise, "we plumb forgot Jack Haines!"

Martin looked at him, just once, and then off into Mexico.

"Wonder what happened to him!" suggested Sycamore.

"Humph!" grunted Lum.

"Think he got away?"

"Nope," responded Martin, "I know he didn't. The cussed fool was in the solitary for raisin' a rough-house and I forgot to let him out."

"Oh!" said Sycamore, speaking softly, "Oho!" And as the significance of the words struck home he blinked and said no more. As for Martin he fixed his gaze on a banner of distant smoke that rose from a far blue mountain; and when the sun went down he was still riding towards it, his eyes squinting, his jaw set, with never a look behind.

CHAPTER XI
UP AGAINST THE RURALES

The border province of Sonora is just like Arizona, except that it is a little rougher and tougher and the Mexicans hand out the law. If the ruler had not slipped, Sonora would be a part of the United States to-day, but somebody told Mr. Gadsden that Yuma was a seaport and he drew the Line to that point—otherwise it would have gone to Topolobampo and salt water and saved us a thousand-mile haul. But as it is, of course, the Mexicans think that this ruler mark across the map is the place where they turned the proud Gringos back, and they keep a bunch of *rurales* or rural guards along the Line to remind us of the fact. And a *rural* can be just as ugly as he wants to, as long as he doesn't kill the wrong man.

Lum Martin had guarded treasure in Cananea—where the smoke banner rose to the south—and he knew the ways of the land, from *rurales* to the price of drink. There is no protection for the American in Mexico but his gun and his two good hands, for our government does not follow up its citizens. If they insist upon shooting up the town and trying to whip the *gendarmes*, well and good, let them lie and rot in jail—that is what happens to Mexicans in Arizona; but if they will keep the peace and avoid trouble Mexico is a haven of refuge when the north country gets too hot.

Now Lum was riding a stolen pony—branded G Bar on the left hip—and that would mean trouble if the G Bars ever got track of him; but in Sonora they don't ask any questions, as long as you keep out of jail. Strictly speaking, they had no right to ride into Mexico without declaring their property at the customs house; but that would all depend upon whether they met a *rural* or not—and Lum knew how to get around them. So they rode forward unobtrusively, avoiding the public thoroughfare and buying food from isolated Mexican houses, and on the second night they rode into Cananea, the copper city, with their horses still fresh and strong.

Though located in the heart of Sonora, La Cananea is essentially an American town. The mines are owned and controlled by Americans; and so indeed is the townsite, the railroad that leads to the Line, and most of the surrounding country as well. First there is the American town, spraddled out over the northern mesa; then in a low arroyo comes a Mexican town, called the Ronquillo; and above that on the side of the mountain is the maze of trams and buildings and shacks that go to make up the mining plant. The American town is a typical Western boom town, the Ronquillo the usual aggregation of Mexican huts and shacks—but there is one institution in the barren vale of La Cananea which cannot be duplicated elsewhere, and that is the Jockey Club.

The Jockey Club is the most elegant and palatial saloon in Sonora, but it is more than that—it is the Monte Carlo, to boot. According to law there can be no gambling in Cananea and when the governor—who sells the concession—passes through town the games are shut down in order to save his face, but at all times the Club is the great attraction for men with money in their pockets, and the rest come just to look. So, after putting up their horses in the Mexican quarter, where Martin had some mysterious friends, and visiting a saloon or two in the hope of hearing some news, Lum and Sycamore finally plucked up their courage and drifted into the Jockey Club.

It was a busy place, the long bar crowded with miners and mill-men and others with a thirst; and, following the custom of the country, they went up for a drink. Then they wandered about watching the games and, as no one paid any attention to them, they soon forgot their fears and became absorbed in the varying fortunes of the roulette wheel.

"Let's try 'er a whirl!" suggested Sycamore, who had a number all picked out. "The black's lucky—I'm goin' to drop a dollar on that."

The black won. He let it ride, and won again. Then he shoved the whole four dollars out onto the board and left it on eighteen. But the little ball skipped right by eighteen and fell into twenty-two. Sycamore dropped another dollar on the black—and lost; he dropped another, and won; then let it ride and lost both of them.

"Got any money?" he enquired of Lum.

"Nope," responded Martin, who was not playing, "you're losin'—better quit."

"Ump-umm!" objected Sycamore, "I feel lucky to-night—I'll break one of these twenties at the bar!"

Ever since leaving Gun Sight they had been living on Sycamore's money—the gold he had dug up before he left far-away Hackamore and Mr. Sam Slocum—and though he had divided up with his partner he still had some twenties left. So he stepped over to the bar and threw down a big yellow eagle, never dreaming that it could betray him there.

"What's the matter?" he demanded as the bar-keeper looked hard at the coin, "ain't it good?"

"Sure it's good," responded the bar-keeper, glancing out at him sidewise, "good for about forty-two Mexican dobies—but we don't get many of them gold twenties down here."

He threw out a shower of heavy Mexican dollars and as Sycamore stuffed them into his pockets the bar-keeper glanced at him again.

"You must 've come from California," he observed genially, "they say it's all gold in there."

"Umm," assented Sycamore absently, and hurried back to his game. He was busily feeding out his pocketful of dollars and doubling or losing his stakes when Martin crowded in beside him and gave him a quick dig in the ribs.

"You better quit," he whispered in his ear, "it's time to go."

"All right," responded Sycamore, "in a minute!"

He played again, and got another dig in the ribs.

"All right!" he said.

"Well *quit,* you dam' fool!" hissed Martin, "ain't you got no sense?"

At this Sycamore glanced up sharply, and the croupier raked in his stake. One look into Lum's eyes was sufficient—he saw there was something wrong.

"Well, I'm through," he announced, making way for another man. "Come on—let's have a drink!"

They went over to the bar together, apparently in the most jovial humor, but that was far from their mood.

"There's a big black rurale over in that corner," muttered Martin, "that's been watchin' you for half an hour. The bar-keeper that broke yore twenty is the man that gave him the tip."

"All right," answered Sycamore without looking around, "I'll let on that I'm drunk and you take me out the back way.

"Gimme whiskey!" he said to the bar-keeper, and his eyes drooped drunkenly as he spoke.

"And yours?" enquired the bar-keeper of Lum.

"Gimme a thin one," responded Lum.

They drank and ordered another one; and while they were drinking it a squad of four *rurales* filed past the door.

"That means us," muttered Martin, "they don't want no shootin' in here, so they're goin' to pick us up outside. I believe they got a guard by that back door, too."

"Well, take the front one then," whispered Sycamore, "and say, let's take it now!"

He threw down a dollar as he spoke and staggered away, with Martin supporting him by the arm.

"Them fellers outside don't know us yet," growled Lum, "so hurry by 'em and make for that railroad trestle."

Now the Jockey Club is located on one side of an ore tramway that runs down from the mine, and directly across the track lies the Ronquillo, where Sycamore and Lum had their horses. On account of the deep arroyo here the track runs over a trestle just below the saloon, and, once under this, they could plunge into the rambling street of the quarter and lose the *rurales* in the darkness.

Traveling with surprising swiftness for a drunken man Sycamore won the door before the inside *rural* noticed his flight; or, noticing it, could give the alarm. Outside stood the guard of four, their carbines at a rest, but they passed without a challenge. Then they wove down the dusty street, avoiding the glare of the lamps and listening for pursuing footsteps. But either the sergeant inside was negligent or he was deceived by Sycamore's condition, for no pursuit was heard until they had nearly reached their goal—then, with a military *pat, pat,* the guard came double-quicking down the street and they bolted through the trestle like scared rabbits.

Through the gulch and down into the Ronquillo they dashed and in the clatter of their own boots the sound of the pursuit was lost. Though it was early in the evening the quarter was dark and silent, for the peon cannot afford candle-light, and only the baying of curs in leash and the yapping of skinny lap-dogs marked the course of their hurried flight. But this alone was enough to betray them and as they passed a quiet alley Lum stopped suddenly and stepped aside to let the hue-and-cry go past. Outside in the main street a lamp burned dimly, but here they were safely hidden and for what seemed to them an eternity they waited for the search to end. The footfalls came and went; then the dogs ceased barking, and at last with infinite caution they crept out and headed for their corral. There were Round Valley and the swift blue-roan, saddled and only needing to be bridled and cinched, and once upon their backs they could laugh the *rurales* to scorn.

But their escape was not made yet, for a Mexican *rural* is like a Texas Ranger—a picked man—and his business is the hunting of men. Just as they passed along the wall of a house two men stepped out from around the corner and in the dim light of the street lamp they could catch the glint of their carbines as they brought them to a ready. The trim tightness of their trousers and short jackets and the huge felt sombreros which topped their heads left no doubt as to their identity—it was a pair of the lost *rurales*, and they were undoubtedly waiting for them. For a moment they looked to the right and left, seeking some gap or way of escape, but the *rurales* had chosen their ground well and there was nothing to do but keep on. To turn and run would be foolish—and besides, it was not their style.

"Gimme another drink!" commanded Sycamore, reaching out and grabbing at his partner. "No, I mean it," he insisted drunkenly. "You gimme 'nother drink!"

"Aw come on!" protested Lum, falling into his old part, "stan' up here—what's the matter with you!"

At this the two *rurales* left off their wary waiting and approached them brusquely, as was their custom with men who were drunk.

"*Alto*!" they ordered, "Halt!" And each picked out his man and covered him with his carbine.

"What's the matter with you?" demanded Sycamore of the tall sergeant—the man who had been watching them at the saloon, and who now had the muzzle of his gun about two feet from the pit of his stomach.

"Throw up your hands!" commanded the sergeant in Spanish.

"*No, Señor*," responded Sycamore in the same tongue. "Do you think I would surrender to a condemned Mexican? *Seguro que no*—not much! *Mira*, Señor Mexicano, I am an American, see?"

The sergeant saw. About half his work in the past few years had been along the line of cajoling half-drunken Americans into giving up their freeborn rights and prejudices, and he had heard this line of talk before. Also the experience had taught him not to crowd such men too far, unless he wanted a fight.

"You are a little drunk," he suggested diplomatically.

"That makes no difference," broke in Sycamore, advancing closer and waving his arms in protest, and at the same time he called him bad names in Spanish.

"Halt!" cried the sergeant, raising his carbine

suddenly and pointing it at his face. "Stand back, you—"

"Now!" shouted Sycamore in English, and striking up the muzzle of the gun he plucked the heavy six-shooter from his belt and struck his man over the head with it. They grappled then for an instant and the sergeant went down, with Sycamore riding him to the ground. At the same moment there was a flash of light and the loud *whang* of Lum's forty-five. The second *rural* fell clattering upon the rocky ground writhing beneath a shower of belting blows from Martin's pistol and before Sycamore could leap to his feet Lum had stripped him of both carbine and revolver and was starting down the street.

"Come on!" he cried in passing, and Sycamore was not slow to follow. Grabbing up the sergeant's carbine, to keep from getting shot in the back, he wrenched the *rural*'s pistol from its scabbard and sprang after him, throwing the gun over the first dead wall he came to in order to run the harder. At the gate of the corral he came upon Lum wrestling with the fastenings in the darkness and, not opening it at the first try, they threw themselves against the rickety gate-frame and smashed it through the middle. Yet even this took time—and it scared their horses, too—and by the time Sycamore got Round Valley to the gateway the whole quarter was in an uproar. Terrified cries of "*Socorro*!" and "*Ladrones*!" rose from the neighboring houses where women had been startled by the smashing of the gate, and from up the street came the hoarse shouting of men who were gathering about the battered *rurales.*

While he waited, Sycamore cinched tight his saddle and slapped on the single-strap bridle, but Lum was still struggling to soothe his mount.

"Come in here, Syc," he called at last, "and help me ketch this fightin' bastard—no, stay where you are or he'll get out the gate! Oh, hell!" And the noise of his scuffling was resumed.

Meanwhile a sudden patter of hoofs had sprung up from over in the direction of the *cuartel* and Sycamore knew the reserves were coming on the run. Then a shrill woman across the street began to shriek to a purpose.

"*Aqui*! *Aqui*!" she squalled. "*Aqui hay*! *Dos Americanos*! Here there are—two Americans! They are stealing horses!"

And that did settle it, for the mob came up on the run.

"Here they come, Lum!" yelled Sycamore, swinging up on his horse and plunging into the corral. "Git on anyway and I'll drive him out ahead of me!"

"All right," grunted Martin who was fighting to get on a bridle and springing into the saddle he went out the gate like a rocket, guiding his horse by the swing of his body and a sudden slap on one side of the head. After him came Sycamore, riding herd on the snorting roan and just in time to catch the eyes of the *rurales*. On they came with a rush, boring recklessly through the stampeded crowd, and then they all went down the road together, Lum far in the lead on a pony that ran like a scared wolf, Sycamore eating his dust behind and the *rurales* shooting and yelling in the rear. It was a lively race, full of doublings and turnings and wild shooting in the dark, and it never really ended until Lum and Sycamore crossed the Line and took shelter in Arizona.

CHAPTER XII

THE FLIGHT INTO PAPAGUERÍA

It was a hard-looking pair of *hombres* that came up out of Mexico, and they were only a short mile ahead of the *rurales.* A relay of these mounted police had picked up their trail at dawn and only the speed and bottom of their wiry cow-ponies had saved them from a fight. Even after they crossed the Line between the two white but distant monuments they did not take any chances, for more than one man in those parts has been arrested by a bullet and extradited afterwards. It was a good three miles and more before they stopped to water their horses in the sandy river that flows from Mexico north, and even after that they pressed on to a higher ridge where they could look out the land to the south.

"What's the matter with them dogged rurales?" demanded Sycamore querulously, as he sat rolling a cigarette and scowling at their retreating enemies. "The last thing I remember is playin' a dollar on the red and seems like it's been nothin' but rurales ever since. Of course we beat up a couple of 'em and took away their guns and that's why these fellers is so red-eyed over it, but what I want to know is, what did they jump on us for, in the first place?"

"Humph!" grunted Lum, rubbing his grimy growth of beard and gazing wearily out over the deserted landscape, "you ought to know that. Didn't you notice the way the bar-keep was lookin' at you when he gave you dollars for that twenty? Well, you want to keep yore eye peeled for a while—old Sam Slocum knowed we'd blow into Cananea and he had every bar-keep in town on the lookout for them cussed twenties! Seems like, between you and Jack, that money keeps me in trouble all the time!"

"Oh, it does, does it?" sneered Sycamore. "Well, I guess if it wasn't for that little sack of twenties I brought along you would've starved to death before you ever got to Cananea—but if that's the way you feel about it you better gimme back that hundred and twenty I give you!"

"Oh hell!" growled Martin, "they's no use quarrelin' about it—I guess we got to spend 'em, or starve—but we got to make a raise somewheres—either that or git out of the country. Them dam' rurales will be watchin' for us now, and if they ever git us within gunshot we're just as good as dead. And then, if they should happen to put us in jail, they'd turn us over to Slocum and tell him to do his worst. You remember them ten thousand Mexican dollars, don't you, that you put on top of yore powder? Well, they belonged to the Mexican government and was being shipped down here to pay off the soldiers, and such. Oh, we're goin' to be popular, on both sides of the Line, but they'll never git me into no Mexican prison—not so long as I can crook a finger or lift a leg!"

"Humm," murmured Sycamore, gazing about him doubtfully, "what's the chances of Sam Slocum and these rurales gittin' together and wipin' us off the map?"

"Well, if you want to know my opinion—they're good!"

"All right then—what you goin' to do about it?"

That was the big question, and Lum pondered it over in silence.

"I know a mine over here," he said at last, "where they ship out about ten thousand a week—in gold. It would be easy took, too. Then we could make a sneak for a year or so and come back and dig up that Hackamore cache."

"What's the matter with diggin' up the cache now?" enquired Sycamore pointedly. He had never quite forgotten Sam Slocum's words: "Either Lum intends to show you that money, or he don't."

"Huh!" grunted Martin scornfully, "you must want to get caught with the goods. That's jest exactly what old Sam is waitin' for."

"Well, I bet you I can slip in there in the night and git away with anything in Hackamore—where have you got it buried, anyhow?"

"That's all right!" answered Martin shortly.

"Sure it's all right," responded Sycamore with spirit. "I guess I got as good a right to know as you have!"

"Uh," said Martin, "very likely."

"You won't tell me, hey?"

"Nope. Likely to git us into trouble."

Lum rose up from his seat on a rock to indicate that the matter was closed. "Come on," he said, crippling stiffly over to his horse, "let's git agoin'! I'm so hungry for somethin' to eat I could steal leavin's from an Apache!"

"Well, where you goin'?" demanded Sycamore sullenly. It was a long time since he had had anything to eat too and the subject interested him in spite of his grouch.

"Let's foller them cow-trails," suggested Lum, pointing to the deep-worn ruts that led away to the north, "and mebbe we'll come to a Mexican house—I never been over in this country before."

They followed down the stream for a while and finally came in sight of a wind-mill, with a large barn and ranch house hid away among the cottonwoods that grew below.

"Ump-um, that don't look good to me," said Martin, drawing his horse back under the cover of a hill, "that's a big outfit of Americans. There's a reward up on us now, sure, and if them cowboys ever git after us we're done for, that's all. Let's hit west and see if we can't find a Mexican house."

"Let's hunt along through these willers first and see if we can't shoot a rabbit," wailed Sycamore. "My stomach is shrunk up till it wouldn't hardly chamber a liver pill—I tell you I'm sure hungry! Say, there's a jack over there right now—and I'm goin' to kill 'im, too!"

He rode in on the unsuspecting jack-rabbit, dropped quietly off his horse and potted him with his carbine, but when he started to build a fire Lum objected.

"I'm hungry too, Syc," he said, "but somebody might've heard you shoot, so let's move on a ways and git where we won't show no smoke."

They moved, as fast as the weary ponies could travel, and then, going down among the willows, they lit a small fire and broiled and ate the rabbit.

"Ah," sighed Sycamore, licking the grease off his fingers, "I begin to feel like a man again. Now if—" he paused and reached quietly for his rifle, and Lum rose up and shifted his gun to the front. A muffled and distant drumming, changing rapidly to the clatter of hoofs came to their ears, and the next moment a tall Texas cowboy with a carbine across his saddle came riding along the trail. Evidently he was looking for something, for he was leaning over to see their tracks—but when the trail ended abruptly and he looked over and saw them watching him his manner changed suddenly to a pose of affected ease and he pretended to be pleasantly surprised at their presence.

"Wy hello!" he called, "is that you, Bill? I thought it was some dam' Mexican out beefing another—" he paused, and rode in closer. "Well, excuse *me,* gentlemen," he said, looking them over warily. "I thought you was a friend of mine," he added, looking at Lum.

"Nope," answered Lum, and the cold uncompromising way in which he said it seemed to discourage the Texan right there.

"All right then," he said, turning his horse about, "heerd yore gun go off, you know—and thought—mebbe—" but what he thought, though of small consequence, was lost in the thunder of his retreat.

"That feller was lookin' fer us," muttered Martin, as they hurried out to bridle their horses. "I've seen them stage plays before—and we'd better drift for the Line."

They drifted and shortly after they had crossed they saw a big cloud of dust come scurrying down the valley like a cyclone, with a bunch of cowboys at its front.

"This country is gittin' too hot for us," grumbled Lum, and putting spurs to their jaded horses they turned their faces to the west. For over the granite mountains that loomed before them lay the desert and Papaguería, and if any man followed them there it would show that he wanted them bad.

Moreover they would know he was after them as soon as they saw his dust, for Papaguería is not a white man's country. Nowhere in the world is there a place where a man can look farther and see less—and even the desert-bred Papagos find the country too barren for them and move about uneasily from place to place. In the winter they live in their *rancherías*, small villages of adobe houses perched upon some hill or ridge in the neighborhood of a tank or spring, and there they tend their ponies and cattle and watch the great plain below. In the spring they move to the mountains to bake mescal heads and water their cattle; and in the summer, when the heat is fiercest and the thunder-caps pile up in the sky, then they flock out to pick cactus-pears from the giant *sahuaros* or, if they are ambitious, to tend their poor fields of corn if the black clouds will give down rain.

It is a desperate country, truly, unwatered for hundreds of miles; but desperate men may not question their destiny—they must go where they are driven. With a band of cowboys behind them and vengeful *rurales* across the Line there was no other place for Sycamore and Lum Martin to flee to, so they turned their gaunted horses to the west.

A desolate Mexican ranch house near the Line furnished them with food that night, the occupants staring out at them fearfully, too tongue-tied to name a price. There was nothing in the house but jerked beef and a stack of *tortillas*, but Lum bade them bring it all out—everything they had to eat—while Sycamore made them rich with a couple of his Cananea dollars. Then they bought corn for their horses, and a flaccid pig-skin to carry water, and rode on towards Papaguería.

Two days later, coming up out of a level plain that was dry as the floor of an oven, they cut a series of pony trails heading north and came in sight of San Ignacio. Their way had led over broken land and ridges, green with sticky creosote bushes but desolate of human life; then it had taken them past high, granite mountains with long washes of sand and boulders reaching far out into the plain, their courses marked by iron-wood and mesquite trees and palo verdes, yellow with April flowers; and then it had led through sinks of silty sand, a soil so rich that the coarse *galleta* grass stood three feet high by the trampled trail and delicate evening primroses and star-eyed daisies gazed up at them as they passed—but the water-holes lay a day's journey apart, in mud-holes and stagnant tanks, and if Sycamore had not been desert-born they would have passed them and died of thirst.

But far to the north, where the railroad gives the desert life, the tribe of the Browns had struck root and produced a hardy stock—and even this barren waste looked good to Sycamore, for he had lived in it all his life. To Round Valley it was like a return to the old range where he had run wild among the rocks and every time he passed a clump of *galleta* grass he bit into its wiry top. The flowering tips of mesquite trees tempted him at every step, and at night he grazed at his rope's end until he mowed a circle clear. It was different with Lum Martin and his roan—they were thirsty all day long, and only followed along because they knew no other way to go.

At first sight the *ranchería* of San Ignacio was only a dark shadow on the top of a knoll. Behind it there rose a clean-cut mountain, its broad flanks richly forested with giant cactus; then as they drew nearer there appeared below the village a sunken tree-top of almost transparent green—the cottonwood by the well. Then the dark spot across the hill-top broke up into checkers of black—the shadows beneath sunstruck brush *ramadas*—and suddenly the adobe houses stood out from the mud-color of the hill, each sheltering its square of treasured shade, and in the black doorways there appeared the figures of women and children, staring out at the unusual guests. Not once in a month, or a six-months, did a white man come to San Ignacio; and then he was not pressed to stay, for the Papagos do not welcome strangers, as Sycamore knew full well.

Once well in view the two wanderers came on

slowly, and as they watered their horses at the guarded spring the women-folks stepped inside. Then the little ones followed, reluctantly, leaving nothing but the barking dogs; and at the top of the trail an old man who came out and sat down to wait.

"Just let me pull this off," suggested Sycamore, as they mounted to make the ascent. "I know how to git around these Papagos—been raised among 'em. I'll talk with the old Captain up there in Spanish—he'll let on he can't understand English—but all the time he'll be listenin' to what we say to each other, and you can bet there'll be somebody that'll savvy every word—the kids go to Indian school. So look pleasant and don't make no breaks and we'll git a bid to eat."

They mounted the hillside slowly, by a trail that was worn deep by human feet, and as they reached the summit the old Indian rose up to meet them. He was a sturdy figure of a man, supple, with shoulders still square and straight and a great display of muscles in his sun-browned legs. Unlike the younger men, who stood at a distance, he showed no traces of the new regime and wore nothing more than a shirt and breech-clout, with his hair hanging down to his shoulders. As for the boys, they were dressed like ordinary agency Indians, in tight-fitting, lace-topped overalls, shirts with fancy armlets, turned-up hats, brogan shoes—and a bristling haircut withal. But one look into the old man's resolute face told Sycamore who was chief, and he addressed his remarks to him.

"Howdy," he said, as he touched his hat in salute, "are you the Captain here?"

For a minute the old man looked them over, their haggard bearded faces, their gaunted horses, their superfluity of arms, and his wrinkled face became set.

"Uh!" he grunted, "*no intiendo Americano*!"

"*No le hace*," answered Sycamore easily, "that's all right," and he asked again in Spanish.

"*Sí*!" responded the old chief, and at that Sycamore got down off his horse. The pipe of peace is gone now, along with the tomahawk and the blanket, but a cigarette helps take its place and passes the time away, for an Indian cannot do business in a hurry. So Sycamore and Lum rolled a cigarette apiece and passed the makings on to El Capitan. They smoked then, gazing about at the yapping dogs, the staring "boys," and the flat-roofed adobe houses that went to make up the town.

"Umm," commented Sycamore to Lum, "the old man has got a big town here."

"That's right," agreed Lum, though he ill liked the part he played, "and he's got lots of water in his well." It was the only good thing he could say for San Ignacio, and he had to say that quick.

"This house here's the dandy, though," went

on Sycamore, jerking his thumb at a large, well-kept adobe with a broad brush veranda in front, which was evidently the chief's. "Keeps it nice and clean, too."

He smoked a while after this, looking dreamily off into the distance, and then the old Captain relaxed.

"Where you go?" he asked in Spanish.

"Very far!" answered Sycamore, waving his hand in a broad gesture towards the west.

"Uh!" grunted the old man. Then, after gazing hard into his face: "Where you come from?"

"Very far!" answered Sycamore again, pointing his hand toward the east, "Cimarron Valley—Gun Sight!"

"*Sí*, *Sí*!" nodded the chief, a smile creeping into his eyes, "I know!"

"You been there?" enquired Sycamore eagerly.

"*Sí*," responded the Captain proudly, "Cimarron—Chiricahua—San Carlos—Sierra Madre—I know!"

"Huuu!" piped Sycamore in well-simulated wonder, "that is very far from here! What you go for?"

"Me scout!" asserted the old man, tapping himself on the chest, "go fight Apache!"

"Aha!" breathed Sycamore, and this time it was in genuine admiration, for a man who has fought the Apaches and come away alive is never without honor in Arizona.

"You bet—me War Chief Juan!" declared the old warrior, lapsing for the first time into English. "Me fight Geronimo—Chihuahua—Naiche! Me chief—Papago scouts—lieutenant Johnson!"

He plunged now into a long and discursive account in Spanish of General Crook's last big campaign against Geronimo, dwelling with much particularity upon the part played by the Papago scouts in running down a remnant of the renegades who had sneaked off the night of the surrender. For eight months they had followed on the trail, down through the Mexican Sierras and back to the White mountains in Arizona, and not until they were within a hundred miles of Fort Apache did they overtake their enemies. Many were the tricks and stratagems resorted to by the Chiricahuas to throw them off the track, but on through the burning deserts and up over the pathless Sierras followed Chief Juan and his tireless tribesmen, for they were the hereditary enemies of the Apaches, with a thousand raids to avenge. And at the end, seeing that they could not escape and to save their warriors' pride, the renegades headed for Fort Apache, there to surrender to the white commander. But even in that the Papagos foiled them and, cutting in ahead, they compelled them to lay down their arms or answer with their lives.

It was a long story—as told by War Chief Juan—and Lum allowed his eyes to wander towards a shed nearby, where some women were cooking meat; but Sycamore followed it closely with many an appreciative grunt of admiration and wonder—and at the end he held out his hand.

"You big Captain," he said in Spanish, "*muy bravo*, *muy coyote*—you white man's friend—no?"

"*Sí*, *Señor*," assented the old chief proudly, "I am the white man's friend!"

"Good!" cried Sycamore, reaching out his hand, "you be my friend too!"

"*Stawano*!" echoed the chief who was so brave and crafty, and without more ado he offered his hand.

They sat down then and lit another cigarette, while Martin squirmed uneasily and took up the slack of his belt. But after the smoke was over the old man glanced towards the cook shed and spoke again—to Sycamore.

"You are hungry, my friend," he suggested benignly.

"Yes," answered Sycamore, "a little!"

And at that Lum Martin snorted. "A little!" After living on jerked beef and tortilla crumbs for two days! But Sycamore knew his man.

"Very well," said the chief, rising to his feet, "we will eat." He moved off a step or two. "And bring your friend, too!" he added. But he turned his face away.

CHAPTER XIII

THE GIRL AT SAN IGNACIO

There has been a lot written, off and on, about good Indians and bad Indians, but Sycamore Brown had known both kinds and he was willing to take a chance. There have been some awfully bad white men in Arizona, too, and he had met a few. Just at the moment he was suffering with a man's size appetite—a ravenous, gnawing hunger that left him faint and weak—and when he saw the feast before him he loved old Chief Juan like a brother. No *pinole* mush in a pot, no strip of scorched meat in the ashes—it was a *meal,* served on a table like a white man, and the girl who set it out seemed like an angel come down from heaven. There were stewed beef and white-flour *tortillas*, and coffee—and more, and more, and more! The beef was cooked with mesquite bean meal and a strong dash of Mexican *chili*, and to make it all the better it was subtly flavored with garlic!

But the girl! She was tall and dark and willowy, with a clean blue dress and hurrying, whispering, brown feet that twinkled out as she walked. Never for a moment did she look up from her task; she never spoke; and Sycamore concealed his glances, for it is not good form among Indians to give attention to their women-folks—but somehow above all the rest he was conscious of her, as if she were the queen of the feast. And what a feast! After he had left off, from shame, the meat was removed and the girl brought a brown bowl of *pitahaya* syrup, the sweet, fig-like fruit of the giant cactus boiled down and flavored with wild herbs—and with it a fresh stock of *tortillas*. So he ate on, with many protests and polite compliments; but Lum ate sullenly, feeding himself grossly and with eyes only for the food. It was bad, for Indians are ceremonious and, like many a white-skinned brother, they love to press more food upon a welcome guest, overcoming all his protestations and begging him to eat his fill.

But at last the meal was ended, the cigarettes brought out and while the women cooked more for themselves they lolled by the table and smoked. And now El Capitan came back to his guests, his tales of war being spent, and enquired the news of their journey—where they had come, at what waters they had stopped and how they had fared on the way. To this Sycamore answered truthfully, dwelling in detail on the lay of the land and the condition of each spring, but as he talked his mind leapt on ahead, devising the proper answers for the questions that were bound to follow.

"And now you go on to the west?" enquired the Capitan.

"*Sí*, *Señor*," assented Sycamore, but he said no more.

"It is a country that I know well," continued Chief Juan. "Very dry—very desolate. Very few Americanos go into it—and many of them become lost."

"*Sí*, *Señor*," agreed Sycamore, "I can easily believe it—but our business is urgent and we cannot turn back for that."

"Some mine, perhaps," suggested the old man. "There are two of them to the north."

"No," answered Sycamore, "it is no mine."

"What then?" enquired Chief Juan, and Sycamore saw that the time to talk had come.

"*Amigo*," he began with impressive gravity, "I know that you have been a good friend to the white man, for you have helped fight against his old enemies, the Apaches. And you have shown yourself a good friend of mine. So I will tell you of our mission, for I know you are a true man, and perhaps you can give us some assistance.

"We have come out here, Señor Capitan, in search of two Americans—two desperate fellows who have broken out of the Gun Sight jail and escaped into this desert land. Have you heard of any such men?"

No indeed, the Capitan had not—but who were

they, what had they done, and how would one know them by sight?

"Have patience," answered Sycamore, crossing his legs and assuming such an air of the story-teller that the women paused to listen, "have patience, and I will tell you all, from the beginning. I am a deputy sheriff, as you see"—he showed his badge, which was still pinned to the underside of his vest—"and my friend here is the same—and what I say I know.

"Last fall at the time when the mesquite beans were ripe a train was robbed on the railroad. The strong-box on the treasure car was blown open and much money was taken out and hid. Two men were the robbers, but no one knows who they were. All winter the officers of the railroad hunted for them and tried to find the money, and two months ago they arrested one man and put him in the jail. But if this man knew anything about the treasure he would not tell; and last week his *compañero* came to the jail, broke it open, shot the jailer and set him free. Then they both mounted horses and escaped into Mexico. But the rurales chased them out again and four days ago they were seen by cowboys near the river San José. Now all the deputy sheriffs of Gun Sight county are out looking for them, and, hearing that they had fled to the west, my friend and I have come out secretly, hoping to catch them unaware and perhaps to win a reward."

"A reward!" exclaimed the old chief, pricking up his ears at the word.

"Yes," responded Sycamore, "have you heard of any?"

"Ah no," said Captain Juan. "We are far from the railroad—my young men do not ride so far—we have heard no news for a month. But the train-robbery! *Caramba*, we have heard of that! *Sí*, *Señor*, a Mexican came through from Tucson and told us all. The robber laid one hundred thousand *pesos* on the strong-box—he put a charge of dynamite beneath—then *ploom*—he blew up the whole train and scattered the dollars for miles! *Que caramba*, what a desperate fellow! And now he has come out here?"

"So we are told," answered Sycamore, blushing beneath his beard to find his fame so great.

"And what do these robbers look like?" enquired Chief Juan eagerly. "Perhaps I might undertake their capture if I were sure of a big reward!"

"The leader," said Sycamore fixing his mind's eye on the villainous Jack Haines, "is a tall, dark man, with a long, drooping black mustache and restless black eyes. He wears the clothes of a gambler, striped coat and pants, a soft black hat and fancy, hand-made boots, and rides a big bay horse with a Texas saddle and spurs. Have you seen any man like that?"

"No indeed," answered the Captain, his eyes

beginning to glint, "but if he should come here later I will know him well."

"Very good—but if you should happen to encounter him do not try to take him yourself, for he strikes as quick as a rattlesnake and does not care who he kills. It will be better, Señor Capitan, to let us know and we will come here and capture him."

"And the reward?" enquired El Señor Capitan shrewdly.

"Of that we do not know—for we have been away from towns for a week. But if there is one, and you help us to capture these outlaws, we will give you an even half of what we get."

"Good!" exclaimed the old man, "very good—but how can we find out about the reward? Perhaps some other men may hear of it before us—and if there is none, then why should we trouble ourselves?"

"What you say is true," agreed Sycamore, "but I have a plan to propose. I have heard how fast the young men of the Papagos can travel across the desert. Now my friend and I are short of ammunition and tobacco, and we are willing to pay—send one of your boys to the railroad, let him buy the tobacco and cartridges, and then tell him to buy some newspapers—all that have been published for a week. Then we can read them over secretly, and if the railroad has offered a reward you can send out runners to all the Indian villages and find out where these desperados have hid."

"*Stawano*!" cried the old chief, leaping up, "good! I will send off a boy at once!"

"One thing more!" called Sycamore, hurrying after him. "I have here a piece of gold money, worth twenty American dollars, that I will give to your boy when he goes so that I can have the change to pay him. But if he should show it to white men they might think he had stolen it and detain him, so tell him to go to a Chinese store first and buy me two red silk handkerchiefs with it. The Chinamen are great hoarders of gold; and besides, they are afraid to make any trouble. Then tell the boy to buy me four boxes of cartridges like these at an American store, and two dollars' worth of smoking tobacco. Do you understand?"

"*Sí, Sí, amigo*!" answered the Capitan, beaming upon him in admiration, "*muy coyote usted*—you are very smart—in two days the boy will return!"

He hurried off then, clasping the outlawed twenty in his hand and chuckling at the "coyote" ways of his American friend. Soon he had his young men running to round up the ponies and before the hour had passed a trusty messenger was astride the strongest and galloping off towards Tucson—but then, with true Indian circumstantiality, Chief Juan came back to a lapse in their conversation.

"You told me, my friend," he began, coming

back to where Sycamore was sitting on a stone outside the door and listening to the girl's voice within, "you told me what the leader of these two men was like. Now tell me about the other—the one who blew up the train, and broke open the jail, and helped his friend to escape. What kind of a man is he, if I should see him?"

For a moment Sycamore hesitated, not knowing whether to describe a man like himself, or some other; but of a sudden the voices of the women were stilled and he knew that they were listening. Lum Martin, gaunt and dour, had left him to look after the horses; he could picture the demure Indian girl within the shed as she waited upon his words and a sudden desire came over him to win her heart by some romantic tale.

"This other man," he began, "is different from his companion. He is a young man, with blue eyes and fair hair, and rides a sorrel horse with white points. I have heard that, being deceived by a former friend, he confessed to robbing the train; but when his leader was arrested and put into jail he repented of his treachery and so broke open the jail and set him free. Nevertheless, he is a dangerous man and quick to shoot with either hand, so I hope you will not have trouble with him."

"And is he the man who blew up the train and scattered the bags of money?"

"So they say, but the country is all in confusion

and no man knows anything aright. There are some people who claim that he is a short, stout man, very brutish to look at, like a Mexican *cholo.* And others claim that he did not rob the train at all—that it was robbed by the town marshal of Hackamore and the money sent off to China. But we are deputy sheriffs and have only our orders, which are to bring them back, dead or alive—and that we are bound to do."

"And this tall black man—the leader—what is his name?"

"In Spanish his name is Mart*een.*"

"And the other?"

"His name in Spanish is Moreno."

"Aha!" The old chief sat silent now, conning over all the facts in his mind.

"And what is your name, *amigo*?" he asked at last.

"My name in English is Sycamore, but in Spanish *aliso*, a tree."

"Good!" commented Chief Juan, and sat contemplating him in amiable repose.

But if Sycamore had satisfied the chief he was far from meeting the approval of stern-eyed Lum.

"What are you tryin' to do?" he demanded when he had beckoned him down to the well, "give the whole snap away? How do we know that old boy won't jump us at night—or send word in by a runner? What yuh want to talk so much for?"

"Well, we got to eat, ain't we?" argued Sycamore. "I noticed you was doin' yore share! And I had to tell the old man somethin' or he'd never 've took us in. He knows right well we got no business out here—and if we ain't officers he knows to a certainty we're horse-thieves! You can't fool these desert Papagos—they've stole a few horses themselves."

"What's to keep 'em from stealin' ours, then?" snapped Lum with peevish haste.

"Nothin'—except the good will of the Capitan."

"Well, he don't look good to me—I'm goin' to sleep out to-night."

"All right," answered Sycamore. "But I'll tell you right now the man never got very far in Papaguería that didn't stand in with the *capitans*. The first night you sleep out by one of these *rancherías* and don't go in and say 'howdy' to the Capitan yore horse is goin' to turn up missin' in the mornin', and it'll cost you money to git him back. But suit yoreself—I ain't got no strings on you. I'm goin' to stay with old Chief Juan myself."

"Yes," observed Lum with a loose laugh, "I noticed you had yore eyes on that gal!"

"You're a dam' liar!" flared back Sycamore, and then stood aghast at what he had said. But Lum did not take the words seriously—he only laughed and turned away—and Sycamore blushed red beneath his beard. A sullen anger at the whole world came over him and he sat off by himself, thinking. At supper he kept his eyes on his plate and ate little, and when Lum finally spoke to him about some trivial matter he only glared at him and scowled down into his plate.

"What's the matter with you?" demanded Lum when they were alone again, "you're all bowed up over somethin'!"

"Uh!" grunted Sycamore.

"Must be that gal!" suggested Lum, and then Sycamore gave full vent to his spleen. He cursed his old friend and called him names, and when no insult would make him fight he stalked away and left him. Somehow the outburst seemed to lift a great burden off his chest and leave him so he could sleep.

CHAPTER XIV

A RUNNER FROM INSIDE

Lum Martin was about the most unsociable brute on earth. As Sycamore went to bed with him that night he wondered how he had ever endured his presence, to say nothing of throwing in with him as a partner. In the first place he would look down his nose for days and never say a word, and when he did open up it was only to get off something raw. Old Chief Juan was a professional entertainer alongside of him—if he didn't have anything to say he would sit around and look pleasant, anyhow. And another thing about Lum—he was so doggoned dirty! The bed that adorned El Capitan's spare room was an elegant affair—it had clean white sheets, scared up from somewhere, and the craziest crazy-quilt for a counterpane that was ever made by woman's hands—but after old Lum had rolled into it it might as well have been a hog-wallow!

There was no doubt in Sycamore's mind now about the girl—she had been to an Indian school somewhere and learned the white man's ways. Bronco Papagos don't eat off of a table, with a table-cloth—and what do they know about crazy-quilts? That blue dress that she wore, with the white collar, that was the clothes they wore at school—probably hadn't been home long—just long enough to wear out her shoes. Well, she looked right pretty, anyway, and shoes would kind of cripple her up—she couldn't walk so free. But she was sure bashful—never looked up nor said a word, and probably spoke just as good English as he did. Well, well—and Sycamore dropped asleep.

The next day was the longest in his existence. At daylight he was roused by a dog that brushed up against his door, and scratched himself, and whined. Then a baby began to cry somewhere, and the boy that tended a family of goats turned them out of a near-by corral with a great shouting of "*Chiva*" and "*Andale.*" He got up then and went down to look at his horse, which was being kept up in a corral and fed on cut grass from the rocky hillside, and corn that he bought by the basketful. It had been a hard trip on Lum Martin's stolen roan, and Round Valley was a little gaunted, but he was just as fit as ever and Sycamore picked up a rough stick and curried him till he shone. Then he rubbed his nose, scratched him under the chin and fed him a dried-up *tortilla* that he had held out the evening before.

After that it was breakfast, and hating Lum for his table-manners; dinner, when the girl was away somewhere; and supper, when she never so much as looked at him. In the evening they went to bed at dark to save candle-light, and so it wore on till the next day. There was some hope now that the *muchacho* would be coming in from the railroad and Sycamore went out under the shady *ramada* to watch for him. What kind of an ant's nest had he stirred up, anyway, by breaking open that jail? There would be prisoners skipping out in every direction and deputies riding after them and probably a big posse sworn in to chase up fellows like him. And where was it all going to end? That was what interested him.

Well, it would all be told in the newspapers, and after they had read them he and Lum would know what to do next. But the outlaw business didn't look good to him anymore, there was too much chasing around connected with it—and nothing to show for it, anyway. He bent a malevolent glance upon old Lum who was solemnly chewing his cud in the shade—if it hadn't been for him he would still be punching cows up in the Pima country, or riding messenger maybe. That was a nice country, up along the Gila, and lots of Indians too; but none of them like this girl. Those Pima girls all seemed to come short and chunky, but she was as willowy as a rope. She wasn't so black, either—looked like she had some Spanish blood—

"There he comes!" spoke up Lum.

"Where?" demanded Sycamore, breaking a two days' silence.

“Over yonder,” answered Martin, pointing to a film of dust in the north-east pass.

“Humph, supposin’ it should turn out to be a bunch of deputies!”

“Somethin’ in that, too—I’m goin’ to saddle up!”

Sycamore was about to follow when old Captain Juan came to the door of his house and looked out at the moving speck.

“Boy come back,” he said, and sat down quietly to wait. Sycamore lingered a minute, looking at him. Somehow he liked this old buck Indian. He seemed to take life so easy—never gave any loud orders—and yet he was boss of the roost. He was a gamey old cock, too—it was a dirty shame to lie to him, but that is all in the outlaw business. A man can’t turn train-robber and general bad man and expect to have any friends—ump-um, nor to tell the truth, either. So ruminating, Sycamore turned away from the old man and went down to saddle up his horse.

“What you goin’ to do if the runner has picked up the news,” he enquired of Lum, “and tells him who we are? If they’s a reward up he’ll come pretty nigh takin’ us!”

“Not while my gun-hand works,” answered Lum. “But I’m for pullin’ out as soon as we git the stuff. It’s only fourteen miles to the Line.”

“Well, you can pull if you want to, but I’m

goin' to play out my hand. Might as well quit sociable if you can—might need 'im for a friend sometime."

At this a saturnine smile twisted the wry countenance of old Lum, but he needed Sycamore for a friend right then and the evil thought never found speech. Having saddled up and hung their carbines in the scabbard they stayed at the bottom of the hill waiting, but when the messenger came in he passed them at a gallop, Indian fashion, and rode up the hill to the Capitan.

"Come on!" said Sycamore, and spurred along after him so that they arrived at the top together.

The whole village was out to receive the runner, for excitement was too scarce in those parts to allow any of it to slip by, and so they gathered on the crest of the hill, the women throwing the long hair back from their eyes and staring at the bearded strangers, the young men lolling on each other in groups and making gutteral comments and the children and dogs chasing about and getting under foot everywhere. A single glance satisfied Sycamore that the messenger had no idea of their identity. He received them with a grin and, promptly untying a flour-sack from behind his saddle, he handed it over to the Capitan and stood aside expectantly. The chief unrolled the sack deliberately and, squatting down, spread its contents upon the ground. There they were—

the four boxes of cartridges, the big package of tobacco, nine or ten dollars in change—and the newspapers!

Sycamore's first impulse was to grab them up and run his eyes over the headlines, but ceremony is everything with Indians and he waited the old man's good time. Now first the Capitan counted the boxes of cartridges, then he looked at the package of tobacco to see that it had not been broken, then he counted over the money to see how much was left.

"How much for the cartridges?" he demanded in Spanish, and so on, until all was accounted for. Then he spoke sharply to the boy in his own tongue; there was a rapid fire of gutteral words and the messenger in great confusion suddenly remembered the two silk handkerchiefs and produced them from his pocket.

"Ah!" grunted the commander-in-chief and having straightened out the finances he presented the accounting to Sycamore.

"Four box cartridges—four dollars!" he said, flashing up four fingers for the tally, and so on until Sycamore counted the change and announced that it was correct.

"*Bueno*!" declared Chief Juan and motioned him to take his property.

But this was not the end of Indian etiquette as Sycamore had learned it on the Gila—there was still the messenger to be paid.

“How much shall I pay the boy?” he enquired, still holding the money in his hand.

“Five dollars!” answered the chief, after exchanging a few words with the messenger.

“Good!” said Sycamore, and counted it into the runner’s hand. Then by a sign he held him until he could open up the package of tobacco, from which he gave him two sacks, the good-will gift, or *pilón*.

But still the amenities were not satisfied—there was the Capitan to be considered next.

“*Señor Capitan*,” began Sycamore, still holding the money in his hands. “Now that we have all we need and our horses are rested my friend and I will go. I owe you for the food and bed, and for the corn to feed our horses. How much shall I pay?”

“It is nothing, my friend,” replied the old man, with a dignified wave of the hand, “nothing at all—you are very welcome.” And so they argued it back and forth as custom in all lands has decreed.

“Very well, my friend,” said Sycamore at last, as Lum gave him a dig from behind, “I will thank you then for your hospitality—but before I go”—he shook the money together in his hands and measured out a half of it—“your young men and women-folks have worked hard—they have cared for our horses and cooked our meals—take this money and give them a *fiesta*, or let them spend it as they see fit.”

At this all the people began to talk and laugh and shout out comments, for very few strangers came into their midst and fewer yet turned out to be such ready spenders. Thereupon the old chief accepted the money gladly, and Sycamore turned to his purchases. The ammunition he handed back to Lum who was nervously standing guard by the horses and then, while the latter stood aghast at his prodigality, he took a good quarter of their precious tobacco and presented it to Chief Juan.

"For heaven's sake, Syc," he called, "break away and let's be movin'—are you goin' to give away everything you've got?"

"I guess it's mine, ain't it?" rejoined Sycamore, thrusting the remainder of his plunder into the sack. "Keep yore shirt on—what's the matter?"

"Well git down to business—something is liable to drop!"

"Not while we're all happy," responded Sycamore lightly, "come on—them horses will stand—let's find out about the reward!"

As he picked up the newspapers and spread them out before him the chief made a motion of dismissal and his people retired to their own homes—for he was indeed El Capitan. Then he came forward and gazed in breathless silence at the talking sheets of paper. There were six papers of uneven dates and all more or less disheveled, but as he sorted them over a certain scare-head seemed fairly to jump at Sycamore.

He stopped and began to read—slowly and muttering the big words to himself, for he was no scholar—and then he began to exclaim.

"Well—by the holy—jumpin'—Listen to this, Lum! Bravo Juan got loose in that jail delivery and killed two men! He stole the jailer's gun and shot his way to the Line! There's a thousand dollars reward on 'im!"

"Thousan' dollah?" enquired Chief Juan, pointing at the place with his finger.

"*Sí, Señor*—for a Mexican!" answered Sycamore, throwing the paper down and grabbing up another. "Well—listen to this! 'REIGN OF TERROR IN GUN SIGHT COUNTY! Fleeing prisoners strike terror to hearts of ranchmen—country up in arms! It is reported that the legislature now in session will provide for a company of rangers!' "

He threw that paper down and went through the rest, scanning nothing but the head-lines. "Here it is!" he cried as Lum stooped down beside him. " 'ARIZONA RANGERS ORGANIZED! Governor appoints Lee Ruggles Captain—authorized to select twenty men—and four sergeants—pursuit of Brown and Martin will begin at once!' *Aha!*"

Sycamore rose up suddenly and pointed with his finger to a line.

“Well, what is it—what does it say?” fumed Lum, whose keen eyes always blurred when it came to reading fine print.

“Read it!” whispered Sycamore, nudging him in the ribs.

“Aw I can’t read it!” confessed Martin, “what does it say?”

“Full description of us—thousand dollars apiece—”

“Thousan’ dollah?” enquired Chief Juan, reaching out his hand for the paper.

“*Seguro*!” answered Sycamore bluffly, passing it over, “sure! Thousand-dollar reward for one Mexican—name Bravo Juan! You see here—tells what he is like—short man—Mexican *cholo*—small-pox marks on face—knife cut here!” Sycamore drew his finger across his face to illustrate the slash and started to fold up the paper, but the old man motioned him to stop.

“You wait,” he said, clutching fiercely at the corner of the paper, “maybe you tell lie. My girl read—she know!”

He turned and shouted her name in Papago and instantly—almost too instantly—the girl of Sycamore’s dreams stepped forth from behind the brush screen.

“Ah-Nh!” said the old man, beckoning her sternly to his side, “you read this!”

He pointed directly to the description of

Sycamore Brown—wanted for breaking open the Gun Sight jail—and as she cleared her throat to speak Lum Martin swung quietly up on his horse. But Sycamore only stood his ground, for he had sworn to play out his hand. But the fine print seemed to blur her eyes too, for after she had read a line she stopped and looked up at Sycamore.

"What say?" demanded her father, pointing peremptorily at the place, "you tell me—in Spanish!"

" 'One thousand dollars Reward!' " read the girl, and then in hesitating, school-girl lisp she continued, "For one Mexican named Bravo Juan—a short man—"

"Small-pox?" demanded Chief Juan, indicating spots on his face with his finger.

"Yes," she answered, and Sycamore swung up on his horse. The girl's intentions were good, but actors are born, not made.

"You can keep the paper," he said, "but I must go. *Adios*, Señor Capitan! *Adios*, Señorita!"

He swung his horse to follow Lum, who had one hand hooked into his belt, but for all his haste he did not forget the silk handkerchiefs. He had intended to give one to old Chief Juan as a gift of friendship, and keep the other himself—but some things are changed by the fates.

"Many thanks, my friend," he said, speaking

apparently to the amazed Capitan. But when the red silk token left his hand the wind of his flight seemed to draw it aside and it fell at the girl's brown feet.

CHAPTER XV
BULLION

With a thousand dollars reward on their heads and Lee Ruggles organizing a company of rangers it did not require a cloud of dust on the horizon to send Sycamore and Lum into Mexico. Lee Ruggles had been a sergeant in the Texas Rangers, with a record for getting his man, and he could find some more just like him to make life precarious for them in Arizona. Also a thousand dollars is a lot of money, for which many a man will kill his best friend or take a chance himself. No, there was nothing to do now but to lose themselves in Old Mexico and wait for the hunt to pass.

There were rangers in Sonora too—the dreaded *rurales*—but they were few and far between, and what was a *rural* or two anyway? Had they not matched themselves against two of them at Cananea and put them on their backs? Yes indeed, and got away with their guns too—though that would only swell the count against them if they ever happened to get caught. But that they would never do—no, they promised themselves to shoot it out and die in the last ditch fighting, rather than surrender now. So they rode down through

Sonora, avoiding the towns and highways; and so hardy had the Americans been who had gone before them that no man tried to stop them or to find out whence they came.

They were *Americanos*, that was all, on their way and with money to buy—though that made little difference with the simple-minded peons. If there was food in the hut it was given them to eat; and if they had money, then they could pay for it. But even such hospitality as this—where poor, half-starved Indian peasants freely shared their slender hoard—even such hospitality became a little monotonous when it was nothing but corn *tortillas* and beans. A good beef-steak with a quart of coffee was more to their way of thinking, and when Sycamore let his mind dwell upon the money he had taken—the big sacks crammed and jammed with it, and silver all over the floor—and then upon all the material things that those sacks of money would buy he fell to cursing his luck and calling for a halt. But Lum was determined to stay hid and they were almost to Hermosillo before Sycamore went on a strike.

"Lum," he said, after a peculiarly villainous meal at an Indian's *jacal*, "I ain't goin' another day south—this Mexican grub is killin' me. Them *tortillas* would founder a mule—it's just like eatin' paper off the wall. So either I quit you right now or we turn east and then hit for the Line."

"Yes," sneered Martin, whose disposition was not improving any under the strain, "you'll hit for the Line, all right; and then you'll come hittin' back again—if somebody don't shoot yore fool head off. What's the matter with you—can't you stand a little hard eatin'?"

"Sure, if they's any sense to it—but what's the use of gittin' so far from the Line? These people down here is nothin' but plain Injuns—they can't even talk Mexican—and when it comes to cookin', well, I never knowed a round-up cook that could beat 'em when it comes to spoilin' good grub! A two-bit meal at a Chinese restaurant would be like dreamin' you was in heaven, after this, and I'm goin' to hit back towards my old chuck-line and git a square. Just because we butted into the Jockey Club at Cananea and got into trouble with them *rurales* is no sign we can't drop into some of them minin' camps without gittin' nabbed. And I'm gittin' so dam' tired of this crawlin' around, and hidin' out, and doin' nothin' that I don't care much what happens to me as long as I git some grub and a clean shirt. So let's figure out what we want to do and then go ahead and do it!"

"Well," said Lum, "you're always huntin' for trouble and excitement—what's the matter with robbin' that Tecolote mine then?"

This was Lum's one fixed idea now, when he wasn't hell-bent for the interior of Mexico, but

Sycamore had had enough and would not agree to it. The mine which so tempted Lum was hid away in a little range of mountains, half way between Cananea and the Line, and it sent out a shipment of gold every week—a big one, convoyed by a guard and two *rurales.* As Martin himself had once acted as this guard he knew all the details of the shipment, and he knew the very place where it ought to be held up in order to make a clean get-away. This was a pile of rocks at the mouth of the cañon, behind which they would be perfectly safe—but it wasn't the hold-up that worried Sycamore, it was getting into trouble with the *rurales.* Having been run out of Arizona by the mere rumor of the rangers he was loath to outlaw himself in Mexico—especially as they had a small fortune in bills buried somewhere in the vicinity of Hackamore.

"What d'ye want to rob that mine for?" he demanded petulantly. "Ain't we got troubles enough on our hands without gittin' them rurales after us?"

Lum smiled.

"I thought you was tired of cra-awlin' around and do-in' nawthin'," he drawled sarcastically. "Why don't you be a sport—or quit the game?"

"Well, I reckon I can stan' it if you can!" retorted Sycamore hotly. "Come on then, and see which of us weakens first!"

He whirled his horse in his tracks and headed

north-east, and a week's ride brought them in sight of Tecolote. It was a month and more now since they had fled from San Ignacio and more than once he regretted that he had ever crossed the Line. The desert was his stronghold—his home since he was a child. He knew it as the Indians knew it—where the water lay and how the trails led out and when it was safe to cross. Mounted on his swift horse, Round Valley, he could distance the best valley horse that the rangers could ever find—yes, he need have no fear, if the Indians would be his friends. But all his plans were spoiled by Lum, who clung to him like a burr. More than once he had deliberately quarreled with him—for he was crazy to get free—but no affront seemed to offend him, and now he was having his way again. Somehow, in one way or other, Lum always had his way—and he always got folks into trouble.

"Well, there's yore mountain," observed Sycamore, as they halted on a rise of ground and looked out across the grassy plain. "Where's yore mine at and how're you goin' to work it?"

"It's on the fur side," motioned Lum. "We'll watch the cañon till we see the rurales go up and then lay for 'em in the mornin'."

"And what'll we live on meanwhile? Supposen to-day should be Sunday—we don't know what day it is—and supposen the dam' pack-train went down yesterday—what're we goin' to chew on while we're watchin' from them peaks?"

"Say," said Martin, "if you're goin' to begin beefin' already we might jest as well cut this out!"

"All right," assented Sycamore, "that suits me down to the ground. Let's slip into one of them minin' camps over by Cananea and buy a little tobacco."

"Huh! What you goin' to buy it with—another one of them twenties?"

"Well, I don't know why not! Supposen you'd hold up that pack-train and git ten thousand in gold—you couldn't buy nothin' with that, could you?"

"Oh, dam' a kid, anyway!" grumbled Lum. "You're always kickin' about somethin'—what yuh want to do?"

"Well," began Sycamore, and there he stopped. He looked over to the east where Cananea threw its smelter smoke against the sky—and remembered the *rurales*; he looked to the north and west, where the mountains of Papaguería stood out like picked gun-sights along the horizon, but the whole country might be full of rangers by now, and there was a thousand dollars on their heads. "Oh, hell," he said at last, "let's rob the mine—but what you goin' to do then?"

"When we get that bullion," explained Lum, "we'll have somethin' to buy with. People will think we're prospectors and they'll be no questions asked. Then we can go over into Chihuahua and live like kings for a while."

"Ah," commented Sycamore, "that sounds more like. Come ahead then, let's pull this job off quick."

They pulled it off quick. The second day after they began their watch the pack-train came up loaded from Cananea, and with it two *rurales*. On the next morning it came tinkling down again, the *aparejos* empty and the bell-mare stepping off free. Then as the led-mule laden with the treasure swayed past their ledge of rocks a masked man leapt down in front of her and covered the guards with his carbine.

"Throw up your hands!" he cried in Spanish, and as the *rurales* rose up in their stirrups the shadow of another man fell across their path and they beheld Lum Martin, a pistol in each hand.

"Throw up your hands, you sons of dogs," he snarled, "or I'll send you both to hell!"

There was something in his harsh voice that convinced them that he meant it, and they surrendered before they knew why. A *rural* is supposed to fight—and given a chance he will—but Lum was not the kind that give chances—he would have killed them before they could draw.

"Now onbuckle your guns and let them drop in the road," he said, and inside of a minute he had the entire party lined up along the rocky trail while the pack-train went on untended.

Meanwhile Sycamore was busy with the led-mule, slashing the taut lariats with his knife and then dumping the whole pack into the dirt. It fell with a thump that was good to hear—a thump and a rumble—and the iron-bound treasure box came tumbling out of its wrappings.

Yes, there it was, a small solid box, held shut by a heavy padlock. Sycamore lifted it and felt the weight of gold; he shook it and heard the bars chunk together—then he raised a big rock and slammed it down on the padlock. Three times he returned to the assault—but it would not yield.

"Shoot it off!" growled Lum, whose prisoners were getting restless, and Sycamore grabbed up his high-powered carbine, backed off and blew the lock to pieces. Then he tore off the latch, threw back the cover and laid bare the precious ingots. There was the gold, seven bars of it, just as the assayer had cast them after each day's clean-up—some bigger than others but each one heavier than lead.

Without a word he divided them swiftly—three heavy ones against four lighter ones—and wrapped each parcel in a sack. The canvas pack-cover served for outer wrappings; he bound the ingots together with lengths of lariat and swung them up on his shoulder. It was a heavy weight—fifty pounds at least—and he grinned beneath his mask as he thought of all that gold.

"All right, Bill," he called to Lum, and while

Martin sent the prisoners away with a stern warning he scurried back to the horses. By the aid of the long canvas wrappings he bound each bundle securely behind the saddles, and then they were up and away. They did not hurry, for it was not necessary yet. The better to cut off pursuit they had taken all the horses and left the *rurales* afoot; and so, with the riderless horses running before them they ambled off towards the Line, loaded down with the spoils of war. It was a clean get-away, with no pursuit, and midway in the grassy plain they threw away the *rurales*' guns and left their loose mounts standing.

Twice now they had met those Mexican man-killers and twice they had come off with their guns—and as they rode on their way they laughed. A Texas Ranger would have fought them with rocks before he would have thrown up his hands, but the Mexicans—well, they were different—they were not hired to get killed. But as they drew near the Line they began to wonder about Lee Ruggles, and whether he was on their trail, though Martin was so swollen with pride that he swore he did not care. Their belts still bulged with the ammunition that Sycamore had bought, and as for rangers—well, they might have been rangers themselves if they had stayed with their former job!

It was mid-afternoon when they sighted the monuments, and not a man in sight. There were cattle grazing about on the plain and the trail showed a shod horse's track, but the country before them was vacant, where before it had given up men. Sycamore had a distinct memory of the hawk-eyed Texan who had ridden in on them there—if he should come after them again with his bunch of cowboys he might have something to show for his trouble, since a horse cannot gallop far weighed down with gold.

"Say, Lum," he said as they turned off towards the west, "what're we goin' to do with this boodle? If anybody should happen to take after us we'd have to unload—or fight!"

"Jest leave that to me," suggested Lum, who had suddenly become important and paternal again, "there's an old ranch right square on the Line down here—we can talk it over there."

They rode on in silence then, for Sycamore did not like this "leave-it-to-me" pose, and as he followed along behind he muttered to himself and wondered what Lum thought he was going to do. It was well along towards sun-down when they reached the ranch, a tumble-down group of adobe buildings hid away in the bottom of a rocky cañon not a hundred yards south of the Line. Evidently the man who had lived there had had something on his mind, for he had set a white stake to the north to show where Old Mexico began—and that he was on the safe side of the Line. Who he was or what had become of him they did not know; but the place suited them, for the hills were to the north of them and they could look out over the rolling plains and keep watch for their friends, the *rurales.*

"Now I'll tell you what we'll do," said Lum, as soon as they had unbridled their horses and staked them out to feed. "We'll jest take this gold out somewhere and hide it—and then we'll lay low for a while."

"Huh!" grunted Sycamore, disapproving on general principles, but as he could think up no valid objection he proceeded to untie his bundle. "All right," he grumbled, "but let's have a look at it first—I never even got to see that other boodle."

He unwrapped the gold as he spoke and spread it on the canvas before them—seven gleaming ingots with the marks of the rough casting still upon them—and as they lay there he hefted them one by one and gloated over their weight.

"By Joe, but that's a heavy boy!" he cried, picking up the biggest bar. "Jest take ahold of it, Lum, and see how it weighs f'r its size."

"Aw, quit yore foolin'!" exclaimed Lum, impatiently snatching it away from him and throwing it back in the pile, "first thing we know a bunch of rurales will hop in on us and find us playin' like a couple o' kids. Here, wrop them all up together and come arunnin' while I look out a place to plant 'em!"

He seized the broken remnant of a shovel that some camper had left by the fire and hurried off up the gulch, but Sycamore followed reluctantly. This was not what he had expected. And Lum was trying to get some advantage of him—he could feel it in his bones. All this hurry—all this bustle and bossing around—it was exactly the same as when they had robbed the train. Of course it was all right to bury the boodle, but why not divide it first and let each one bury his own? Sure! Why not? Wasn't it fair—wasn't it just the same? And suppose they did bury it all in one hole—what was to hinder old Lum from coming back and digging up the whole cache? And burying it somewheres else? Sure! That was his game!

"Say, Lum," began Sycamore as the enormity of the deceit came over him, "what's the matter with dividin' this up, and each man bury his own?"

Lum laid down his shovel and looked at him.

"What's eatin' you now?" he enquired.

"Oh, nothin'—only we got to divvy up sometime!"

"Sure! But let's pick a time when the rurales ain't right on top of us!"

He took up the shovel and went to digging as if the matter was settled, but Sycamore was not so easily put off. The memory of other times when Lum had done this same thing came over him and his blood was hot with revolt.

"*I* don't see no rurales," he grumbled looking out along the horizon. "And I'm goin' to have my share!" he burst out, throwing the gold down and tearing away the covers.

"Oh, you are, are you?" said Lum quietly.

"Yes I am!" answered Sycamore defiantly. "I'm tired of bein' treated like a kid. I guess if I'm good enough to do all the hard work I'm good enough to git my share!"

"When did you ever do any hard work?" enquired Lum coldly.

"When!" cried Sycamore in a passion. "Why dam' yore black heart, didn't I blow up that express car and git away with the money? Didn't Jack and me do all the work while you was playin' cards in town? You took that money and got away with it and God knows if I'll ever git a cent of it, but they's one thing I want to tell you right now—I'm goin' to git my half of this if I have to fight for it!"

He stepped back as he spoke and his hand dropped down to his belt—but Lum only pretended to laugh.

"Well, sho, sho, boy," he said, chuckling and dropping back to his cracker speech, "what yuh gittin' mad about? Who said you couldn't have yore half? But how're you goin' to divvy? There's seven of 'em!"

"All right," growled Sycamore, still watching him suspiciously, "I don't care how we divvy as long as I git a whack. If you want the three big ones you can have 'em—if you don't you can have the four little ones!"

"Umm," purred Lum, still chuckling to himself, "you're gittin' generous—make a good poker player!" He sorted the gold bars out deftly—hefted them—and took the big bars. "All right, pardner," he said, "fly to it. Now what yuh goin' to do?"

"I'm goin' to take this gold off and bury it," answered Sycamore, wrapping it up warily with one hand. "And I'll tell you right now," he added, "I don't want nobody snoopin' round!"

CHAPTER XVI

ALL KINDS OF TROUBLE

As Sycamore backed away with his treasure he watched Lum as one dog watches another when he is making off with a bone. Now that the breach had come he was afraid of Martin, for he knew what he was capable of doing. In a movement so quick that the eye could hardly see it he might draw and shoot him dead. Not that he expected a gun-play, but his fighting instincts rose up within him and warned him to beware. Sycamore had never forgotten that time when he had asked where Jack was and Martin had showed his hand. Lum had needed him, up to now; but he might want the bullion worse. Certain he was that his partner had been using him, as a boss hobo uses his "kid"—but this time the work was too raw.

At the first turn of the rough cañon he halted and stood waiting and, taking that for a signal to move, Lum gathered up his treasure and started the other way. When he had disappeared Sycamore waited a minute—then he turned and ran in a mad frenzy to hide his gold—to keep it away from Lum. He thought of Martin trailing him, the next day or the next week, marking down each foot-print, looking under every rock and prowling, prowling, until he found the cache. Sooner or later they would quit each other now—and then Lum would make a point for his gold. But how to fool him, how to circumvent him—that was the question. If he buried it in the sand the fresh earth would betray him, and among the rocks—well, the rocks were best.

The bottom of the narrow cañon was a dry watercourse, full of slippery ledges, and pot-holes where past torrents had rushed and rumbled. On every ledge Sycamore paused and scanned the hillside for his rock—one that he could lift and then put back into place—and he kept on till he found it. Then he set it gently aside, opened his jack-knife, and dug a hole in its bed. Every particle of dirt as he scooped it out was saved and stored in his hat—he laid the ingots in the hole side by side, then changed his mind and took out one. Once more he lifted the rock and restored it to its bed—stood off and looked at it, and shifted it a little more. Then when it was fitted to a nicety he located it by a dozen landmarks and tiptoed back to the gulch.

An Apache scout, trailing him up the cañon, would scarcely know he had turned aside, for the solid rock did not show his tracks. Further up the gulch he hid the hatful of dirt and then with his tongue in his cheek he wrapped four flat rocks in the canvas and buried them deep in the sand. This was for old Lum's benefit, if he should try to steal his cache; and in order to show a little cheap woodcraft he combed the ground over with a piece of brush and covered the place with leaves. It was nicely done, but Lum would find it—trust him for that—for it lay at the end of the trail.

With a grin for his own sagacity Sycamore picked up his bar of gold and went loping off down the cañon. When a man's life depends on his horse he is likely to be uneasy away from him, and Lum was not a very trustworthy partner. It was curious about Lum—the minute he ceased to trust him he remembered a hundred of his treacherous deeds, and his mind was filled with fears. He knew now—what Sam Slocum had told him long before—that Lum had never intended to let him share their hidden treasure. First he had got rid of Jack Haines—left him to rot in jail—and now it had come his turn. And who could doubt, if it came that way, but that Lum would leave him for the crows!

At the mouth of the cañon Sycamore peered out fearfully, his gold hid away in his pocket and the other hand on his gun, but Lum had not come in from his burying. It was a chance for Sycamore to get to his horse and he was not slow to take it—then he slipped the bar of gold into his saddle-bags and tightened up his cinch for a ride. Something was likely to drop any time now, and it was just as well to play safe. Something to eat now, and he was ready for anything—he untied their sack of jerked beef and divided it half and half.

At this point Lum Martin came suddenly into view.

"Here, what you doin'?" he demanded as he saw Sycamore chewing on some meat, "robbin' the grub agin'?"

"Never mind," returned Sycamore, chewing defiantly at his jerky. "I divided that meat up, too—I reckon a man can eat his own grub, can't he?"

He turned as he spoke and began to tie the bundle on his saddle, and instantly Martin changed his tactics.

"What's the matter with you, Syc?" he complained. "What's come over you all at once? Don't git mad over nothin'—you ain't goin' to quit me, are you?"

"That's what!" answered Sycamore, swinging up on his horse and hitching his pistol to the front. He turned Round Valley towards the west, but Martin leapt forward with an oath.

"Here!" he raged, laying his hand on the bridle-rein, "whar d'yuh think y're goin'?"

"Let go that rein!" answered Sycamore his voice quavering with sudden passion, "let go or—" he dropped his hand to his gun and Lum instantly let go his hold. "Now you leave me alone!" menaced Sycamore, reining his horse away. "I ain't huntin' for trouble, but don't you try to run it over me, Lum Martin, or I'll kill you as sure as hell!"

"*I* ain't tryin' to run it over you!" protested Lum, throwing out his hands in appeal. "When did I ever make any such play? You must be crazy, Syc—I ain't got nothin' ag'inst yuh!"

"Ughr!" sneered Sycamore over his shoulder. "I'm glad to hear it. You can keep that stuff you stole!"

"What stuff?" cried Martin following after him.

Sycamore stopped his horse and looked back.

"The stuff you got from me and Jack," he said. "I know you aim to beat us out of it!"

"It's a dam' lie!" raged Lum. "I do not!"

"Well, where's it buried, then?" challenged Sycamore, swinging around and facing him. "It's all right for you to talk, Lum Martin, but I know you're tryin' to do me! You may think I'm a kid, but I cut my eye-teeth some time ago, when I see how you ditched Jack Haines. No, sir! If you want any more trains robbed you'll have to do it yoreself! To hell with ye—I've got enough!"

"Well, go on then!" flared back Lum. "Go on and report to yore boss! How do I know you ain't a stool-pigeon, out workin' for ol' Sam Slocum?"

"What?" cried Sycamore, spurring angrily back and facing him. "What's that you say?"

"I say you're a stool-pigeon!" screamed Lum, shaking his fist and dancing, "a stool-pigeon!

Oh, you can look, but I knowed you—I knowed you the first time you come in! That was pretty smooth—breakin' open the jail and lettin' me out—but I noticed the first thing you asked me—you wanted to know where that boodle was hid! That's Sam Slocum's game, the crooked dog, but you can't make a monkey out of me—I've done that kind of work myself!"

For a minute or more Sycamore sat his horse and listened, vaguely wondering if Lum had gone crazy. His simple mind was baffled by the turmoil and the raging—all he knew was that Martin still accused him of being a stool-pigeon—the rest went by like a fog.

"Hey!" he yelled, breaking in on the jarring clamor, "what're you talkin' about, anyway?"

"I'm atalkin' about *you!*" shouted Martin.

"Well, key down then—I can hear you—and everybody else within five miles! Keep yore shirt on—do you want to call the rurales?"

At the word the light of reason came back into Lum Martin's eyes and he looked down, almost ashamed. Months of hating and brooding, months of base scheming and unreasoning malevolence had turned him upon himself until he was almost insane. But now that he had shouted it out, now that he had expressed his puny suspicions and had been answered by an uncomprehending stare, the unworthiness of his attitude came over him and he felt suddenly rebuked.

"Aw, let it go!" he exclaimed, half apologetically. "What's the difference? They ain't no use quarrelin' about it!"

"Well, if you think you can call me a stool-pigeon," burst out Sycamore in his turn, "and get away with it, you're mistaken—that's all I got to say! It's mighty funny, after all I've done for you, if I can't ask for my share of the boodle without havin' to pull off a gun-play! You must think I'm a good thing, the way you try to work me. You take the whole business on that first hold-up and then git mad because I want my half of this. And then on top of that you call me a stool-pigeon!

"Didn't I hold up the jail and turn you loose? Didn't I refuse to testify ag'inst you and keep you from goin' to the pen? Well, then, I want you to take that back—don't you call me no stool-pigeon—"

"Oh, that's all right, Syc," broke in Martin soothingly. "Don't hold every little thing ag'inst a feller. I was excited, can't you see, and I didn't know what I said. Git down, and come on over here—I know you're on the square!"

"Aw—" began Sycamore, and then he flung down off his horse, "Now lookee here, Lum," he said, "they's no use talkin' around about this—either you tell me where that Hackamore boodle is buried and let me in on the deal, or I quit you and quit you cold! Now which'll it be?"

For a moment Lum Martin stood irresolute,

looking at him. He needed Sycamore for a partner. More than that, he wanted him where he could watch him. At the same time he wanted to keep that secret to himself. But how could Sycamore know—? A crafty look came into his eyes and he answered softly, in that soothing tone which he used when he spoke with intent to deceive.

"Come on over here by the house," he said. "Let's sit down and have something to eat—and while we're eatin' I'll tell you where it is."

Already the sun had set behind the mountains; the soft evening glow was in the air and the hills stood out strongly against the sky. It was a time for peace, not for strife, and Sycamore dropped his bridle-reins and slumped down against the mud wall which once had been part of a house. Then each of them drew out a strip of dried meat and fell to paring morsels off the end, and as they cut and chewed, old Lum began to talk. He explained his reasons for silence—the detectives were after them and one man was safer than three. He alluded to Sycamore's betrayal—how he had been taken in by Sam Slocum and his gang—and his fear that it might happen again. Then he swore Sycamore never to tell—nor to visit the place without him—and told him where the treasure was hid. It was all very mysterious, but whether the boodle was where he said it was is another question.

The lazy sunset glow was still in the air—there was just light enough to show a man his gun-sights—when suddenly in the midst of their confidences they heard a rock scrape on the hill.

"What's that?" whispered Sycamore, craning his neck to look, but Lum who sat where he could see merely touched him and pointed to his carbine. Without a word Sycamore handed it over to him—and then he stayed his arm. Silhouetted against the northern sky he saw the burly figure of a horseman—it was Dillon, the Gun Sight sheriff, and he had a gun in his hand.

"He hasn't seen us," breathed Sycamore. "Let's git to our horses and run!"

"Nope—he'd wing us," answered Lum, and took a quick aim across his knee.

Bang! spoke out the gun, and the red flame leapt out against the twilight. For a moment they sat breathless, looking. The man was gone and his horse was running away. At that moment they rose up, and at the same instant a rifle spoke out on the hillside—and then another—and then Dillon's! They answered back, shooting as they ran for their horses, but the bullets seemed to come in on them like a shower. A sudden blow sent Sycamore on his face—he looked up and saw Lum go down—then as the rush of feet sounded near him he leapt up and made for his horse.

"Hey, Baby! Hey, Baby!" he called, and Round

Valley never flinched. The blood was running down his sleeve as he swung up into the saddle and his right arm felt numb and weak, but he landed with his spurs in action and Round Valley was off in great bounds. Then the shots began again—the sullen bang of six-shooters and the rattle of magazine rifles—and the bullets smashed through the bushes. There was a shouting and a scamper of horses and a long run out across the plain, until at last the night fell about them and Round Valley came to a halt. As he stood trembling in the darkness Sycamore dropped off and felt his horse over for a wound—then listened for the sound of pursuit while he hung his arm in a sling.

It ached, that arm, and the riding irked it, though the wound was in his back. Somehow as he ran a bullet had caught him stooping, ripped up his shirt and passed through the heavy muscles of his shoulder, coming out to the right of his neck. That was the blow he had felt—then the blood had welled out, the bullet-slit had closed, and now it was his arm that hurt. But it would have to keep on hurting, for there were deputies behind him, and at dawn they would pick up his trail.

He lingered a while, to get his bearings and decide what was best to do, and at last he turned to the west. The memory of San Ignacio, far away, came back to him, and of the Capitan, and the girl in blue. There was a thousand dollars on his head and he was wanted on both sides of the Line—but if they would not befriend him, nobody would, and he was lost for sure.

CHAPTER XVII

IN THE CITY OF REFUGE

Between the watchers by day and the dogs at night no man ever got within a mile of San Ignacio without his presence being known. With Sycamore Brown it was ten miles, for he came in the daytime, and at five they recognized his horse. Then there was a great running to and fro, a mustering of arms and sending away of women and children, for Chief Juan knew now who his guest had been and how he had been deceived. So, like prairie-dogs on their mound, these wild children of the desert scampered back and forth; and when his men were well placed the Capitan sat down to wait.

As for Sycamore he saw none of it, for his wounds were sore and the fever was in his brain. His eyes looked back when they opened at all and he lopped down in the saddle while Round Valley picked out his own trail. Three days of riding across the desert, three nights of restless sleeping and hitting the trail at dawn, and the rider was ready to drop; but Round Valley was still smooth and sturdy and every time he passed a bunch of desert grass he reached down and grabbed a bite. It was for that purpose that Sycamore had taken off his bridle and left him with nothing but a rawhide halter on his nose, for feed is short by the water-holes and he dared not turn him loose at night. But the long days were pleasant to Round Valley—he forgot the spurs and hurried from grassy flat to mesquite browse; and if there were grain-fed horses behind him they were weak and gaunt, for there was nothing for such as they to eat.

At the well-hole Round Valley drank his fill, but Sycamore was too weak to dismount and rode on till they topped the hill.

"*Camastamos*, *amigo*," he said to the chief, and Capitan Juan gazed at him coldly.

"Where you come from?" he demanded abruptly.

"*Muy lejos*—very far!" answered Sycamore with a weary droop. "I am hurt, Capitan—shot in the back—and the flies follow me like a torn sheep. But take me in and feed me, for I am a good man. *Sí*, *Señor*, very good—I am worth a thousand dollars to those who follow behind."

He paused and wet his lips, waiting, but El Capitan did not speak. His eyes scanned the sick man over, from his boots that were getting worn to his greasy shirt and unkempt beard—and then it came back to the tied-up arm and the handkerchief that served for a sling. It was a red one—red silk—and the Capitan had its mate—a gift of friendship.

"Here, *muchachos*!" he called at last, and his young men came running out. "Take this man from his horse," he said, "and put him in my house—and to-night we will have a council." So it was that Sycamore found a place to rest his head, and when they had given him a big drink of water thickened with the bitter-sweet mesquite meal he dropped off to sleep, satisfied to abide his fate.

He was awakened at last by the sound of Chief Juan talking in a loud and sonorous voice; and as his Indian talk became more and more oratorical he realized that he was making a speech. The village council was in session in the "town hall" and as the debate went on from slow and measured speech to arguments and chorused shouts it suddenly occurred to him that he was probably the object of their contention, since his fate was in their hands. He roused up now and listened intently and from the tumult of their Papago he suddenly picked out the Mexican word "*Huero*"—white, or light-complexioned. That was the name they had applied to him the first day he came among them. Again and again he heard it spoken, and suddenly the Spanish phrase "*mil pesos*"—thousand dollars—struck out from the torrent of their vehemence.

So that was it—they were talking about that reward, and whether to give him up. Higher and higher raged the strife, for Indians do not spare each other in the council; and then suddenly old Chief Juan spoke out again, at first slowly, then with animation, then rising to a wild flight of eloquence which brought out a chorus of applause. A rapid-fire of questions followed, all answered by the Capitan, and then with a rumble of comment the council broke up and dispersed.

But now another argument rose up in the old chief's house—women's voices, and the Capitan answering back. It was the women-folks, back from their hiding, and as he listened through the adobe wall Sycamore was sure that he heard the girl. Then of a sudden their voices drew nearer and Capitan Juan opened his door. A tallow candle held in his hand revealed the grim wrinkles that lined his face, but he gazed upon Sycamore kindly, though he scowled at those behind.

"Did my young men put medicine on your hurt?" he asked, and when Sycamore answered "No" he frowned.

"Let me see it!" he said, and at the sight of the festering wound there were exclamations from both the women.

"Oh, it is too bad!" cried the girl, in Spanish; and the wrinkled old squaw who was with her spoke pityingly in her own tongue.

"Hunh!" grunted Chief Juan, looking at it closer. "When you get shot?"

“Three days ago!” said Sycamore and fixed his eyes on the girl.

“Let me look at it!” she said in English, the precise English of schools and books. “I have studied to be a nurse—perhaps I can help you.” She turned the torn shirt aside and gazed long at the bullet-holes and the swollen and angry flesh between them; then she rolled up the sleeves of her dress and spoke rapidly to the woman and to her father.

“My father will take off that dirty shirt,” she said at last, “and I will go get some hot water.”

“Yore girl speaks awful good English,” remarked Sycamore, hoping to please his host, but the grim old chief only grunted and ripped up his shirt with a knife.

“My daughter too smart,” he said in Spanish. “She no like Indian ways. No like Indian house—Indian Country—nothing! Indian schools—*no good!*”

He gave a vicious jerk with his knife and Sycamore almost fainted from the pain, though he pretended that it did not hurt. To a man who had followed Geronimo his wound was probably a mere scratch; but it hurt him, all the same, and he was glad when the girl came back.

Wherever it was that she had studied nursing they had taught her to be hygienically clean. First she took his filthy shirt away and laid out one of her father’s best; then she poured a few drops of medicine into the hot water and as she began to bathe his hurts Sycamore recognized the familiar odor of carbolic.

"That's good stuff," he remarked, as the old chief went out in disgust. "Used it on a horse once."

"Ah yes," answered the girl with a patient smile, "it is good—but not for everything! I have no medicine here—no peroxide of hydrogen—no listerine—no surgical dressings—nothing. It is not much use to know what to do, unless you have something to work with."

At this first start at a conversation she seemed suddenly to forget her reserve and while the old woman, who acted the part of duenna, squatted down and watched her intently she poured out the story of her woes.

"We had such a good hospital at the school where I went," she sighed. "Everything was white—and clean—and the doctors were very kind. They said I would make a fine nurse. My chum is a trained nurse now—she gets twenty-five dollars a week—but I could not finish my course. My father told me to come home. There are sick people here too, but I have no medicine—nothing but this bottle of carbolic.

"I will have to open this wound," she broke off, touching the hurt gently with her finger-tips. "It has closed too soon. After it has drained for a few days it will heal from within."

“All right,” answered Sycamore, “you’re the doctor!” But when she went out for a knife he gazed after her in awe. What kind of an Indian was this—and what was peroxide of hydrogen, anyhow? And those big words! It was the kind of talk he had heard a Boston school-marm use when he was learning his A B Cs up on the Gila.

“Say,” he said, when she came back, “excuse me, but where was this school you went to—up on the Heely? I come from near there myself!”

But he never got to ask her if she knew Jim McGrew, the Chula Vista store-keeper.

“You musn’t talk too much, and get excited,” she said, moving him gently about on the bed. “Now hold still—it will hurt a little—and I will talk to you by-and-by.”

With a quick twitch she opened up the wound and as the blood and corruption ran out she soothed him with comforting words—very soft and pleasant, but long, awfully long. Then for a long time she bathed the place, and when Sycamore woke up from a doze there was a bandage across his shoulder and the room was dark and still. He stared a while at the blank nothingness, shifted his sore arm, sighed and dropped off to sleep. Somehow after all his riding and fighting it was good to have someone taking care of him again, the way his mother used to do. He was tired of Lum Martin and the men he had run with—weary of the stealing and robbing, and the jockeying in which he always got left—yes, it seemed as if this old Indian and his girl were the only real friends he had. Perhaps he was cut out to be an Indian himself, after all, for the white man's ways were too many for him.

But there is no rest for the wicked, once the Arizona Rangers get on their trail—no matter how good they are in their sleep. The morning after Lum Martin was taken two men set out after Sycamore and, not having any dust to go by, they followed his horse's tracks. The desert was new to both of them; but they had their orders, and there was five hundred dollars apiece in it if they won. So they rode on, a day's march behind him, and at noon the Capitan saw their dust. Then instantly he sent his young men flying to bring up the horses and just as Sycamore was being bathed and bandaged and fed good things by hand the old man burst into his sick-room and ordered him to get up and ride.

"White men come!" he cried, "far away. Pretty soon come near—you go off now."

"Go where?" enquired Sycamore, trying vainly to rise.

"My boys go—bring horse. Pretty soon they come back—you go with them."

"*Stawano*," moaned the sick man, motioning away his nurse, "you saddle my horse—but I can't go very far."

He sat up in bed then, but his strength had

left him—he knew he was sure to get caught.

"*No, amigo,*" he said, as the old chief urged him, "I cannot ride to-day. But bring me my rifle—and leave the door open—"

"No, no!" cried the girl, putting her hands against him, "you must not fight and hurt yourself! I will hide you here and my father will protect you—he will tell them you have gone away!"

"No good!" grunted Chief Juan. "They will search the houses—and Indians no fight white men!"

"That's all right," sighed Sycamore, sinking slowly back on his pillow. "You bring me my guns. I got to take a chance," he added, to the girl. Then he lay there for a while, thinking, and finally he called in the old man.

"*Amigo,*" he said, "those men are officers. Perhaps if you give me up they will pay you a thousand dollars!"

"Hunh!" grunted the Capitan, gazing at him grimly.

"And then again, maybe they won't, eh? They may keep it for themselves, no?"

"*Sí, Señor,*" assented the Chief Juan with a wise nod. He had known of such things before.

"Very well," said Sycamore, "what will you do? Will you give me up?"

For a long time the old war captain looked

out across the shimmering plain where two dark spots appeared below the horizon.

"No, my friend," he said at last. "I think you are a good man—and I will hide you. But listen—I have a plan—*muy coyote*! I mount one of my young men upon your horse—he ride west. Officer follow—he ride again. Pretty soon—officer lost. Then boy bring horse back. Now come these men—come to my house. 'Man gone!' I tell them. Is it good?"

"*Sí*, *Señor*," assented Sycamore, "*muy coyote*! But tell the boy not to beat my horse—and if he brings him home fat I will pay him more."

Sycamore lay quiet now, thinking of the ordeal to come; then he roused up suddenly—he had forgotten the bar of gold!

"Say," he called to the girl, who was watching outside the door, "ask your father to bring me my saddle-bags for a minute, will you?"

The Capitan came in hurriedly, the saddle-bags in his hand.

"Here they are, *Señor*," he said, "just as they were given to me! But the boy is waiting to go!"

"One moment!" responded Sycamore, and dove down to the bottom of the sack. Yes, it was still there—the golden-yellow wedge—and he gazed upon it lovingly while the old man took back the saddle-bags and sent the boy on his way.

"*Señor Capitan*," he said, as the old chief returned. "These men who are coming may kill me or take me away to jail—who knows? Here is a bar of gold. Take care of it for me—and if I should not return accept it as a gift of friendship."

"Very well, my friend," answered the Capitan, and without another word he went out and closed the door. It was dark then, for the Papagos have not got as far as windows, and all that he could see was a streak of light, and the girl, looking out the crack. For a long time he lay there watching her and fiddling with his pistol. It was awkward for a right-handed man—this trying to shoot with the left. And in bed, too, where he would have to raise himself up. But if it came to a show-down he would have them in the door, and the room was as dark as a cave.

"What do you see?" he asked at last.

"Two men—about a mile away. They are dressed like cowboys and are coming now at a gallop."

"Must have seen my horse goin' out," commented Sycamore. "Say," he added a moment later, "ain't you afraid to stay in here when they come? Them fellers may get excited and shoot."

"No," she replied, "I am not afraid—but if you do what I tell you they will never know."

"All right!" mumbled Sycamore, "I can't do no shootin' while you're here, anyhow. But what's the idee?"

"Never mind!" she answered with sudden reserve. "When they come to the door you hide yourself good under the bed-clothes—I will do the rest. And now don't talk any more—they will soon be here."

All was quiet then till a sudden subterranean thud of hoofs announced their arrival at the top of the hill. They parleyed with the old chief—first in English, then in Spanish—but his answers were mostly by grunts.

"Who was that man that rode away from here?" one of them demanded at last.

"Indian boy!"

"*No, Señor*," spoke up the second man abruptly. "I know better! What color of a horse did he ride?"

"White horse—*palomino!*"

"That's the one!" exclaimed the second voice in English. "Come on—that's him, all right! Let's git after him!"

"No, wait a minute!" protested the other impatiently. "This old feller is a friend of Brown's, and we know he's bad hurt—how do we know he ain't hidin' around here somewheres? Come on—let's take a look first!"

"All right!" said the second man gruffly, and at a swift sign from the girl Sycamore flattened himself out in the bed. Then without a word of apology to the old chief or to his people the rangers began to go through the houses, pushing open each door as they came to it until they were almost to the hiding-place.

"Here's one we ain't been through yet," said a harsh voice on the outside, and as Sycamore covered up his head he felt the girl leap in beside him and cover herself with the quilt. Then the door burst open—there was a pause as the man peered in—and the Indian girl raised her head, about which she had bound a white band.

"What do you want?" she asked in her gentlest English, and with a hurried jerk the door was closed.

" 'Scuse me," mumbled a voice on the outside, and the man's spurs clanked as he strode hurriedly away.

"Come on, Lee!" he called. "Let's git a move on—there's nothin' here!"

There was a silence then, and the sound of a distant conference, and then the subterranean tramp of horses' feet again. For a minute more the girl lay quiet, her breath coming quick and hard—then she slipped out of the bed and stood watching by the door—and the next moment she was gone. Sycamore could hear the whisper of her feet as she whisked into her father's house—but though he listened long it was hours before she returned.

CHAPTER XVIII

DESERT WILLOW

There are still living in our midst people who claim that modesty is woman's greatest charm. It is an old idea, fast dying out perhaps in these days of boudoir street costumes and chewing-gum, but still not without its element of truth. The Indians of the wilderness still believe in it, and let no one think that because their daughter's cheeks are dusky they are not quick to mantle with the blush of shame, for they are slaves to all the proprieties.

Among our people, at certain times and upon special occasions, there is still to be found a hold-over from primitive days, the duenna. She is a gay creature, renewing her youth at balls and week-end parties under pretense of keeping a discreet eye upon the conduct of man and maid. But every Indian girl has her own duenna, a stern, censorious creature who follows her day and night and is personally responsible for her conduct. Far up on the mountains among the piñon trees, out on the desert at the harvest of mesquite beans and *pitayahas*, along the hillsides when the mescal hearts are being gathered up and roasted—there the Indian maiden may go, to do her share, but always with one of her elders.

Nor are the Indian standards of modesty and decorum lower than our own. Their men may be rough and brutal of speech, but the girls are instructed from their earliest youth to be chaste and quiet and modest, so that when they come to womanhood they may attract a good man for a husband. So it was that the daughter of old Chief Juan was abashed at her own deportment, and when at last she returned to her patient it was in the company of her chaperon.

If Sycamore had any thoughts to express, any words of thanks for the service she had performed, he was restrained by her obvious embarrassment and the droop of her quivering eye-lashes. There was something about her presence that subdued him and he allowed her to depart in silence. But with old Chief Juan it was the other way.

No sooner had the officers disappeared in the distance than the Capitan slipped into his room, his seamed face wrinkled deep with a crafty grin.

"What your name?" he enquired, laughing dryly to himself.

"You man that blew up train—stole money?" he enquired next, and when Sycamore answered in the affirmative—knowing that an Indian's testimony is not competent in the courts—the old man fairly beamed his approbation.

"Good man!" he grunted. "*Muy coyote*—my

friend!" He tapped Sycamore lovingly upon his sore shoulder and squatted down by the bed. "Where you get gold?" he whispered, making a picture of the bar with his hands, and when Sycamore told him of the robbery he chuckled and his eyes gleamed at the thought of the loot.

"*Muy coyote*, *amigo*!" he said again, "but this is bad—this hurt!"

"Yes," agreed Sycamore, "I cannot shoot now, nor ride. But you are a crafty man yourself, Señor Capitan—and this is your own country, you know it well—tell me now, if I give you money, can you hide me until I am well?"

"*Seguro*!" grinned the old chief, "sure—if you place yourself in my hands!"

"Then bring me the bar of gold!" answered Sycamore, "and I will give you half of it!"

"Very well!" said the Capitan, and while he was cutting the bar in two he unfolded his cunning plan.

"*Mira*, *amigo*," he began, "you know me! Big warrior! I fought Geronimo—I fought Naiche—I fought Apache—Apache *muy coyote*! I fought with soldiers too—learned soldier ways—very well, here is my plan! Soldiers have glass—" he ringed his fingers about his eyes—"you know—look far! Very well, I send boy to Tucson—buy glass for you—you watch far away. Boy buy cartridges too—everything you want. Newspapers too, no?" The old man grinned at this. "*Stawano*!" he continued. "To-morrow morning I send my women to mountain—dig up mescal flower—bake. My boys go too—hunt rabbit—catch cactus-rat—climb high up. You go too—my women cook for you—boys watch for signal fire. Every time I see white man come—I make smoke! Good! No?"

Yes, it was good. Sycamore liked the plan, and in the morning they were on their way—the boys scouring the country ahead for rabbits, the women walking behind and leading the horses that packed the provisions and blankets. Captain Juan himself helped place him on a particularly gaunt and low-spirited cayuse and as they dragged along up the rocky cañon Sycamore had a chance to see some real Indian hunting. Armed with their bows and arrows the ten or twelve "boys" of the party advanced up the cañon in a half circle, beating the brush as they went and driving all the rabbits they could into the sandy wash that was cut down the middle. Then when they had started two or three they closed in on them; the dogs were sent up the wash; and as the rabbits ran or tried to sneak through the surround they were shot or speared with long lances. Loud shouts and whoops of laughter went up as the hunters either killed or missed, and when some rabbit ran up the hillside the arrows flew from the bows as rapidly as shots from a repeating rifle.

Behind the drive the women plodded along

with their burdens, their long hair whipping about in the desert wind and their red and blue dresses making bright patches of color against the gray hillsides. Already on the southern slopes the first mescal yuccas had thrown up their flower-stalks; tall candelabra, from which a thousand lily-white bells hung gleaming in the morning sun. Along the dried-up water-course the smooth-barked palo verdes stood out green and flamboyant beside the graceful desert willows, whose slim ethereal leaves seemed hardly to cast a shadow. Higher up on the mesas and rocky benches the giant *sahuaros* reached out their tortured arms, and all about in a hundred menacing forms the lesser desert cacti rose up like bristling pin-cushions.

It was a wild country to the eye, with bold fire-blasted cliffs rising naked against the cloudless sky and all nature barbed with spikes and cruel spines; but even in such a land a man might be satisfied for a while if his enemies would leave him rest. So thought Sycamore Brown as he watched the Capitan's daughter glide on before him, her little feet shod in moccasins now to protect them from the thorns, her blue dress kilted up for the long journey and on her head an earthen-ware *olla* neatly balanced on a coil of cloth. That was for him, that *olla*, and as the morning wore on and he became weak and feverish she was careful to give him a drink but something had come over her now, for she would not linger and talk. It was as if she had turned wild again from going out into the mountains; and as she walked on ahead she conversed with the others in Papago, leaving it to the old woman to follow beside his horse.

Half way up the rugged cañon they came to the mescal pits, deep holes sunk in the side of a knoll near some water-holes in the rocks and surrounded by dead coals and ashes. Here in a grove of mesquite and desert willows they made their camp and while the other women took butcher-knives and baskets and scattered to bring in the mescal heads the girl and her duenna built a brush shelter and laid him beneath its shade. Then the old woman left to drag down wood and start a fire in the pit and the girl mixed him *pinole* gruel from a sack of ground parched corn.

Now that the Indians were away her manner was suddenly different—she smiled now and sat down under his shade, conversing amiably in school-book English. High up on the mountain-side the boys were lighting fires among the rocks and as the thin blue smoke rose up Sycamore asked if it was a signal.

"Oh, no," she answered, still smiling indulgently. "They are burning rats' nests. Then when the rats run out they shoot them with their arrows. You are not an Indian, so you do not understand."

But Sycamore knew more than she thought but

he pressed the matter no further. He knew that most Indians that catch rats have a barbarous custom of roasting them in the ashes *au naturel*, and eating them with the jackets on.

"I do not like these Indian boys," she went on, seeing that he did not approve. "Those young men have all been to school. They have learned to read and write and speak good English, but when they come home they forget. They will not talk in English nor follow the white man's ways. They are lazy—they will not make nice houses when they know how to—I do not like that. Some boys are trained for carpenters, some for mechanics, some for gardeners and farmers—now there they are, catching rock-rats!"

She paused and looked up at them again, and at the old woman sweating at her work in the pit.

"I had a teacher in my school, Miss Kellogg, and she told me that is not right," she said, pointing at the squaw's heavy labor. "She said that men should do the hard work and let women make the home. That is what they teach us there. They teach us to cook and sew and keep the house, and everything was so nice! Oh, I did so love to work in the laundry—we had stationary tubs, and drying rooms, and electric irons!"

"Electric irons!" exclaimed Sycamore, startled out of his calm. "What are them?"

"Why, didn't you ever see an electric flat-iron?" she enquired naively.

"Not that I know of—sent most of my clothes to the Chink. How does it work?"

"Well, it is just like an ordinary flat-iron that you put on the stove, but instead of that you connect it with the electric-light socket and that keeps it hot all the time. I used to do Miss Kellogg's shirt-waists for her—she had such beautiful things!"

Her voice trailed off into silence as she contemplated her lost past and Sycamore lay quiet and watched her. He began to understand now why the Capitan's daughter was so somber, and why there was always a patient wistfulness in her smile. From electric flat-irons to San Ignacio was quite a change.

"My father does not like the Indian schools," she began again, as her thoughts came back to the present. "He would not let me go—but the agent took me when I was a little girl. He took some of those boys and girls, too."

"And are they educated?" asked Sycamore.

"Yes, they are educated too. But we are too far from the railroad—there is nothing for us to do. So we become wild again." She sighed and looked away. "But I will never forget," she said. "No, I never will—I promised! That is why I like to talk with you," she added quickly.

This was a new idea to Sycamore, but he took it quietly.

"Well," he said at last, "that's all right—I

like to hear you talk. Of course I don't speak good English—nothin' like yourn, anyway! I'm somethin' like them boys up there—never learned much when I went to school—but I sure like to hear you use them big words."

He quit there, for he saw she was blushing—the Papago boys did not talk to her that way. There was silence for a while, and then he came out with a question—one that had been a long time in his mind.

"Say," he said, "I don't like this speakin' to you like you was a stranger all the time—you know, I don't like to holler 'say' at you—what's the matter with tellin' me yore name?"

She glanced at him now with a certain growing interest in her eyes, and then she turned to the hillside.

"Do you see that tree over there?" she asked, pointing to a desert willow that swayed dreamily in the wind. "My Indian name is for that, but you could not pronounce it. But I have an English name, too. Miss Kellogg gave it to me—she called me Frances Willard."

"Frances Willard!" repeated Sycamore. "Well, that's a pretty name, but what's the matter with Desert Willow? The boys named me after a Sycamore tree and I never made no kick."

"No, but you don't understand. When I went to the school I was ashamed of my Indian name—it was so hard to say—and I told them it was Desert

Willow. Then Miss Kellogg became my friend and she was so kind to me and read me things out of books—stories of great men and women and the wonderful things they had done. Washington was the greatest man, and then Lincoln—but the greatest woman was Frances Willard. Her picture was in the school-room—I used to look at it on the wall—and one day I told Miss Kellogg and she changed my name to Willard, on the book. She always called me Frances, but in Spanish it is Francisca."

"Ah!" cried Sycamore with sudden enthusiasm, "that's the name for me—Francisca! But say—I ain't had much schoolin'—who was this Frances Willard, anyhow? Seems like I heerd about her somewhere—but what did she do?"

"Frances Willard was the great Temperance reformer," recited Desert Willow, her eyes fixed as if she scanned the page. "She devoted her life to the cause of prohibition and to teaching children the del-eterious effects of al-coholic stimulants."

"Oh!" commented Sycamore. Then he looked at her a while. "Say, Francisca," he said, with a twinkle in his eye, "did you learn all that in school?"

"Learn what?" asked Frances Willard, her sweet voice quavering as she sensed some barbed jest.

But Sycamore was kind.

“Never mind,” he said. “I like to hear you talk—even if I can’t understand them big words.”

“Oh, do you really?” stammered Desert Willow blushing through the brown of her cheeks. And then she got up and helped her duenna pack wood, for Papago boys don’t talk that way.

CHAPTER XIX

A WEEK WITH THE RAVENS

The next day passed like a dream for Sycamore—and the next—and he forgot the rough world outside. In the evening they raked out the coals and fire and filled the pits with mescal; then they covered the hole with grass and dirt and let the sweet hearts mellow in the steam of the heated rocks; and on the fourth day they dug them out and had their feast. From the village down below came Captain Juan and the rest of his people and, each with a leaf of the fibrous root in his mouth, they sat around the fire and sucked out the honeyed sweetness. It was a great feast, full of shouting and laughter and jokes in the Papago language, and Sycamore joined in the merriment; but if he dreamed that the world had forgotten him he knew better when the runner came in.

Two days in and two days back, changing horses and riding them down, the *muchacho* had performed his mission and followed on to make his report. First he spread out his purchases—clothes, tobacco, cartridges and medicine, and an army officer's glass in its case. Sycamore took the remainder of his money and paid him well; then he divided half his tobacco with the revelers; but the proceedings did not interest him—he was thinking about what was in those papers. Not since he had heard the sudden shots and had seen Martin fall as he ran had he heard a word of news. Was Lum dead? Was he caught? Had he confessed?

He tore the papers open with his free hand and scanned them by the fire; and as he read his face fell, so that the Indians paused to notice him. Lum was not dead. He had been shot in the leg and captured—he had confessed everything! No, he had confessed to robbing the *rurales* and had showed his captors his gold! So that was lost, and old Lum had weakened, after all!

But what was this? "Mexicans Offer Reward!" Sycamore read it over slowly, until he saw his name in print—then he galloped through it blindly and came back to pore over it again. There was a reward up for him in Mexico—five hundred dollars for him alive—a thousand dollars for him dead! And offered by the commander of the *rurales*! What a bunch of barbarians they were!

Sycamore paused in his reading and thought a while, for this was serious. There was no shelter for him now across the Line. But they would never catch him crossing into Mexico—ump-um—that was too much of a temptation for someone to shoot him in the back. It was Papaguería now, or nowhere; and it was a good thing he had given Chief Juan half his gold—the old boy would have a chance to earn it. But here was more news! Well, well, that was Lee Ruggles that had come after him!

"The notorious Syc Brown escaped, but Captain Ruggles and Ranger Lally are on his trail." It was the rangers and the *rurales* now, and that was bad—he might take a trip across the Line yet.

Sycamore was turning the paper over for further news when he glanced up and saw Captain Juan talking with the runner. It was in Papago, but somehow he knew that it concerned him—the runner had picked up some news and the old chief was excited.

"*Mira*, *amigo*," he said as Sycamore came over to join him. "This boy has had some trouble. Man who sold him glasses looked at money—he say money no good. Then he asked him, where you get? Boy no talk—pretty soon go away. Man run after him—give him glass—take money. Pretty soon other man come—boy leave town quick—this man come behind!"

"What kind of man?"

"Little man—gray hair—*big eyes!*" answered the runner.

"Yes, I know him!" exclaimed Sycamore turning to the chief. "Railroad man—*muy coyote*! It's that—, Sam Slocum!" he said to himself in English, and went off to sit down and think. They were all after him now—the rangers, the *rurales*, and Sam Slocum. There would be man-hunters, too, more than likely. And more than likely they would get him. He was crippled now; his right arm was still useless; and an Indian was riding his horse. Ah, if he only had Round Valley—and his pistol-hand would work!

He called the Capitan over to him again and took him off to one side.

"*Amigo*," he said, "I am in trouble. These men come after me, to kill me or put me in jail, and I can neither shoot nor ride. You must hide me now, where they will never find me, and when I am well I will go away. You are a crafty man and this is your own country—where can I go now to hide alone?"

"Alone?"

"Yes, and no one must know the place but you; for this little gray man is a devil—he can read what is in your heart. Look out for him, my friend, and tell all your people not to talk. And if any white men come—any hunters, any prospectors, even other Indians—look out for them; they will be working for this little man with the big eyes. But it is not because I am a bad man that he wants to catch me. This is the reason. He wants to make me show him the money—the money we took from the train."

"And is it much?" questioned the old chief eagerly.

"Yes, my friend, very much! Four big sacks full!"

"Hah!" sighed the old man, his eyes gleaming at the thought.

"Four big sackfuls!" repeated Sycamore slowly. "But hide me well, *amigo.* You know me—I do not forget!"

"*Seguro*!" muttered Chief Juan, bowing his head in thought. "Be assured, my friend, I will hide you well."

Among the Indians of the desert there is one thing that is never forgotten, and that is water. On the highest peak that rose up like an arrow-point behind the village of San Ignacio there was a *tinaja* among the rocks—a tank, hollowed out of the granite and known only to Captain Juan and the ravens. In the summer, when the great thunder-caps hovered over the peaks, it was filled with rain-water but it was hid so close that not even the mountain sheep came there to drink. But in the morning while his people returned to their village the old chief mounted to it by a secret way, leading a reluctant horse, and before noon Sycamore was hidden away like a chuckawalla lizard in a crack of the mighty cliff.

Far below him lay the Indian village, a patch of dark shadows in the sun, and beyond stretched the limitless desert. In the cave that opened up behind him was his blanket and a supply of food, and an *olla* to carry water from the tank. Besides this there was nothing but his arms and the officer's glass. It was luck that had brought that to him, for the world is full of cheap telescopes; but he had told the runner to buy the best and it had cost him the last of his money. Somehow there seemed to be a curse on those twenties—he was glad in his heart to get rid of them—but this glass was worth the price.

He focussed it and rested it against his barricade of rocks. Yes, he could see the village, and see it plain. There was the little square where the Indians danced at night; there was the big adobe house, where the men of the council met; the mud houses clinging to the lower slope; the crooked trail and women coming up from the well—and the round brick oven where they baked their bread. There were children playing about, and dogs, and men—he could tell the old Capitan by his clean white shirt and his hair cut short at his shoulders, but it was too far away to read faces. Yet there was one who baked at the oven that he could tell by the way she walked.

All the afternoon he lay quiet behind the pile of fallen rock that made his cave like a cliff-dwelling; then as the bats came out from its depths and the light died out from the desert he picked up his red-painted *olla* and made his way back to the water-hole. It was a slim pool, full of mosquito wigglers and rank with stagnant odors, but good as tank-water goes. Such as it was, he took it and went back for the night—and in the morning he went down again. All that day he lay looking down on the village, lonely as a lost soul, and at evening he saw Sam Slocum come in.

First there was a puff of dust in the north-east pass, then a signal fire from some Indian on a neighboring point, and then two horsemen growing larger and larger until they watered their mounts at San Ignacio. Sycamore watched his man as he moved about, accompanied by an Indian guide, and he knew that the struggle had begun. Lum Martin was caught, and Jack Haines was in jail, but neither of them would say a word. He knew it—otherwise Sam Slocum would let him go. But he was the former stool-pigeon, the easy mark, and they needed him to make out a case.

So they came after him, for he was the only man except Lum Martin who knew where the treasure was hid—and Lum would never tell. When they had shot him Lum had made a confession; but even then he was foxy, for it was not of robbing the train but of holding up a treasure train in Mexico. Now he was standing pat on the Sand Tanks affair and Sam Slocum was raking hell for a witness. It was a good time for that witness to crawl into his hole, because old Sam knew he was close by. He stayed right where he was in San Ignacio that night and all the next day, and

Sycamore knew he had found out something, for he never wasted any time. The next day he started off towards the west, and the Indian fires signaled his departure to all the world beyond—but at evening he came slipping back again as if to catch his man in a trap.

So it went for a week, until Sycamore's arm was healed and his strength wooed back. But though the arm was healed it was not the same. It hung by his side, white and feeble, and for hours at a time he stood upright in his cave and practised draw-and-shoot with his left, in case it should come to war. Already his young blood called for action—for his horse, to mount and ride away—but the old chief made him no sign. Then on the eighth day, when his food was all but spent, he saw the white cloth on the flat roof of the Capitan's house and went down to meet him at the mescal pits.

"You see little big-eyed man—look through glass?" enquired Captain Juan, smiling grimly as he delivered the food. "*Muy coyote*—that man. He knows you are near San Ignacio."

"What does he say?" asked Sycamore.

"I no talk to him," explained the old man, "no talk *Americano.* He talk to my girl—speak *Americano.*"

"Uhr!" grunted Sycamore. "And what does he say?"

"First—he say Sycamoro no good—bad

man—rob train—kill people. Then my girl say no—Sycamoro good man."

"Ah!" commented Sycamore, as he noted the detective's finesse.

"*Sí*!" nodded the Capitan as Sycamore shook his head. "I scold my girl—she talks too much—speak *Americano*—no good!"

"Um," assented Sycamore. "What else did he say?"

"Then he tell girl—Sycamoro good man—have bad friends—rob train—kill people—hide money. Ranger man come—kill Sycamoro. Little man no come to kill—come to look for money."

"Well?"

"Little man want to talk."

For a minute Sycamore sat silent, pondering on an answer.

"Where's my horse?" he asked at last.

"Boy make smoke yesterday," answered the Capitan. "Twenty mile—over there." He pointed to the west.

"You tell boy bring my horse here to-morrow! Where are the two men that chased him?"

"Two men lost—horses fall down—three days over there!" He pointed to the north and smiled.

"*Stawano*!" said Sycamore. "You bring my horse to-morrow. Next day I talk with little man—then I go."

"Where you go?" demanded the old man sharply.

"*Muy lejos*," answered Sycamore with a sigh, "very far!" And he waved his hand towards the west.

CHAPTER XX

SAM SLOCUM

All that night Sycamore turned uneasily on his stony bed, thinking of Sam Slocum. He knew what Slocum would say and he was resolute against him. Yet if he refused to come in, if he refused to show the treasure or give evidence against Lum Martin, then like a flash the detective would turn against him and hound him to his destruction. And Sycamore had not been an officer for nothing—he knew the ruthless creed of the man-hunters and the lure of a big reward. If money and men could do it, then Slocum would get him—and there were the rangers, too. Who could tell who was behind these rangers that the legislature had been so prompt to create? The papers said they were organized to catch Bravo Juan and clear the Territory of outlaws—but would not a word from Sam Slocum put half of them on his trail?

Yes, it was dangerous to turn against Slocum; yet freedom was dear to him, and the kiss of the desert wind. He could never endure a prison—no, it was better to die in the open. But Sycamore did not aim to die. Who was Lee Ruggles that he should fear him? Had he not ridden his horse down and lost himself in pursuit of Round Valley? Who were these Texans and Cimarron Valley cow-punchers that he should be afraid? The desert was his home—they could never get near him. One word from old Capitan Juan and the Papagos would all be his friends—and besides there was Desert Willow!

What did he care for their cities and towns as long as she dwelt at San Ignacio? But to go to jail—to lie there, waiting to betray his friends—to stand up before them all and be branded for a stool-pigeon—and then, maybe, go to the pen or be extradited into Mexico—that was not for him! Rather would he flee from place to place, a renegade, an outlaw, a border coyote—as long as she was in San Ignacio, and he could get to see her. So he made up his mind, and slept; and the next day he went down to the mescal pits to await the coming of Round Valley.

High up on the rim of the cañon he hid behind a pile of rocks and long before the Indian boy came in he had picked him up with his glass, coming in by a dim trail from the west. Yes, it was the same old Round Valley and he was just as fat as ever—a good horse, the rangers could never catch him! The moment he laid his hand on his neck something impelled him to swing up in the saddle, and something else impelled him to be gone. What did he want to see Sam Slocum about? He was likely to put up some job on him or talk him into giving up.

"You tell Capitan little man no good," he said to the boy. "You tell him I go now!"

"*Stawano*!" answered the runner, and as Sycamore rode slowly back up the mountain to get his food and blankets he went bounding off down the cañon with his message, and a chunk of the white man's gold. But Sam Slocum was not a man to be balked so easily—he had learned the ropes at San Ignacio, and when Sycamore looked down from his cliff dwelling he saw the white flag, spread out on the Capitan's roof.

"Meet me at the mescal pits," it said, and Sycamore did not dare to disobey. So when Sam Slocum and Chief Juan came galloping up the cañon they found him waiting behind a pile of rocks, over which the muzzle of his carbine was thrust out as a signal for them to halt.

"Jest leave yore guns on yore horse," he said to Slocum, and as the detective came forward he looked him over grimly. Ten days on the desert had not improved Slocum's appearance at all, and there was an ugly glint to his eyes that told Sycamore he was good and mad; but a detective has to be all things to all people and Slocum tried to be polite.

"I don't see why you need to be afraid of me," he observed as he halted in front of the gun. "You know I've always been your friend—and I've always treated you white, too!"

"*I* ain't afraid of you," answered Sycamore coldly.

"Well, what you want to run away for then?" demanded Slocum angrily. "Why don't you come down and talk like a man—what you hidin' behind that rock for?"

"That's my business," retorted Sycamore, who did not want to show his game arm. "What can I do for you, Mr. Slocum?"

"Now say, Syc," pleaded the detective, "what's the use of getting chesty? Haven't you known me long enough to trust me? I've come clear out here from Tucson, just to get a chance to talk with you, and if it hadn't been for this man here and his daughter you would have gone away and left me—and after you'd said you'd meet me, too!"

"Well, I ain't got nothin' to talk about!" declared Sycamore hotly.

"Ah!" cried Slocum, raising his eyebrows, "but maybe *I* have! Maybe there's some news since you saw the evening paper!"

"Well, what is the news then?" sneered Sycamore. "Lum Martin confessed?"

A black look passed over the detective's face at this but he became resolutely calm. There was no use in quarreling with Sycamore.

"Jack Haines has confessed!" he said, folding his arms and blinking his big round eyes. "And Lum Martin has been indicted!"

"Well, what do you want me for then?" queried Sycamore.

"I'll tell you, Syc," began Slocum, lowering his voice confidentially, "it's like this. We all know that this man Haines is a bad man. He was a member of the Sam Bass gang back in Texas, has killed a number of men, and is a dangerous character to have running around loose. We know, if it hadn't been for him, that train would never been robbed. He put you boys up to it, and we're afraid to have him at large. Now we can go ahead and promise him immunity and have him swear Martin into the pen—but that isn't what we're after, and for two reasons. The first is, we don't want Haines out; the second is we don't want Lum sent up. We want him to give back that treasure.

"All right now—here's the point. We know that both Haines and Martin have taken advantage of you. You were only a kid—you didn't know what you were doing—and they just used you for their own advantage. Now here's the proposition. You come in with me and testify against both of them—we send Haines to the pen for life and turn Lum loose when he digs up those sacks. You'll never spend a day in jail; we'll treat you well; and when it's all over, if you do what's right, we'll give you a good job as messenger. That's how much we think of you, Syc. They can talk all they please, but I know you're honest!"

"Sure!" assented Sycamore, nodding his head emphatically, "sure I'm honest!" But that was as far as he got. The issue somehow seemed to be clouded. Sure he was honest, but what was a man to do? Sell out his friends? Stool on his partners?

"Nope! I'm sorry, Mr. Slocum," he said at last, "but I can't do it!"

"Well, why not?" cried Slocum, exasperated at his flat refusal, "what's the matter with the proposition? By God, boy, if you knew how hard I've worked to get you off; if you knew how I've opposed my own people, and the sheriff, and the rangers, and all of 'em, you'd show a little consideration! What's the matter with you, anyway?"

For a minute or two Sycamore stood behind his rock trying to frame up some suitable answer—some reason that the detective would not instantly seize and turn against him—but the words would not come. He knew what he wanted to say, but he could not stand up to old Sam at talking.

"Well," he said, "well—I don't want to testify against Lum."

"Oho! So that's what's biting you, is it? I suppose you think Lum is your friend, hey?"

He leered at Sycamore so exultingly, expressing by every move such a world of information to controvert him, that Sycamore did not dare to answer. Maybe old Lum had worked him a little, but that was no reason for stooling on him.

"You think he told you where that loot was buried, don't you?" sneered Slocum, returning to the attack. "You think you're going to get a whack at it, don't you, Mr. Brown? Well, I just want to tell you that we've tore the whole house down since you left Hackamore and dug the ground up deep—and there wasn't any loot there! None whatever!"

Sycamore's face fell at this, for Lum had told him where the treasure was buried—he had said it was under the house.

"That's the kind of friend you've got!" jabbed Slocum, as he savvy where the blow had gone home. "That's how much old Lum thinks of *you,* after all you've done for him. He never intended to give you a cent of that money, and he never will! He's saying now that he's sorry he gave you that gold—you was always flashing it everywhere and getting him into trouble. In fact, he told one of the boys in jail he intended to kill you that very night he was caught—down on the Line there. Only waiting for you to go to sleep, was all. You don't know how lucky you are, boy, to be alive!"

"No!" growled Sycamore, and then he fell silent. Old Lum had certainly lied to him—there was no getting out of it, not if they had dug up the adobe house. And that was kind of bad—what he had told that fellow in jail. Lum was looking awfully snaky that night, too.

"So there you are," said Slocum, suddenly fixing him with his compelling eyes. "Now come on out of there and have a drink with me and we'll fix this deal up right!"

He pulled out a flask as he spoke and so natural did it seem to fall in with him that Sycamore was well on his way before he gathered the full import of his act. He was going out to throw in with Slocum. Yes—and before Slocum had come he had sworn he would never do it. He had steeled himself against the man, knowing full well that he meant him evil, and now—Sycamore stepped back behind his rock and picked up his handy carbine, and the hot metal seemed to give him strength.

"Oh, I don't know," he said, reappearing again in his old place; and so suddenly did he rise up that he surprised a very foxy and Svengali look on Slocum's face. "I don't know about that," he repeated, striving to reassure himself. "What's the deal, anyhow? No, I don't want no whiskey!"

"Oh, hell!" exclaimed Slocum, taking a drink himself. "What's the matter with you?" He gurgled the liquor in his throat, and Sycamore's mouth watered, but he refused the bottle resolutely. That look he had surprised in Slocum's face had given him a scare—he realized that the man was dangerous.

"I don't know about you, Sam Slocum," he

said, speaking slow and gazing at him coldly. "Maybe you're puttin' up a job on me."

"Nope," said Slocum, suddenly matter-of-fact again. "I'm putting up a job on Lum Martin."

"Well, you'll never git me in on it—because I won't testify against him. So if that's all you want we might as well quit talkin'."

"Why won't you testify against him?"

"Because I won't, that's all! I got a plenty of doin' the stool-pigeon act for you, Sam Slocum!" cried Sycamore with sudden bitterness. "I got a plenty of havin' you and them tin-horn detectives of yourn make a monkey out of me and then go off and laugh. You thought you was pretty smart when you got Roy Hackett to come into Hackamore and sell me suits of clothes, but you can't cap me into the same game twice—not with no bottle of whiskey!"

"Oh, I can't, hey?" queried Slocum, turning suddenly mean. "Well, maybe we'll cap you into it with a thirty-thirty bullet then! If you knew how many rangers and deputy sheriffs I've got stationed around here, just dying for a chance to pick you up and get that thousand dollars reward you'd sing a different tune, maybe. Who the hell are you, Syc Brown, to put on all this dog? I've got the goods to send you to the pen for life—for train-robbery and breaking open that jail—and I'll do it too, if you don't come through with this evidence! I've made you a fair offer and you can either take it or leave it, but lemme tell you one thing, young man—if you throw me down after all I've done I'll get you if I have to bring you in feet first. You don't seem to appreciate kindness and consideration—so I might as well tell you you're surrounded and just the same as my prisoner anyhow!"

The detective added this last on the spur of the moment, but it failed of its desired effect.

"And suppose I shoot a hole in you with this thirty-thirty," suggested Sycamore, shoving his gun to the front and cocking it. "What then?"

He was very cool now and the mists had cleared away—fighting was where he shone.

"Don't do that," answered Slocum, catching his breath as he faced the rifle, "because it won't do you any good. Now there's no use making these wild plays, Syc," he went on in shame-faced acknowledgment of his over-play, "I haven't got a man within twenty miles of here—so put up your gun and listen. Here's the proposition. I came clear out here to get you to testify. If you refuse I'll have to go back to Gun Sight and close up the deal with Jack Haines—then you're no good to me at all. So don't think you can come in later. All I want you to do is to tell the truth—and if you do we won't forget it. Now how about it? Don't be a damn fool all your life, Syc! These fellows have done you dirt and old Lum was just fixing to kill you—you don't owe them anything. Come on now—will you do it?"

Sycamore puckered his eyes up doubtfully and turned them away from his tempter. By every rule of reason he ought to yield, but his heart was set against it. He was not educated—he could not talk with Slocum—but something told him it was wrong. Then the old shame came back to him, the shame that had mantled his brow when they called him a stool-pigeon at Hackamore, and suddenly his mind was clear again.

"No!" he said. "No, by God! You can say what you please, but I won't stool on nobody!"

"All right," answered Slocum, turning grimly to mount his horse. "All right, Mr. Brown; you'll talk different through a pair of bars!"

Sycamore grunted and watched him off.

"Yes," he muttered with a sly smile. "Sure! But you haven't caught me yet!"

CHAPTER XXI

ACROSS THE LINE

It is a generally accepted fact that the exercise of all the Christian virtues at once is liable to interfere with the success of even the most accomplished detective. He must be honest, or criminals will not place their trust in him; but when the aforesaid criminals have refused to come through with the dope the morals of the affair are likely to seek a lower plane. Samuel Slocum was a very successful detective—or had been, up to the time he took the Lum Martin case—and, but for the temperamental accident of Sycamore Brown's refusing to wait to see him and pulling off the interview a day ahead of time, there is no doubt that he would have had a few men so placed that they could capture him if he refused to come in.

The fact is that Sam Slocum needed Sycamore and needed him bad. He had to have him. Some of the things he had told Sycamore were true, and some were not; but, except for the mere accident of the time they met, he would certainly have had him surrounded. As it was he might make it yet, unless Sycamore got across the Line. So he sent his horse scampering down the cañon to call out the reserves, and Sycamore took the hint to hunt for higher ground.

The trail where the Indian boy had come in was his natural route of retreat and he put three or four miles behind him before he crept up on the ridge, but even in that short time things had happened. There was a big smoke rising up, and at first glance he thought San Ignacio was burning, but a long stare through his field-glasses assured him that the village was safe. It was a signal fire, up on the top of a hill, and the man who was piling green brush on it looked very much like Sam Slocum. Evidently he had been taking lessons from the Indians.

Sycamore scanned the horizon for some of the men it was to summon, but the only dust he could see was that of two men coming in from the east. He laughed as he turned back to his horse—that was pretty good, what Sam had told him down at the mescal pits, about his being surrounded, and just the same as a prisoner. If Round Valley couldn't make those two horsemen look like a fly-speck on the rim of the world he certainly had lost his speed. So he swung up and they jogged on towards the west, Round Valley grabbing sustenance as he traveled and Sycamore sitting light in the saddle. It was a trick he had learned—never to slump down in his seat or shift his weight about but to balance himself in the stirrups and travel with the horse.

Behind him lay San Ignacio and the signal-smoke, getting smaller; in front the long, crooked trail and a V where it slipped through a pass. The mountains were strung along to the north; and the south was vacant, for there lay Old Mexico and the Line. It was a dry country down there, dry and barren; a man would find it hard picking if they ever chased him across. But he was going to the west, where the boy had been before, and every Papago in the country would know his horse and greet him for a friend. The next village was right in that pass there—

He stopped and got out his glass. Yes, there was a dust ahead, and it was certainly coming his way. Two men—white men—and riding hard. He rested his horse and waited a while, until he could make them out. They were tall men, with Texas sombreros, and one of them rode a gray horse—Lee Ruggles and Lally, the ranger! Sycamore looked out the country to the south and found it deserted—well, he would have to make for the Line. So he turned and struck out across the open towards a big white monument he had seen, and even then he did not hurry.

The breeze came up from the west and sent little wind-devils whirling and swirling across the plain to lose themselves in the distance. He noted them idly, his face turned back towards the west, where the rangers were spurring after him, and even then he was not afraid. By the time they came within gunshot their horses would be rode down, and Round Valley would show them some speed. But suddenly a certain wind-devil caught his eye—it was coming from the east, and coming fast—and it was heading for the Line!

Then it was that Round Valley felt the quirt, and the streak of dust he left behind him could be seen for many a mile. Already the white gleam of the monument rose before them, when another dust-streak sprang up due east of it—and he could see the man as he rode! But the way still lay open before him, and it was a way that he wanted to go. Ignoring the distanced rangers Sycamore swung his horse to the west again and rode quartering for the Line. Never mind the monument, any place on the Line was good enough for him now—and he wouldn't stop when he got across, either.

A spit of dust rose up ahead of him and he knew that somebody was shooting at him. Once more a bullet struck, and he saw that it came from behind. A third shot—and it landed closer to him—what if the man should get his range? The man to the east was riding hard, but Sycamore knew he could beat him—he turned Round Valley for the Line. So they raced, Sycamore riding south, the other man coming west and whipping at every jump. Nearer and nearer they came to the place where he had to cross, but just as Sycamore whipped out his pistol to fight the other man's horse went down and threw him into the dirt. It had been a long ride and the poor brute had done his best, but the pace had been too swift.

Up jumped the rider and ran back to get his rifle, but it was too late—Sycamore had crossed the Line and was fogging on to the south in a cloud of dust and dirt. Nor did he let that cloud subside until he was good two miles into Mexico, for a rifle will shoot far these days. It was strange to Sycamore, where all these men had come from. Surely they could not live out there on the desert, but they had sprung up like wind-devils in an afternoon breeze—sprung up from nowhere—and every one of them after him!

There was something very sobering in the thought. When a man gets to be so valuable that five men will chase him to the Line it is likely to give him pause. Of course a thousand dollars is a lot of money—but he was worth more than that to somebody. The thought of his meeting old Sam Slocum down there by those mescal pits gave him the shudders now and he decided to make a long jump west before he cut back to the Line. But meanwhile, not to show his hand, he halted upon a hilltop and waited for the night. Very carefully he rubbed down his brave horse, Round Valley, and tied him out to feed and then, resting his glass across a ledge of rocks, he looked back at his thwarted pursuers.

They were all standing in a bunch now, six or

seven of them, and among them he could make out Ruggles and Sam Slocum. The Capitan was there too, and another Indian, and they were all talking together. Then as he watched he saw one of them hold up a white cloth and motion him to come in. But the idea did not appeal to Mr. Brown. The further he could keep away from those people the better it made him feel—especially after that long-distance shooting—so he sat tight and made no sign. A conference followed, while Ruggles watched him through a glass, and then Sam Slocum seized the white cloth and rode towards him.

It was contrary to the rules of war but Sycamore could not help that—he scrambled back for his carbine and shot at him, flag and all. There was another conference then and finally Lee Ruggles took the flag. He came on slowly, stopping to look through his glass, and as Sycamore made no more hostile demonstrations he rode up to the foot of the hill. Having tied his horse in a gulch where it could not be harmed Sycamore rose up from behind his pile of rocks and motioned the ranger to come near. He had known Lee Ruggles over at Gun Sight and had liked him fine, but it was just as well to be careful, so he waited behind his rock.

He came up then, a tall, bronzed man, clear-eyed and smiling through a two weeks' growth of beard.

“Hello there, Syc,” he hailed, “what ye scairt about?” And then he laughed.

“Hello, Lee,” responded Sycamore, his fighting-face relaxing as he guessed the cause of the merriment. “Was that you shootin’ at me?” he enquired with a sheepish grin.

“Shore was,” answered the ranger. “ ’Bout two miles away—but I had you on the run all right—you threw the dirt in the air a thousand feet high.”

He came up to the base of the rock and sprawled out on a boulder, and then for a few minutes they talked about the chase. There was nothing of the sleuth in Lee Ruggles, he was just a plain “go-gitter” who hunted men as some people follow the hounds. But in a way he was a sleuth too, for he knew how to humor his man. Sycamore was hot and peevish, as exemplified by his shot at Sam Slocum, and it was better to let him cool down a little before they began to talk business.

“Well, what you goin’ to do now, Syc?” he said at last. “That is, if it’s any of my business.”

“Thinkin’ about a little pasear down through Sonora,” lied Sycamore.

“The rurales will git you,” suggested Ruggles. “Better come in with me.”

“Nope.”

“What’s the matter?” laughed Ruggles. “ ’Fraid of the grand jury?”

“Nope—I don’t like that man, Sam Slocum.”

"Well, come in with me then, and I'll git the thousand dollars reward!"

"Nope. I'll take a chance in Mexico."

"All right. Say, Sam Slocum says he wants to talk with you!"

"You tell him to go chase himself, will you? You tell him that if I ever git him in range again I'll shoot him right where his suspenders cross!"

"Why, what's the matter, Syc? You don't seem to like old Sam very well!"

"No," grumbled Syc, "the old rat tried to git me in a hole and nab me—and now I got away I intend to stay away. Them rurales may run me down and kill me, but that won't do Sam Slocum any good—he'll never git me for no witness!"

"Hmm," mused the ranger. "And that's jest what they'll do too, Syc—them rurales will shore kill you. They's a squad of 'em down in there somewhere—and you know how that reward reads—they can't hardly afford to take you alive."

"Well, that's all right," answered Sycamore evasively. "I'm not huntin' for trouble, and at the same time I won't be took. If I got to shoot somebody it might as well be a Mex."

"Well," said Ruggles, "that's right friendly of you, Syc, and the rangers will shore appreciate it—but it's goin' to be bad news for Sam. You know he's kinder lottin' on gittin' you for a witness."

"Well, he won't do it—that's all."

"All right then—I reckon I'll be gittin' back. But say! There's a girl up there wants to see you!"

"A girl!" repeated Sycamore in astonishment. "What girl?"

"Injun girl. Lives over at San Ignacio. Guess you know who she is—the one that hid you when me and Lally was there." He was watching his man very carefully now, for this was the last card in his hand. If Sycamore would consent to see Desert Willow she might talk him into surrendering—it was for that purpose that Slocum had brought her down.

"What's she doin', way down here?" enquired Sycamore suspiciously. "Did Sam Slocum bring her down?" he demanded quickly. "Well then, you tell her I won't see her!"

He was angry now and suddenly put out with himself. The idea of Sam Slocum talking that girl over and calling her in on the play! What could she have to say, more than advise him to surrender? And the idea of bringing her clear down there!

"You tell Sam Slocum," he said, "that he'd steal milk from a sick baby! You tell him from me that he's a sneakin' whelp and I won't have a thing to do with 'im—no, nor with anybody he sends!"

"All right," answered Ruggles with philosophical calm. "Anything else I can do for you?"

“Sure,” responded Sycamore, after a moment’s thought. “Tell old Capitan Juan to come down here, will you? Keep me from gittin’ lonely!”

“All right, Syc. So-long. If it gits too hot for you down there we’ll always be glad to see you, you know!”

He grinned and went back to his horse, but as he was riding away he turned and hollered back.

“Say! Bravo Juan is down there somewhere! Bring him along with you!”

“All right!” answered Sycamore. “How about the reward?”

“You can have it!” roared Ruggles. “Hunt ’im up! We want ’im bad!”

“I’ll do it!” muttered Sycamore to himself. For the moment he was an officer again, and his fighting blood rose to the chase. “Yes, I’ll do it!” he said; but after that he fell silent. Who was he to run down Bravo Juan? There was an equal reward on his own head, and they wanted him just as bad. Bravo Juan was a murderer and a cut-throat but he preyed only upon the weak and defenseless. *He* had stolen from a corporation. Even now they were laying new traps to catch him. No, he would do well to save his own skin—let Bravo Juan go to the devil!

CHAPTER XXII

A BIG CIRCLE

When Capitan Juan arrived at the foot of his hill Sycamore could see that he was in a bad humor. He jerked his horse about and spurred him with both heels at once and as he climbed up to the top Sycamore could hear him cursing to himself. Perhaps a drink or two of whiskey that he had got somewhere was responsible for these outward demonstrations, but there was another and a deeper cause. His daughter had crossed his will, and he had sensed the reason.

"You like my girl?" he demanded, after Sycamore had rolled him a cigarette, and upon a non-committal grunt from that young person he burst into a torrent of Spanish oaths. "White man—Indian girl—no good!" he cried. "Very bad! I no like! Papago girl—Papago boy—all right! No?"

He fixed his audience with a glittering eye and Sycamore responded with a prompt, "*Sí, Señor*." He was not looking for trouble with the Capitan.

"My girl no good!" stormed the old man. "*Muy mala*! *No vala nada*!" Then, suddenly changing his ground, he demanded: "Why you no see her?"

"This is no place for a woman!" answered Sycamore diplomatically.

"Yes! But why you no want to? You no like my girl?"

"*Quien sabe*!" responded Sycamore, shrugging his shoulders like a shuffling Mexican, "she was very kind to me—when I was sick."

"Yes, but—you want to marry her?" The old man came out with it brutally, after the manner of his kind, but Sycamore was equal to him still.

"I cannot marry any one," he said. "I am a fugitive—I run from place to place—that is why I sent for you. I want you to tell me where to go."

"Ungh!" grunted the Capitan, and sat for a while in silence. Sycamore could smell the liquor on his breath and he kept quiet, for a drunk Indian is a bad man to handle. "You see two hills?" the Capitan said at last, pointing to a pair of buttes in the west. "Indian sign there"—he picked up a long, pointed stone and set it on top of a rock—"like that! You go where it point—find water—hole in flat rock. Very well. Next day you go west—forty mile—find Indian village—like this!"

He drew him a map in the dirt with the point of his second finger—his first finger had been shot off by the Apaches; then he extended the map, showing village after village in Mexico and others across the Line.

"You go," he said. "You tell Capitan—you my friend—Capitan Juan! All right!"

He was smiling again now quite amiably, and as Sycamore sat studying the map the Capitan gathered a few sticks for a fire. As they burned he drew out a small piece of white cloth—it was a fragment of Sam Slocum's flag of truce—and spread it on a smooth rock. Then he picked up the charred sticks one by one, quenched the live ends by spitting on them, and painted a rude picture on the cloth. At the top was a man on a horse; below, two hands hooked together; and below that a picture of his own hand, with the index finger gone.

"You see?" he said, pointing to the first figure. "This white man—wear hat. Horse white—all same yours. Two hands—shake—means 'my friend!' This here—my mark!"

Sure enough! It was an Indian letter—the kind they used to write before the white man came. Sycamore folded it up carefully and tucked it away in his pocket—and it served him better than a U.S. passport in the month he was below the Line. That was the month of June, the time of the *pitahaya* harvest, and the Papagos were scattered out across the desert gathering the prickly pears. A detail of mounted *rurales* took up his trail and followed with blood in the eye; but the Indians were always against them and, though they chased him from village to village, they failed to get the reward.

The season was against them, too, for in a pinch Sycamore would hide out for a day or two, hooking the ripe fruit from the tops of the towering *sahuaros* and feeding it to his horse in place of water. A cake of mesquite-meal bread, a sack of jerky, and a canteen of water for himself, and the *pitahayas* would last them for days; but in the end this simple life palled on him. He was no Indian, though he had taken to Indian ways, and the solitude made him lonely. Yes, he was lonely as a dog, and as he fled he swung in a circle that led him back to San Ignacio.

That is the way the fox flees when he runs before the hounds, and no matter how far afield his way may lead it takes him back to his den. San Ignacio was the only home-place that Sycamore knew now, and ever since he had parted with the Capitan he had been uneasy over his words. It might be the custom, for all he knew, for Papago fathers to arrange marriages for their daughters, but the old man's talk did not point that way—or, at least, not his way. Of course Sam Slocum had taken advantage of her simple heart to convert her to his side—and doubtless she was prepared to urge him to come in—but that was by the way and took no place in his mind—it looked as though Capitan Juan was trying to marry her to a Papago!

The more Sycamore mused upon her grace

and beauty, the more he remembered her tender ministrations and the music of her voice, the more he was obsessed by a desire to see her and the more his wobbly circle turned back towards his heart's desire. After a month in the open his right arm was strong again and he could draw and shoot as before; Round Valley was freshly shod with a new set of cowboy shoes—there was nothing to stand in his way now but the fear of the hard-riding rangers. But who were Lee Ruggles and his rangers? No better men than himself, and not so good! He knew that country like a book, and he could shoot it out with any of them! No, he was not afraid—and to prove it he rode one night to within a mile of San Ignacio.

There was something awesome and spooky about San Ignacio at daybreak. It was as dead and deserted as the tombs—and yet Sycamore had his doubts. If Sam Slocum knew he was in love with the girl he knew he would come back to see her; and there might be a ranger there, hid. For a long time he watched the town through his glass; then as nothing stirred he circled it and looked for tracks; when he found them all pointing one way he rode in and watered his horse. Yes, the town was deserted. The doors were all shut and fastened and there wasn't a dog to bark at him. Once more Sycamore looked at the tracks and he found that they were headed for the hills—the Indians had taken everything that they possessed, rounded up their ponies and cattle, and moved up into the *pitahaya* belt.

Yet who would need a guide with that broad trail before him? He followed on up the cañon, past the mescal pit and the pot-holes and out on the ridge to the north; and from there he swept the lower country with his glass. Along the level bench-land that lay at the foot of the range the giant cacti stood like an immense planted field of pickets and, passing in and out among them, he could make out a pinto horse. Then he picked up other horses, and the smoke from a cañon fire—that was their camp, where the women were boiling down syrup. But even this did not satisfy him and he lay hid until he made out Desert Willow.

She was moving along a ridge with her duenna and he could tell her by the way she walked. Upon her back was a great carrying basket and as she mounted towards him she reached up to the tops of the *sahuaros* with a long pole made of giant-cactus ribs; then she stooped to pick up the fruit and glided on. Even at her heavy labor she was lithe and graceful, too fine a figure of a woman to be wasted on such a task. But that was the Indian of it—probably the men were all off in a side-cañon somewhere, brewing up *tizwin* from the cactus syrup and having a general drunk.

Sycamore picked out a landmark and started towards it, riding across country over the ridges, and at last, quite unexpectedly, he came upon Frances Willard. She was standing on a hillside resting and when she looked up and saw him she started and turned away quickly. Then without a word she raised her basket and hurried back to her duenna. It was then that Sycamore remembered certain rough and evasive answers which he had given to the Capitan, as well as his flat refusal to see her when she had come clear down to the Line. But his was not a shrinking nature and he followed along above her until he could flag the chaperon.

This amiable old woman, who answered to the name of Tia, had helped nurse him during his sickness and he had rewarded her with a nugget of his stolen gold, as well as with other tokens of good will; but now that they were caught out alone the duenna refused to respond to his advances—his grins and signs were useless, it was plain she did not approve.

"What do you want?" murmured Desert Willow at last, still turning her face away.

"Oh, nothin' much," answered Sycamore. "Where's the old Capitan?"

There was a silence then, and he perceived he had touched a sore subject—her father had probably scolded her about him.

"Well, how are they comin', Francisca?" he enquired, with a cheerful assumption of friendship. But still there was no answer. They stood there, looking down or glancing out through their heavy hair, with the tense immobility of wild animals that think they are hid or, knowing that they are discovered, still cling to their protective pose. If they fled, he might follow after; if they went on he would fall in behind; so they stood still and waited.

"Huh!" grunted Sycamore at last as the implication became plain to him, "reckon they're scairt of me!" He reined his horse away as he spoke and spurred savagely on towards the camp and then suddenly Frances Willard came to life.

"Don't go over there!" she called, motioning for him to stop.

"Why not?" demanded Sycamore, turning in his saddle.

"There's a man there!" she answered mysteriously.

"Huh—may be the very feller I'm lookin' for!" returned Sycamore with a devilish swagger. "Old Sam Slocum, eh?"

"Oh, no, no! Not him! It's—" she paused and looked away bashfully.

"Well, who is it?" enquired Sycamore, riding back and ogling her with masterful eyes. "Some ranger—or something like that?"

"No, it's—it's only an Indian boy—but—"

"Oho!" said Sycamore. "So that's it! Some feller that's workin' for 'em—some feller to give 'em a tip, eh?"

She did not answer this directly but by a droop of the head seemed to give a guarded assent.

"All right," nodded Sycamore, leaning nearer to her, "and I'm much obliged to you, sure. I seen you with my glass from the ridge yonder—and kinder come over this way, you know. You been a pretty good friend to me, Francisca. How're you gittin' along?" he enquired impulsively, and at this sudden sign of interest her breast heaved and she cast her eyes to the ground.

"Oh I am so 'shamed!" she wailed at last. "I did not mean—I thought—"

"Aw, that's all right," answered Sycamore comfortingly. "I knew old Sam had not got around you. But never mind all that—say, gimme one of them cactus-pears, will you?"

She reached it up to him instantly and an expert chaperon might have noted a slight clutching of hands as the desert fruit was exchanged, but Tia was looking away.

"I'm kinder 'shamed, too," confessed Sycamore as he peeled the bright red pear. "You been mighty good to me, Francisca, and I—well, I sure appreciate it. But I was feelin' powerful mean that day you come down to the Line, and—well, I didn't want to see you. I'd do most anythin' for you, Francisca—you jest ask me sometime—and, well, I was afeerd if you asked me to come in I'd weaken. Gimme another pear, will you?"

She passed him another *pitahaya* and as their

hands met she gazed at him with eyes so soft and lustrous that there was no longer a secret between them.

"Say," said Sycamore, coming down off his horse, "lemme help you work, will ye?" And while they were behind a mesquite tree he caught her in his arms and kissed her.

CHAPTER XXIII

G BAR LALLY

Perhaps it was because he himself had something to conceal and therefore failed to make the proper advances, but it seemed to Sycamore as he rode into the Indian camp that he was not quite as welcome as formerly. The old Capitan in particular was short-spoken and distant, and a running fire of comment from the young men of the party made it evident that he was not popular with the rat-eaters. Not since their first camp at the mescal pits, where Desert Willow had tended so carefully to his wounds, had the *muchachos* regarded him kindly, but their remarks, now, in Papago, seemed caustic.

Sycamore had been very careful to ride on ahead, and he never so much as glanced at Francisca when she came in, but somehow the news of his arrival had preceded him, and evidently some word of his indiscretion. If he had not squared himself with old Tia he had certainly tried to, and Francisca was not doing any talking,—perhaps some envious rival, skulking along the ridges, had noted his devoted attentions, or for that matter simply seen his *palomino* horse from a distance and made a bold guess at the rest. At any rate his presence and conduct seemed to be well known and, as near as he could judge from their language, quite as generally disapproved.

It is the custom of the desert Papagos to abandon their villages in summer and move with all their belongings to the mountains. This is partly because their wells and clay-bottomed "tanks" go dry and fail to provide sufficient water for their stock; but it also takes them up out of the hot, flat desert and puts them near to the *pitahayas* and mescal plants. It is also the occasion of the annual cactus-wine festival, when the syrup of the *sahuaro* fruit is mixed with water and fermented in great earthen *ollas* and, after four days of religious ceremonies, most religiously and uproariously consumed.

On the beginning of this festival the women are in the habit of retiring, since they do not take part in the grand drunk, and waiting the sober to-morrow—or next week. Whether he had arrived at the beginning of the festival, when his presence might interfere with the magic of the ferment, or at the end, when the men were recovering from their jag, Sycamore did not know. He only knew that he was unwelcome and, after getting his supper and buying some corn for his horse, he chose a time when no one was looking to slip quietly out into the darkness.

A long period of dodging and hiding had made

him preternaturally careful, so that he refused to sleep in a house or even near other men. He was worth a thousand dollars—dead—in Mexico, and human nature is indeed frail. He had found it so, and though the Papagos had always shown themselves his friends he did not subject them to any breaking-test temptations, especially while he was asleep. So on this occasion he reverted to his Mexico practises and retired about a half a mile from camp. Here, in an open space where the desert grass stood high, he unsaddled by a bush and prepared to spend the night. First he fed Round Valley his corn and picketed him with a long rope to the bush; then he spread his saddle-blankets down for a bed, took off his boots and hat, and settled down to pleasant dreams.

At intervals during the night Round Valley would drag the rope across his face or come up close and stand on three legs while he dozed, but all these little attentions were appreciated by Sycamore because they kept him alert. And Round Valley played his part well, for if any wild animal or Indian pony came near, he would snort and pull on his rope. The false dawn came, a faint rosy exhalation in the east, and as his horse began to tug at the bush Sycamore got up, picked up his saddle and bed, and moved to where there was feed. Then it came on dark again, the black dark that precedes the sun, and he sank into a dreamless sleep.

But there is no real rest for the wicked—Sycamore rose up suddenly from his blankets and stared off towards the east. It was daybreak now and the first gorgeous rays of light were touching the saw-toothed summits; all the mystery of the desert and the calm of dawn was present there—but Round Valley sensed something more. He looked up from his feeding and snorted, and then he stood intent, his ears pointing to the east. If he had fallen to chomping again Sycamore would have dropped back to sleep in a moment; as it was he sat still and waited. All was quiet; he slipped on his boots mechanically and buckled up his belt—then suddenly he sprang to his feet and grappled with blanket and saddle. A distant clack—the clank of iron on granite—had come to him from the east, and Round Valley snorted again. Then in an ague of haste Sycamore ran to him and threw on the blankets; up went the saddle, cumbered with carbine and field-glass and saddle-bags stuffed with food, and with a quick tug at the rope he went skulking low for cover. That sound was the thud of an iron-shod hoof—and Indian horses don't wear shoes!

Behind a bushy palo verde tree he halted and twitched out his glass; then he put it up quietly and stood ready to mount and ride. It was Lally, the G Bar man who had turned ranger, and Sycamore knew he had come to get him. A good-looking Papago boy that he had seen around camp the day before was with him and they were slipping up on the camp. Slowly they rode along by him, a hundred yards or more up the hill, and as old memories and a sudden hate rose up in him Sycamore jerked his gun from its holster. No G Bar man could run it over him, and as for that rat-eating Papago kid, nothing would delight him more than to reward him for his treachery with a bullet. He threw up his carbine and stood watching them, but somehow that wasn't his style—he couldn't shoot a man from cover. Very slowly now they forged ahead, their eyes always to the front, and as the ridge of a hog-back concealed them Sycamore swung warily up into his saddle and took the back trail at a walk.

That is the common trick of hunted animals—to crouch and let the hunter pass and then slip off to one side. Men who go out after deer often find where they have been eluded, and now and then a man-hunter fails as well. G Bar Lally was a ranger, but the office did not render him infallible—not even with an Indian guide. Sycamore walked his horse for safety; then he jogged him as he hit into the back trail; and finally with a wry grin on his face he leaned forward and struck into a gallop. These smart Teehannos with their double-cinch saddles and little tin badges were not so bad as they looked. Sycamore was not even in a hurry to get away from Mr. Lally. It was a free country, and a fine large one too; but if any one man thought he could chase him clear to the Line he was entitled to one more guess.

The trail which Sycamore followed was an open one and it did lead towards the Line. Now that the rangers had discovered him there was no other place to go—they might box him up in some cañon or shoot down his horse in a pass—but that was different from being afraid. In the mountains a man can be ambushed or surrounded, and even the low pass ahead of him was dangerous; but out in the open country with an even break at the start he would match Round Valley against any of them. He galloped on until he got out of the giant cactus and then with the rocky bench-land behind him and the flat sandy plain under foot, he pulled down to a fox-trot and kept a close watch behind.

He was a good four miles out in the open and well on his way to the south pass when Lally broke out of the brush. Like most Texans he was a rough rider, having been told that there would be horses after he was dead, and the moment he clapped eyes on Sycamore he was after him at a gallop. But Sycamore was thinking of the long ride still ahead, and of a possible ambush at the pass, and he refused to gallop through the sand. So they led off across the barren desert, streaking in and out among the scattered creosote bushes, until Lally had closed up half the gap. Encouraged by this he began to whip and spur and, fearing to allow him within rifle-shot, Sycamore headed for the pass at a lope.

The memory of the chase that Sam Slocum had given him was still fresh and black in his mind and he rode furiously until he reached the divide. But there were no rangers there to waylay him. He swept the broad floor of the desert with his glasses and smiled as he found it bare. He had a free way into Mexico—and there was only one man behind. Should he flee now, while the fleeing was good, and show him a cloud of dust to the Line, or stand up to him like a man and shoot it out then and there? It did not take Sycamore long to come to a decision; he was tired of being chased around by swelled-up officers of the law—he would give Mr. Lally a lesson.

Quickly putting his horse behind a rock which rose up like a citadel near at hand he scrambled to the top of it and settled himself in a crevice; then, raising his sights to the limit he held a coarse bead on the ranger and pulled the trigger. Several seconds passed, while he pumped up another shell, and then the bullet fell short. Again he fired, holding higher, and the ranger swung low in his saddle; once more he drew down on him remorselessly, not caring whether he got man or horse, and again the tall ranger ducked. But he came on, regardless of consequences, flailing his weary horse with the quirt, and Sycamore held a dead center and fired. There was a pause, while the bullet sought its target, and then horse and man went down.

A cloud of dust rose up and hid them and then, from far ahead in the road, the man got up and looked about. His hat was gone and he limped as he walked but his fighting spirit was not dashed. With vengeful haste he rushed back to his horse and tried to get him up, but Sycamore had blood in his eye now and he pumped forth a hail of bullets. They were none too carefully aimed but they kicked up just as much dust and as the third of them struck in front of him and went singing away into space, G Bar Lally broke and ran. He did not even stop to grab his saddle-gun but hit for cover forthwith, and Sycamore grinned broadly as he scrambled down from his rock.

He was grinning halfway to Mexico, and he didn't hurry either, but as he ambled on towards the Line the laugh died out and vanished. It was all right to scare up G Bar Lally and leave him afoot in the desert; but G Bar was a ranger, an Arizona Ranger, and a fighting, vindictive cuss to boot. Also Captain Lee Ruggles might resent his unprofessional conduct in downing one of his pets and send out a couple more. And they might be mean and ornery enough to linger around San Ignacio and nab him when he came to see his girl. She was his girl, all right, and she swore she never would marry one of those no-account Papago boys anyway—but how about getting to see her? Perhaps after all he had made a tactical mistake—it might have been better to let Mr. Lally think he was afraid of him and give him a heat to the Line.

Yes, it undoubtedly would. For Lee Ruggles did resent the slight to the service and he watched San Ignacio the way a hawk watches a squirrel-mound. It was easy enough for Sycamore to edge in on the town, but to get away from it—that was the proposition. And Lally tried every low-down, sneaking trick he knew of to ambush him and shoot down Round Valley—or was it Round Valley he was shooting at? Then there came about a spirit of friendly cooperation between the rangers and the Mexican *rurales* and the Line began to lose its attractions. In fact, from the Parnassus heights of love Sycamore was cast down to the seventh hell of remorse, and as he fled from place to place he began to wonder what it was all about and how he was ever to escape.

Not a word of news could he learn; he had no idea whether Lum Martin had been sent up for life or turned loose to dig up his money—and for that matter he did not care. What he wanted was a look from Francisca's dark eyes, a smile from her sweet sad lips and the music of her voice in his ears. Then Lum could keep his money. But there was a reward up on both sides of the Line, and the Indians were not so friendly any more, and—well, he had a man or two on his trail to boot. A thousand dollars is such a pitifully large sum to some people—they will knife a man in his sleep for the half of it, or ambush him when he is talking with his girl. There was a scar-faced Mexican in particular who dogged his steps in Mexico, and even took a chance across the Line, though there was a reward up for *him* in Arizona. And Sycamore, had saved his life, too. Yes, he had turned him out of jail, only a month or so before he was going to be hanged. That shows how much gratitude you can expect from a Mexican—the ingrate was Bravo Juan!

Bravo Juan had visited a ranch house at sundown, forced an old woman who was there to cook him up a meal and then, after eating it, had shot her down in cold blood. That is the kind of an hombre Bravo Juan was, and yet when he came across Sycamore down in Sonora he had tried to call him brother. Just because there was a thousand dollars up for both of them the low-browed felon had presumed to think they were equals! He had wanted to shake hands and burn the makings of a cigarette, and when Sycamore had refused to throw in with him he had got ugly and tried to betray him. For Bravo Juan was a cunning brute—he committed all his crimes in the United States and the *rurales* would not arrest him. In fact, it looked as though he was working for them, or at least for their thousand-dollar reward.

Well, that is the way things were going, and between the rangers on one side and Bravo Juan and the *rurales* on the other there was no rest for Sycamore Brown. His clothes became worn and ragged, his hair and beard unkempt and long, and there was such a wild, hunted look in his eyes that everyone knew him at sight. He was the outlaw *Americano*, the man who robbed trains and mines and paid for his food with gold. Even at the most distant goat-ranches where the *paisanos* lived on cheese and *tortillas* and dwelt as isolated as rock-rabbits, even there the wide-eyed natives recognized him, for the news of his crimes had gone everywhere. Also the news of the reward—five hundred dollars alive, a thousand dollars dead—and a thousand *pesos* would make a peon a king.

There was no safety for him anywhere, not even in the humblest dwelling, and his stolen money seemed accursed, for it tempted men to kill him. Then at last a black despair settled down upon him and remorse for what he had done. Now when it was too late he repented his wild deeds and longed dumbly to be good, but the officers would have none of him. In vain he sent in letters and made smoke at appointed places—Lee Ruggles refused to treat with him or so much as come out for a talk. No one came to answer his signals, but G Bar Lally established a camp near San Ignacio and waited, with Desert

Willow for his lure. It was all in the year's work with him, but for Sycamore it was a heart-break, a madness, a yearning that gave him no rest as he fought against his fate.

For months the hunt was kept up, first by the rangers and then by the *rurales*, and at every chase he would circle back to San Ignacio. Then of a sudden he dropped out of sight, and the rangers watched for him in vain. One month passed and then another, and Chief Juan sent runners far down into Mexico. He had reasons for wishing to know, but there was no news of the white-skinned *Americano* who had paid all his debts with gold. He had gone and only rumors came back from him—now in the south, now in the east, now far away to the west where the ancient Journey of Death leads on to California. Now he was rumored killed, now denned in a Mexican jail, now raiding the mines in Chihuahua and the Sierra Madres; and then all word was lost and the winter wore on to spring.

CHAPTER XXIV
OUTLAWED

Whether they looked for him with eyes of jealousy and hate or with eyes of love and longing no one saw Sycamore Brown at San Ignacio until the flowers had come. Then as the broad desert was shot with yellow poppies and the flaunting white of primroses, he rode in on the town at dawn. He was changed now, clean-shaven and dressed like a Mexican, with tight-fitting trousers and jacket and a sombrero trimmed with silver braid; but Round Valley was the same, and the Indians knew him from afar.

There had been a time when Sycamore was welcome at San Ignacio, but times had changed and the only face he looked for was nowhere to be seen. The men stood aloof in sullen groups as he rode boldly up the trail, the women peered out from behind half-closed doors; and old Chief Juan, his face set and inscrutable, received him like any stranger. As for Sycamore, if he had expected a more cordial reception he did not show it but greeted the Capitan formally and sat quietly on his horse.

Of all the Indians in Arizona the desert Papagos are the most inhospitable and clannish, and their hearts are easily swayed by jealousy and distrust.

The white man had dared to woo a Papago; he had brought in the officers and the rangers and now even the Capitan, who had taken his part at first and shared his ill-gotten gold, was anxious to see him off. So he sat there, sphinx-like, gazing quietly out across the desert, and Sycamore lopped down in his saddle and waited. You cannot hurry an Indian; he must take his time, and then either he will treat with you or he will not. Sycamore had come a long way to see Francisca, but only through her father's favor could he hope to have his wish. She was hid away somewhere, probably in the adobe house, and there she would stay until her father told her to come out.

Half an hour went by and like a mound of prairie-dogs that have been disturbed by a passing hawk the Indians began to come out. It was breakfast time, and there was water to carry; the women made it the occasion to slip out and look at the *huero*. A small boy came up from behind and when Sycamore turned upon him suddenly he ran squalling into the house. Evidently the Papago mothers were using him to scare their children now. Still he sat there, puffing his cigarettes, and as he threw one away the old man looked up at him quickly.

"What you want?" he said.

"Oh, nothing, nothing," answered Sycamore, shrugging his shoulders.

"Hunh!" grunted the Capitan and looked out over the plain.

"Where you go?" he said at last.

"Nowhere," shrugged Sycamore. "Nowhere. I just came here to San Ignacio to see my friend the Capitan." A light of interest came into Chief Juan's eyes but he was silent. "When I was here before," continued Sycamore, "Capitan Juan was my friend. He took me in when I was hungry—he cared for me when I was hurt—he hid me when I was hunted. *Muy bien*, Sycamore does not forget. I have come to bring a present—but if the Señor Capitan is displeased I will go away."

He reined in his horse as if about to go, but the old chief held up his hand. A memory of a bar of gold came back to him, and he knew that Sycamore had more.

"What is this present," he asked. "Something that is stolen? *Muy malo*—pretty soon come ranger-man—come deputy—take away—put Capitan in jail! What is it?"

"Only a little thing," answered Sycamore negligently. "It is nothing, Señor Capitan—nothing but a gift from a friend. And since the gift is not welcome—" he paused and shrugged again.

"Where you come from?" demanded the Capitan roughly. He was beginning to sense the gold.

"*Muy lejos*," sighed Sycamore, waving his hand

towards the east, "very far!" And then he sighed again.

"You hungry?" enquired the old man, his eyes beginning to burn. "You want coffee? *Muy bien*—get down. Pretty soon—women cook."

So Sycamore found his way back; and out in the brush-covered cook-house he found Francisca, though she never looked up from her work. Old Tia was there also but she turned away from him, and the old chief was low in his mind. The breakfast passed in silence, without a word of praise for the food, and the minute it was over Sycamore rose up and stepped outside. Behind him followed the Capitan, still studying on something in his mind, and they smoked several cigarettes before he could frame it into words.

"*Señor Americano*," he began, "you know my daughter—no?"

"*Sí, Señor*," responded Sycamore gravely.

The old man paused and pondered a long time now, watching him from under his eyebrows.

"You like my daughter—your wife?" he asked at last, but Sycamore had read his black heart too well to fall into such a trap.

"It would be great honor, Señor Capitan," he replied, "to marry the daughter of Chief Juan. She is a good woman and whoever gets her will be lucky, but my mind is set on other things. I am going on a long journey and cannot marry now. I am going very far, *amigo*, and perhaps I may never come back. So I have come to bring you a gift and say farewell to your daughter."

He got up as he spoke and walked slowly over to his saddle-bags, and the old chief watched him like a hawk. Then from the depths he fetched up a little bundle wrapped in canvas and returned to his former seat. The package was small and heavy and he hefted it thoughtfully as he sat idly in the sun. Inside that little roll was a solid ingot of gold—his last—dug up from his cache in the rocks, and he offered it for the old chief's favor. If he invited him in to see his daughter, well and good; if not, a silk handkerchief would do as well. It would pay for all the friendship that he got. So he sat there, waiting, and Capitan Juan stared at him hard. He was a crafty old fox and understood the situation well.

"When you go?" he enquired, his face wrinkling up in a sudden smile.

"*Poco tiempo*," answered Sycamore, meaning any time between ten minutes and ten days, and the Capitan rose to his feet.

"Come," he said, and led the way to the kitchen. There he spoke rapidly in Papago and went abruptly out, while Tia got discreetly busy with the dishes. Desert Willow washed her hands and came to meet him, but their greeting was formal and restrained. They shook hands, glanced at each other shyly, and then sank down on a bench to gaze bashfully at Tia. But this world was not made to order for lovers and Sycamore decided to make the best of it.

"How're you comin', Francisca?" he enquired reaching stealthily for her hand, and while the aged duenna scoured the pots and *ollas* and sighed at her lot in life the lovers drew closer together. It was costing him about a hundred dollars a minute, if the Capitan wanted to nidge, but Sycamore was fully satisfied. He still had the gold in his pocket, too, and he resolved to keep it for a while. So they chattered along, Francisca in her Indian-school English, which she was already beginning to forget, and Sycamore telling boastful stories which no one else had ever heard. The old woman pottered about, dumbly, listening uncomprehendingly to their English and making a thousand excuses to stay, until at last she stepped out for some wood.

"You're lookin' mighty pretty, Francisca," suggested Sycamore, drawing closer as Tia passed out the door. "I come a long ways to see you—and mebby I won't see you again. How about—" He paused and looked at her more closely. "What's the matter, *chiquita*?" he whispered. "Don't you like me no more? You ain't goin' to quit me, are you, and marry one of these *muchachos*? Can't you give me a kiss, sweetheart? You know I stole that other one. No? Well, all right—but what's the matter?"

"I have many troubles," answered Francisca,

turning her downcast face away. "Troubles with my people—troubles with my father—troubles with you. I am sorry now that I went to school—all the time I am dis-satisfied. My father is angry because I will not obey him—the people do not like me—and no one will speak me English! Oh, I am so lonely to talk English—but no one ever comes."

"No, you're plumb wasted out here!" assented Sycamore. "You're too educated for this bunch. D'ye hear from yore old friend, Miss Kellogg, now? No? Well, she's all right and you remember what she said: Don't you throw yourself away on no ignorant *muchacho*—you jest wait till some man comes along that can buy you an electric flat-iron, eh?"

He dived down into his pocket and flashed his wedge of gold, but she only shook her head.

"Miss Kellogg taught me that it is wrong to steal," she said, suddenly fixing him with her sad eyes. "That is why I am sorry—for you."

"Huh! You don't call robbin' rurales stealin', do you?" demanded Sycamore indignantly. "You don't think I'm a *thief,* do you? Ump-umm! When I want anything I take my gun and go after it—but I'm no petty-larceny sneak-thief, not by a long shot!"

"And then you shoot people," continued Francisca, hopelessly, "and live with bad men—and the rangers come out here to catch you. Oh,

I was so ’shamed when Mr. Slocum came! He said you were a bad man and ought to be sent to prison—and then I told him ‘No!’—and he told me all you had done. I was sorry then that I had ever known you—it made me cry—and to-night I will cry again. I was your friend then, and I felt so sorry for you, but—but—”

“Oh, you want me to go away, do you?” suggested Sycamore, getting up suddenly to look out at his horse. “Don’t want to talk with no hold-up, hey?” he enquired sardonically. “This here gold don’t look good to you, now does it?”

He flashed the bright wedge of gold and grinned triumphantly, but she refused to answer with a smile.

“It is wrong to steal,” she repeated gently. “I am sorry.”

“Well,” said Sycamore, sitting down beside her and trying to enter her mood, “I’m sorry, too. It don’t pay—that’s the size of it. There’s nothin’ in this hold-up game—I wish to God I was out of it!” He paused a minute, but there was silence and Desert Willow sat very still. “You’d like me better then, wouldn’t you, Francisca?” he ventured. “Wouldn’t you?” he urged, and Tia came in with the wood.

“Well,” he said at last as the silence became oppressive, “I reckon I better be movin’. Saw yore good-lookin’ Papago friend goin’ out to git the rangers—’n they’s nothin’ around here for me." He rose and waited for her to protest but she did not even look up. "Sorry I ain't good enough for you," he muttered bitterly. "Too bad I ain't an Injun." Then as she sat unmoved he jammed on his hat and was gone.

The Capitan met him outside the door, grinning evilly, and Sycamore handed him the gold. He swept the horizon with his field-glasses, paused to stare at the east, and slapped them back into the case.

"*Mira*," he said, motioning impatiently to the smirking chief. "There comes the Capitan of the rangers on my trail. When he gets here tell him I am tired of hiding. If he will talk with me, make a smoke and I will meet him across the Line."

He tightened his cinch and mounted, and the old Capitan held out his hand.

"*Adios*, *amigo*," he said, but Sycamore glanced at him coldly.

"Never mind," he answered reining his horse away, "but tell the Capitan."

CHAPTER XXV

A FIGHTING CHANCE

It was a black day for Sycamore as he sat on a little hill across the Line and waited for Lee Ruggles. After all his hardships and fighting, his wounds, his flights, his hidings in desert lands, it had come to this—waiting to give himself up! When Desert Willow had been his friend it had seemed a trifle, but now she had turned against him—she could not stand for a thief. But the gold was nothing to him—absolutely nothing. He had given a thousand dollars' worth to her father and never grudged a cent. It was to see her that he had come—she was the girl he wanted—and now she had turned him down. An Indian girl—a Papago! And yet—well, she was the girl he loved.

He sat and watched the signal smoke that rose up from San Ignacio, and his mind leapt on ahead. He thought of jails, and prisons with their fetid air; of brutal associates and wasting idleness, and coming out again an old man. An ex-con, a branded criminal—what hope would there be for him then? And where would he find Desert Willow? She would be an old woman then, a wrinkled squaw, the slave to some rat-eating Papago. No, it was too much! It was too much for a man who had just robbed for sport—for fun, you might say—and because he had fallen in with old Lum. Yet that was the way with the law.

He sat with his head in his hands, thinking. Then suddenly, like one who wakes up from a long dream, he straightened up and looked about. Here was the desert—there was San Ignacio—the girl was still there—why give up? Why not fight it out? Or perhaps he could square himself! Perhaps they would give him a chance! He was young; he had been easily influenced; the judge might let him off, if he would come through with what he knew. Once more he mulled it over, but when he sat quiet and considered the matter again his soul rose up against it.

Stool he never would, not for Slocum nor for all his men; but if he surrendered they would have him at their mercy. They could starve him then, and punish him, and give him the third degree—and if he refused they could send him up for life. Or they could keep him shut up in jail from one court session to another until he perished for sun and air. And good old Round Valley—he would have to part with him—he would never see him again.

So he sat, heart-broken and vacillating to and fro, until Lee Ruggles rode in from across the Line. Ruggles was a jolly fellow—last time he had come out he had laughed and got off jokes—but this time he was serious. No, he was more than that—he was stern-eyed and half-resentful. Maybe the long ride on his trail had not helped to soothe his nerves.

"Well," he said as he climbed wearily up the hill, "I hear you want to come in."

"Might," answered Sycamore. "What can you do for me?"

"Who? Me?" demanded the ranger brusquely. "Not a thing! If you'd've come in when I asked you I'd've let you down easy—now I won't promise you nothin'."

He cast himself down on a rock and rolled a cigarette grimly. The sweat of a long hard chase had dried on his face, and his mouth was set and stubborn. Evidently he thought the chase was ended.

"You're no good to us now," he went on as Sycamore sat limp and silent. "If you'd've come through and convicted Lum Martin we'd've treated you like a king—now you can take yore medicine, like the rest of 'em."

"And supposen I don't come in," suggested Sycamore mildly.

The ranger glanced up at him sharply and left the words unsaid. There was another side to it, of course.

"What has happened to old Lum?" enquired Sycamore, after a pause.

"He got ten years—Jack Haines the same. And Haines is wanted in Texas, too."

"I thought Jack was goin' to testify against him!"

"Nope. They both stood pat."

"Huh!" grunted Sycamore. "That shows what a liar Sam Slocum is—he told me that Haines had confessed. Where's Sam now?"

"Over in California."

"Never did find that loot, did he?"

"Nope. Know anything about it?"

"Not a thing. Never did. So Lum got ten years, eh? And wouldn't come through with it then! By Joe, I bet there was a lot of money in them sacks!"

"Nope. The express company says there was less than nine thousand."

"Well, I know better!" cried Sycamore excitedly. "I—" He stopped, and Ruggles grinned at him quizzically.

"You put it in, eh?" he suggested, and Sycamore bit his lip.

"No, but I bet Lum would never spend no ten years in that hell-hole down at Yuma for a little old ten thousand dollars. Got any more indictments ag'inst him?"

"No, but we might extradite him into Mexico for that bullion robbery. Sam Slocum is workin' on the case. If Lum will come through we can get him pardoned, but if he don't—well, you know what they'd do to him in Mexico!"

"Umm," mused Sycamore, "I reckon I do! But you'll never bluff old Lum. He'll serve his sentence and dig up that money and you'll never see him no more. He'll git away with it all."

Sycamore spoke with a settled conviction, and for once in his life he was right. Lum Martin got three years off for good behavior, was released several days before his extradition papers came and promptly dropped out of sight. A month later he showed up at Hackamore at midnight, worked the hotel-keeper for a bottle of whiskey and disappeared into outer darkness, taking his secret—and probably his treasure—with him. But for all that, it might have been different!

"Pore old Lum," said Sycamore, "he's crazy over that money—but say—what d'ye want me for?"

"Well," the ranger hesitated, "Sam thought you might put something more on him and then Lum would weaken and—"

"Not on yore life!" cried Sycamore. "Nothin' like that! If I come in I don't testify ag'inst nobody—jest surrender and stand my trial like the others. But ten years is an awful long time—"

"Umph!" grunted the ranger, and looked him over pityingly.

"Think I'll git that much?" ventured Sycamore, and the ranger's face grew cunning.

"Don't know, Syc," he said. "Depends on whether you plead guilty or not."

"Huh!" protested Sycamore, making a bold face of it. "*I* never done nothin'—you got no case aginst me, nohow. Who's yore witnesses?"

"Well, I don't know," answered Ruggles slowly. "That's the district attorney's job. My orders are to bring you in."

He stated it very mildly, but Sycamore read something behind.

"Oh, how about that jail-breakin' job?" he exclaimed as a new light broke in upon him. He was scared, now that he perceived the pitfall—they could give him the limit for that!

"Well," admitted Ruggles, "you're indicted for it, all right."

"Oho!" murmured Sycamore, and then he drew cautiously away. "Well, I'm sorry to make you so much trouble, Lee," he said, "but I guess I won't come in."

"Git you anyway!" menaced the ranger, standing up and eyeing him watchfully.

"Not while I'm in Mexico!" answered Sycamore shortly, and he slipped in behind a rock. Even with a good fellow like Ruggles it was just as well to be safe.

Ruggles smiled.

"You're gittin' pretty careful, ain't you, Syc," he remarked and then he stood awhile, smoking. "How about the rurales?" he suggested at last, but still with a quizzical smile.

"Huh!" grunted Sycamore scornfully, "I reckon if I can dodge the rangers I don't need to be scared o' *them!*"

Again the captain of the rangers smiled, and suddenly his face became frank. "By God, Syc," he declared, "if you was straight I could come pretty nigh usin' you! I wish you wasn't such a crook!"

"*I* ain't no crook!" retorted Sycamore hotly. "Who did I ever do? Ain't I got the dirty end of it every time? No, I ain't no crook! That's why I sent for you—I'd like to square myself, if I could!"

"Well, you can't do it!" replied Ruggles shortly. He sat down on his rock again and stroked his mustache thoughtfully. "I'll tell you, Syc," he said at last, "I'll tell you what you're up against. You might get out from under on that train-robbery count, but when you broke open the jail and let out Bravo Juan you got yoreself into a jack-pot. I don't care what yore idee was—you turned that hombre loose on us and he certainly has raised hell. Now there's jest one way to square yoreself and that is—*bring him in!* You catch me that Mexican and put him across the Line and I'll square you with the district attorney!"

"Sure enough?" cried Sycamore, the fighting light flashing up in his eyes. "Can you do it? I'm scairt of them lawyers, Lee—they'll ketch me on somethin' else!"

"No, I'll give you my word, Syc—and I'll tell you how I can do it. It's the Governor that wants this Bravo Juan, and he wants him bad. I've got my orders to get him, and to get him at any cost. If you get sent up, the governor will pardon you out again—but you never will, because the district attorney wants him worse than the Governor. The whole Territory is in on it, and if I don't bring him in pretty soon I'm liable to lose my job. That's the size of it, Syc—now what can you do about it?"

"Well, I'll git 'im!" answered Sycamore, "or die tryin'. He's a treacherous devil—I've had him on my trail for months. But that ain't it—he's a fightin' bastard—I don't believe he'll ever give up. You got to have him alive, have you?"

"Yes, we got to have him alive. He's been murderin' people and defyin' the authorities until these border Mexicans think it's safe. That's why we want to hang him."

"Umm," murmured Sycamore, still pondering on his plans. "Where did you hear from him last? Along the San Pedro, eh? Well, that's a mighty bad place for me—there's a squad of rurales stationed there that knows my horse ten miles away. Where else does he run? Up around Naco? Well, I got to git him away from there, that's all. Yes sir, I can't do a thing around them rurales—I got to git him away.

"I'll tell you, Lee," he said at last, "I reckon I can git him, but here's the proposition. I got a thousand dollars on my head down in Mexico, and Bravo Juan is after it. If I can tole him out of the country I may be able to nab him, but if it ever comes to a shootin' I'll have to kill 'im, that's all. They's no use gittin' the drop on 'im—he'll fight anyway. I reckon I got to jump 'im and wrastle 'im down. Lend me a pair of hand-cuffs, will ye?"

CHAPTER XXVI

BRAVO JUAN

In the ordinary affairs of life Sycamore Brown was just good enough to lose. If he robbed a train he lost the money; if he trusted anybody they threw him down; and if he fell in love he lost out by not being an Indian—but when it came to a fight or the subtleties of a man-hunt he was back in his natural element. Bravo Juan was a bad Mexican and he had friends on both sides of the Line, but Sycamore was out to catch him and to catch him man to man.

He had no illusions about his opponent. Juan was a short man but he was broad and powerful, with a snake-like quickness of action that was more dangerous even than strength. And he was a cunning brute. Time and again he had picked up Sycamore's trail and followed it, never closing with him yet always seeking an advantage, and he had been a hard man to shake off. But now the tables were turned and Sycamore was after him. From coyote he had changed suddenly to wolf and with a glad light in his eye he headed for the San Pedro.

The San Pedro is not much of a river as rivers go. It rises in Sonora and flows uphill, following some peculiar level of its own and writhing around in its sandy bed until it breaks into the Gila. But though it defies all the laws of rivers by flowing north—and all the laws of optics by running uphill—the San Pedro is highly thought of both in Arizona and Sonora. A series of ranches and adobe houses are strung along its bottom on both sides and the cattle-trails lead to it for miles. It is water—and wherever you find water in that country you will always find somebody to talk to. Sycamore cut the river near the Line and, having a method in his madness, he stopped and talked to a Mexican.

Now border Mexicans as a class are treacherous and they have no love for the Gringo; and this man was a friend of Bravo Juan, as Sycamore had discovered to his sorrow. But now the case was different. If the *rurales* discovered him, Round Valley would have another of those long runs to the Line; but if Bravo Juan learned that he was there, who knows, he might follow after him! So Sycamore waxed confidential with the low-browed Mexican and told him where he was going—to the west. Then he drifted on again, and waited.

At the end of the second day he dropped in on another Mexican house, bought some food and some corn for his horse, and moved on towards the west again. So he lingered about, angling for his prey, and on the fifth day he sighted Bravo

Juan through his glasses. He was traveling fast and following on his trail, and in order to get him hooked Sycamore showed himself on the side of a hill as he headed out through the pass. Then he led off, and the Mexican followed behind.

But Bravo Juan was no man-hunter as that word is understood above the Line. He was not the kind that takes after a criminal, runs him down and shoots it out at the end. For a month at a time, when he was trailing Sycamore through Mexican Papaguería, he had lingered in the rear, never openly hostile, never even openly on his trail, but always snooping and watching and waiting for his chance. His presence was like the shadow of some cloud that comes racing up from nowhere and disappears in the great beyond. It kept Sycamore awake in his saddle and made him think about getting shot in the back—but the bullet had never come. Bravo Juan had kept alive quite a while by following a system of his own—he never shot but once and he waited for his time.

Now that he had the Mexican on his trail Sycamore was free to lay his plans and he pointed straight for the desert. There in the barren mountains and across the waterless plains he could isolate him from his kind, jockey him, and bring him to his hand. How to do that he did not know for sure—the first thing was to get him alone. After that he could crowd in and jump him.

For three days Sycamore rode on to the west, until he came to the edge of the desert. Twisting and turning to avoid the thrust of Rocky Mountains the trail led along the Line, now straight as an arrow for miles, now swinging to right or left to come to some hidden ranch, but from La Cienega it turned north into Arizona and Papaguería. La Cienega was a meadow and a marshy spring, a jungle of willows and arrow-weed sucking life from the seep of water, and it lay below the Line. Once it had been a cattle-ranch with adobe houses and a pole corral, but the Apaches had ravaged it too often and now the place was in ruins. It was a camping place where desert wanderers paused to stretch their skins with water before they made their start or, returning, rushed in to slake their thirst.

At the Cienega Sycamore camped for the night and started north at dawn. It was twenty miles across the desert to the first water, a deep tank in the bottom of a mountain cañon, and if Bravo Juan followed he was caught. Not two weeks before Sycamore had camped at this same water-hole, and he knew the very place where he would lie in wait for him. The only question was—would he come? For half a day Sycamore traveled on across the level brushy valley, now so deceptive with palo verdes and mesquites and the yellow of short-lived flowers. If one were to seek a drink of water in that paradise of trees and blossoms he would know why the place was called desert.

But Bravo Juan was crafty—he did not follow that day. Until the sun went down Sycamore watched for him with his glass, but he did not come. Below the Line he was bold enough, but in Arizona he was shy. So he held back, and Sycamore fumed and fretted. All night he lay tossing and restless and at dawn he was up on the peaks again. No Juan—and he did not come that day. Or if he came Sycamore did not see him.

At dusk he watered his horse and rode down out of the cañon, but his sleep that night was troubled. Time and again Round Valley would tug at his rope and snort; some evil spirit was abroad, some being that he sensed but could not see, and as the moon set his terror seemed to increase. Three times he came and stood by his master's bed, breathing hard and staring into the gloom, and each time Sycamore rose up to listen. Then he picked up his blankets and moved, though he did not know from what. The false dawn came creeping in at last, putting a faint halo on the rim of the eastern hills, and Sycamore fell dead asleep with Round Valley feeding by his side. It grew dark again, the dawn crept in, and then suddenly Round Valley stopped chewing and started. Even in his sleep Sycamore noticed it, for his ears were tuned for trouble. There was a pause, a low suspicious breathing, and then with a frightened jump Round Valley left the ground and rushed to the end of his rope.

Up from his blankets leapt Sycamore, clutching blindly for his gun—and the loud, blasting *whang* of a gun was in his ears. Somebody had shot at him—from somewhere. He looked around—ducked—and it belched at him again. Then he grabbed his pistol and shot at the smoke of the gun and a man sprang up and fled. He had crept down a little draw and fired at him over the cut bank, and now he was making for the hills. So startled was Sycamore at his sudden awakening that he stood staring until it was too late—then he recognized the skulking back of Bravo Juan!

As a man who has touched a rattlesnake and come away unharmed curls up his hand and marvels that it is whole, so Sycamore felt himself over and thanked God that he was still alive. Two shots at thirty feet, and Juan had missed him twice. The first time he had shot too quick—the second Sycamore had ducked the bullet. There were no thanks to Bravo Juan. He had crept close to make a sure shot but Round Valley had jumped and spoiled his aim. Good old Round Valley! Sycamore trembled as he burdened him with the saddle and then he was up and away. His nerve was shattered—that was all there was to it—and he wanted to get out of range.

On a little hill about a mile from the mouth of the cañon he stopped and took a drink from his canteen; then he focused his field-glasses and swept the country behind. It was brushy and covered with scattered giant cactus, but bare ridges rose up on both sides like the wings of a corral and prevented a skulking escape. Bravo Juan was there—he was hiding somewhere in the cañon—and if he came out he would have to fight. Nor had the Mexican got off so lightly, for in his haste he had dropped his rifle and Sycamore had brought it away.

As he ate a hurried breakfast his courage grew, and he began to think of war. He had his man bottled up in a box cañon—all he had to do now was to get him out. And he had him reduced to his six-shooters! That was a big start; a pistol is only good for a hundred feet or so, but a rifle will shoot a mile. He could crowd in on him now and pick his horse off, then when he had him afoot he could harry him until he gave up. Up rose Sycamore once more and rode boldly for the ridge, and from there he looked out the cañon with his glass.

The sides of this rough cañon were steep and rocky, and the bottom was piled high with a glut of boulders, but a trail wound in and out among them leading up to the water and between two of them Sycamore caught a glimpse of a bright bay horse. He dropped back over the brow and looked again, and there was Bravo Juan, skulking and looking behind, leading his horse up to water.

So close did the glasses bring him that Sycamore could see the sweat-patches on his shirt, and the gaunt flanks of his mount. They had not been to the pot-holes yet—they were parched dry by their long desert ride—and now they were looking for water. Like a flash Sycamore snapped in his glasses and sprang up on his horse. They should never get to drink—not if he could beat them up the ridge.

As a young buck leaps and bounds over rocks and deep places so Round Valley went plunging along the hillside; then with a heart-breaking scramble he fought his way up to the top. Below, not a quarter of a mile in a straight line, lay the gleam of the hidden water-hole, and on its margin stood Bravo Juan, fighting back his horse with his hat. The surface of the water was still unruffled; it was a case of who should drink first. Sycamore twitched his carbine from the saddle and held it on them quietly—then as Juan stooped to drink he splashed water in his face. Like a mountain lion surprised at a spring Bravo Juan gave one bound and lost himself among the rocks. Startled by the splash and the report the horse flew back, holding his dragging reins up high—and when Sycamore smashed a bullet on the rock before him he whirled and ran away down the cañon. Then to make the rout complete Sycamore followed him with a tattoo of bullets and Juan was left afoot.

A furious hatred, such as he had never felt for a man before, came over Sycamore as he swung his gun back to the water-hole. There crouched the man who had crept up to kill him by night, to shoot him as he lay asleep. He lay within twenty feet of the water with his mouth all made up to drink, but the hot noon sun should beat down upon him and make him pant like a lizard, and still he should not drink. With vengeful care Sycamore drew a fine bead on the hole he had entered and plumped a bullet in; then he sought every aperture in that rock-pile where the Mexican lay hid like a snake and reached for him with a thirty-thirty. It was true that Bravo Juan held the water-hole—and it was a great advantage—but if Sycamore and Round Valley must go thirsty then Juan himself should never drink. Not until the sun went down and his rifle-sights failed to catch the gleam of the tank, not until then would he let this murderer drink. The sun rose higher and higher and Round Valley sucked wistfully at his bit. At noon the canteen went dry, and it was twenty miles to water. But Bravo Juan, in that pile of rocks, was thirstier than he was—perhaps it would make him give up!

So Sycamore stuck, and the sun was within an hour of setting before he turned away. Often he had heard old Mexicans, and prospectors who had been lost on the desert, telling stories of the *visnaga* or nigger-head cactus and its wonderful tank of water. Now would be a good time to find out how bitter the juice was, and maybe Round Valley would drink it. With clubs and a jagged rock Sycamore battered away the wiry spines at the top of one of these desert tanks and cut out a cup-shaped hole; then he dug out the cool flesh, which smelled like a melon but tasted more like turnips, and crushed it until he had water. Not the kind of water that comes out of canteens—but it was wet anyhow, and Round Valley ate eagerly of the sweet, moist flesh. As no evil effects seemed to come from it Sycamore cut open another, and another, and then with his canteen half filled and Round Valley partly satisfied he caught up Bravo Juan's horse and rode down to the mouth of the cañon.

The night was coming on, and it was then that Bravo Juan was dangerous. In the sunlight he could stand up to him, but after dark it would be different. The Mexican was afoot and desperate. No matter how carefully he watched, the devil was likely to creep up on him—and another time he might not shoot so wild. It was a horse that he wanted—a mount to take him across the desert to Cienega—and if he could not get that he might manage to shoot Round Valley and put his adversary afoot. Until the sun went down Sycamore cut open *visnagas* for the gaunted bay and meditated; and then, with both horses well supplied he headed straight out into the desert. There was no sleep for him near the water-hole; but if he could escape the murderer by night he could trail him down by day, no matter where he went.

So he camped in the midst of the desert, with the two horses to keep his guard, and at the first touch of dawn he was up and saddled for the start. The bay he led behind, fully rigged but with the stirrups tied, and at a swinging trot he rode back towards the mouth of the cañon. But he did not need to go that far—as he crossed the Cienega trail he came upon Bravo Juan's tracks, leading off in long strides for Mexico. It was twenty miles, and he had on high-heeled riding boots, but the Mexican had taken his last chance. With an oath Sycamore put spurs to his horse to follow—throwing the bay loose to make more speed and leaning forward as he galloped on the outlaw's trail.

As the miles flashed past he saw the tracks grow fresher—the dew-dampness was gone from their edges and the earth curled up green and rough. Half way, and he saw where the Mexican had rested; then where he had broke into a run, and fallen. The tracks became halting and irregular now; then he found a pair of boots in the trail and bare foot-prints leading on. Juan was a peasant, after all, and when his high boots hurt him he returned to his natural state. But still he kept on and in a sudden panic Sycamore struck the lagging Round Valley with his quirt, for his man promised now to outrun him. They toiled on wearily, mile after mile, and then Round Valley gave out. He stumbled, caught himself, and stumbled again and his eyes turned so bloodshot and staring that Sycamore pulled him down to a walk. Win or lose, he would not kill Round Valley, for he valued him more than his life.

The sun was well up in the sky when Sycamore came in sight of La Cienega. Two miles from the spring a bench rises up from the valley, and there he drew out his glass. No man to be seen—no, not a living thing. He looked again, gazing long at the bunch of willows which clumped up below the spring, and while he was lazily watching it his man stepped out suddenly and stood upright in the sun. Then he walked up to the spring, came back, and squirmed into his hole like a snake. There he was—Bravo Juan—and if anyone wanted him bad enough he could crawl in and bring him out.

CHAPTER XXVII

WAR TO THE KNIFE

For a long time Sycamore sat conning the thicket through his glass—then he skinned his teeth in a vengeful grin and went back to get his horse. It was noon when he reached the mouth of that hole and the air was hot and heavy. Stripped to his overalls and shirt, barefooted and trembling with tense care, he lingered for a minute, listening; then with cautious fingers he picked the dry sticks from his path and crept silently into the thicket. In one hand he held a cocked pistol while the other cleared the way; in the slack of his belt he had a second pistol, and Lee Ruggles' hand-cuffs in his hip-pocket. The time had come when he was to meet Bravo Juan face to face, and he was going after him. All he asked was an even break, and he did not expect to get that.

Bravo Juan was waiting for him, watching to get the first shot, but perhaps he could take him by surprise. Foot by foot he crept down the narrow tunnel, where wild cattle had horned their way in in order to escape the flies, and at every turn he peered around by inches, expecting to get a shot in the face—then suddenly he crouched low and his breath came in a quick gasp. There like an Aztec war-god, grotesque in his brutish ugliness, sat Bravo Juan, leaning against a slender tree, asleep! Across his lap lay a pistol, cocked and ready, and a knife was stuck in his belt. Before him he had made a narrow loop-hole, to look out on the spring, but the heat and the quiet had overcome his watchfulness and Bravo Juan had nodded.

A sudden, fighting fire came into Sycamore's eyes at the sight and he lay for a minute panting. Then as his heart grew strong he gathered himself together and crept in on his man. A clutch at the pistol, a deft jerk at the knife-haft, and he would have the devil disarmed; then for the sudden blow, the grapple, and he would have him in his power. Breathlessly he slipped across the little open, with pistol poised; he laid it aside and rose on his knees—and Bravo Juan opened his eyes! Wide-staring, startled eyes they were, yet heavy with over-powering sleep; and the moment they came open the man-hunter made his spring.

With one hand he grabbed the cocked pistol and hurled it into the brush; he aimed a blow at the gaping jaw while the other hand clutched the knife. Then they grappled and the bushes heaved and crackled as they flung each other about. It was the knife for which they were fighting and Juan clutched at it with his bare hands, but Sycamore wrested it from him and threw him on his face. He was strong and his nerves were strung for the combat, but the Mexican was taken by surprise. Swiftly he twisted the outlaw's arm and pulled it up behind him; he whipped out the hand-cuffs and snapped them onto the wrist—and then Bravo Juan broke loose and rose up like a devil, fighting!

With hands, with feet, with a body that squirmed and twisted like a snake's, he struck and kicked and wrestled, grinding his strong teeth in an agony of effort and spitting with rage and venom. His eyes started out of his head with demoniac madness, his breath came with whistling fierceness, and like a wild cat that cannot be held he bit and scratched and kicked. No man however strong could long withstand it. They wallowed on the ground, rose up fighting, and fell among the bushes; then as he lay on his back Bravo Juan whipped back his manacled arm and struck Sycamore with the flying cuff. He struck again, and Sycamore clutched at his arm while the blood ran down his face. There was a pause, a shuddering struggle, and as he felt his hand-hold weaken Sycamore ducked before the coming blow and grabbed blindly for his spare gun.

It was gone—and the chain-hung hand-cuff stung his shoulder. Again he grabbed for the arm, and as they wrestled his knee struck something hard. It was the pistol, fallen from his waistband in the struggle. The blood was in his eyes now, blinding him with its clot of dust, but he did not need to see. Jerking loose from the uneven conflict he ducked and grabbed for the gun. The sharp, cutting corners of the chained shackles laid his head open as he swung up to strike; and then, in a blind, hateful frenzy he struck out with the revolver and took gashing blows in return. Once, twice, three times, he struck down with all his strength and then the clutching hands fell back and his flailing blows went home.

He had a hard head—Bravo Juan—otherwise he would have been killed. Sycamore came out of a daze and found himself beating a dead man, or a man who ought to be dead. As for himself, the blood was caked over his eyes until he could hardly see and his head seemed big and swollen. But he did not forget his caution. Turning the Mexican on his face he wrenched his arms behind him and fastened the limp hands with the cuffs; then he rose up and shook himself and felt tenderly of his eye. That had been a wallop, for certain, and there were other cuts as deep; but Bravo Juan had suffered worse, for his head was a welter of gore.

Catching him roughly by the shoulders Sycamore dragged the battered outlaw to the spring and there, after taking a drink himself, he slapped water on his face. It was an evil face indeed, seamed and pock-marked and knife-scarred by former battles and bleeding now from fresher wounds—and the mad eyes made Sycamore shudder. For he had to take this murdering brute a hundred miles, by day and night, and if he gave him the slightest chance he would kill him like crushing a bug.

With his back against a tree and his hands shackled together behind its trunk, Bravo Juan sat weak and lolling when Sycamore went for his horse; but when he came back he found the ground torn up and the manacles sunk deep in the flesh. That was the kind of prisoner he had, a wild, desperate brute, knowing full well his fate and fighting to save his neck. But Sycamore had learned his strength and cunning well, and he tied him tight with ropes. Then with Round Valley near to give him warning he lay down in the shade and slept. At evening the bay horse came in, gaunt and famished for water, and Sycamore caught him to carry his master to jail. All that day and night he rested, while his prisoner writhed at his stake; then with grim patience he rode across the desert, avoiding houses as he would the plague, until at last he came to Gun Sight.

But it was not a triumphal entry—far from that. Weak, starved and battered from his fight, with the shirt half torn from his back and one eye swollen shut, he dragged the bay behind him and flogged sullenly down the street. Bravo Juan, with his feet tied beneath the horse's belly and his hands shackled to the fork of the saddle, made all the trouble he could, but Sycamore was used to that; his first big jolt came when a deputy sheriff broke through the mob and told him to throw up his hands.

"Don't you think it, my friend!" flashed back Sycamore, and covered him with his gun. "Now you go on ahead," he said, "you don't come no gag like that. I took this man with my own hands and I don't give him up to no town deputy. Lee Ruggles is the man I'm workin' for and the officer ain't born that can rob me of my prisoner."

So with much jangling and quarreling along the way—for there were men who would have robbed him of his reward—Sycamore rode up to the county jail and surrendered his prisoner to Ruggles. Not even the sheriff of Gun Sight county would do—he stood valiantly by his rights and went to jail with his charge. Then there was a long day of fitful sleep and conferences with the district attorney—and the doors swung open to set him free.

The indictments against him were quashed, both for train robbery and breaking the jail; but as he went out he met Charley Randall, the jailer that Lum Martin had shot in the leg, and Charley began to curse, and limp. There was a man there too whose father had been killed by Bravo Juan, and he must needs speak his mind. So it went, and when Sycamore hired a room and flung himself down to sleep the reporters and gossip-hunters followed him up and bothered him half the night. Then bar-keepers and boon fellows sought him out, anxious to draw a crowd to their saloons and get him to sit and talk; and at the end of the second day, when he had recovered, he had a grudge against the town.

Lee Ruggles was good to him, but he was not effusive. There was a reward coming for the taking of Bravo Juan—and of course Sycamore would get it—but there were men who condemned it utterly and demanded that he be put in jail. Had he not robbed the train? Had he not opened the prison and turned Bravo Juan loose on the community? Well, what right had the captain of the rangers to set him free and give him a big reward? So they talked, wrangling and argufying in saloons and on street-corners, until, far from being a popular hero, Sycamore found himself maligned and execrated and even the object of threats. But Ruggles had given him his word and he kept it. Let the populace riot as it would, Sycamore Brown had delivered up Bravo Juan and he was entitled to the reward. So he gave it to him, with some private words of counsel, and Sycamore hit the road. To hell with those Gun Sight saloon bums—let them whistle for their drinks! He had a date in Papaguería.

CHAPTER XXVIII

THE FINISH

It was a matter of constant wonder to Sycamore the way that Indian girl got on his mind. With a thousand dollars in his clothes, the saloons all open and the freedom of the Territory, the very first thing he did, after buying some presents and a ring, was to hit for San Ignacio. He might not make his winning in a minute, but win he would, and G Bar Lally could go chase himself and take a jump at the moon. If the girl was backward he would stay all summer and woo her till she yielded—there would be no more runs for the Line. In fact, the Line did not interest him anymore, as long as she stayed on this side.

But like many a moon-mad lover Sycamore had overlooked a bet. With white folks the young people say the word, but with the Papagos it is different. To obviate any mistakes the parents make all the arrangements, and the Capitan had been busy. When Sycamore rode in on the village he threw it into confusion. The women ran hither and thither; the men glowered angrily as he passed and Capitan Juan stood scowling righteously in his place.

"What you want?" he demanded, and he

expressed himself so gruffly that Sycamore was roused from his calm.

"I want to see your daughter, *hombre*," he answered boldly, and then as the old man started back with haughty scorn he showed his hand. "What's the matter?" he enquired, glancing about at the gaping crowd, "have you spent all that gold already?"

"What gold?" challenged the Capitan, but as all eyes turned upon him he motioned hurriedly with his hand. "No, no!" he motioned, shaking a finger before his nose; and then, perforce, he weakened. That gold had been stolen in Mexico—and he had kept it for himself. The latter was the greater sin among the Papagos.

"Come with me," he muttered hurriedly, and started for his house. Sycamore followed, but as he entered his heart went down, for there sat the good-looking *muchacho*. Yes, it was the same boy that had led G Bar Lally in on him—and now he was sitting by Francisca.

"You see this boy?" demanded the chief brusquely. "Very well—he marry my girl."

"What?" cried Sycamore, reaching by instinct for his gun. "Married!"

"*Poco tiempo*," added the Capitan, and Sycamore's heart went back into place.

"Oh!" he said. "Pretty soon, eh? And how about you, Francisca?" he asked in English. "Do you stand in on this?"

"*No le hace*!" protested the Capitan warmly. "It makes no difference! This boy's father—me, Capitan Juan—we make! *No le hace*!"

"Oh, I guess it does *hace*!" answered Sycamore coolly. "This is a free country—and under the American law! If your daughter doesn't want to marry this boy she doesn't have to, and I can have you arrested if you make her. Now how about it, Francisca," he asked in his softest English, "do you want to marry this boy?" He waited, but she did not answer. "Because if you do," he said, "here's where I quit. I come clear out here to ask you myself—but—" He paused again, but she did not even raise her head. Then an old man came in, raving in Papago, and for a minute the air was full of it. A jabbering, gesticulating crowd gathered about the poor girl, scolding, arguing, and entreating, but she offered them no response. They turned upon each other, still babbling and making gestures, and then the Capitan advanced towards Sycamore.

"My people," he pronounced, "they say—you go!"

"I will go," answered Sycamore promptly, "if the girl tells me to."

Once more the crowd gathered about her, and then Sycamore thrust them aside.

"Let me talk to this girl alone," he said to the Capitan. "I want her for my wife—let her decide."

"No, no, no!" protested the people, but the Capitan waved them out.

"*Muy bien,*" he said speaking pacifically. "Let us talk together. *Mira*, Don Sycamoro! I am your friend—no? I am your friend—you give me gifts—good! But listen! It is the custom of my people—they have never broken it—that no Papago shall marry a white man. I like you—yes—but you cannot have my daughter!"

"*Muy bien,*" responded Sycamore, "now listen to me. This country is ruled by the white man—no? His laws are the laws. Very well, it is the white man's law that the woman shall speak, and whatever man she takes shall be her husband. I like your daughter. She is educated—she understands the white man's ways—and she has saved my life. So I ask her to marry me. But if she likes this Papago boy better—then I will go."

He stopped and waited expectantly, but Francisca did not look up. Not since his arrival had she so much as raised her head. She was thinking—she had something on her mind—and not until it was decided would she speak.

"*Mira*, Señor Capitan," entreated Sycamore, holding out his hands. "You know me. I am a good man. I have money"—he drew out a wad of bills—"and the government has pardoned my robbery. Now I can have a home—and I want your daughter for my wife."

"No!" said the Capitan sullenly. "No Papago

can marry a white man. The people will not allow it."

"All the same, go and ask them," urged Sycamore. "Call the council together and ask them what they think. Go on, now!"

"No!" grumbled the old man, "no!" But all the same he went.

The room was empty now—except for old Aunt Tia, who never quit her job. Sycamore sat down on the bench and wiped his brow thoughtfully and as he did so Francisca looked up.

"Oh!" she cried as she saw his half-healed wounds, and in that moment she forgot herself. Prayers, threats and entreaties had been spent in vain, but at the sight of his hurts she quickened. "Oh, that is awful bad," she said, looking at his swelled eye closely. "And your head! Those cuts are bad inside—let me look at them!"

Sycamore bowed his head before her and as her firm fingers felt out the festering wounds he thanked God he had stood off the doctor.

"I got them with a pair of hand-cuffs," he explained, "while I was fightin' with Bravo Juan."

Francisca spoke sharply to old Tia, who scuttled off to bring some water.

"Yes?" she said, and then he told his story.

"And did you do it for me?" she repeated, when he had told her of his fight for freedom. "Was it for my sake?" She was silent then while he answered, bathing his bruised head with the water that smelt so gloriously of carbolic. "Oh, I am glad," she breathed at last, but of what she would not say.

The loud harangue of the council was at its height and Sycamore was still telling of his love when suddenly the uproar stopped. A quiet came upon the indignant speakers who were demanding his life's blood in Papago, and it startled him more than their philippics. He remembered his horse and leapt up quickly, but Round Valley was still in his place. It was something far away that was engaging their attention—a pair of horsemen riding furiously—G Bar Lally and the Papago suitor! For a warrior that Papago boy was the real yellow—when it came to a disagreement he always hopped on a horse and came back with G Bar Lally.

Now if there was any man in the world that Sycamore hated and despised it was this same Lally and at sight of him he bristled like a dog, but when the ranger came charging up the hill he had regained his natural calm. He could not afford to quarrel.

"Throw up yore hands!" cried Lally, making a great play with his gun, but Sycamore only smiled.

"You're behind the times, Mr. Lally," he said, holding out a letter with one upraised hand; and as he scanned the official document the ranger grew pale with rage. Then he handed it back and fought his horse while he thought up some other quarrel.

"This boy tells me that you've scared his folks," he raved at last. "He says you come right into their house and tried to steal a woman! Now I've stood enough off of you, Syc Brown, and if you don't git out of here and leave these Injuns alone I'm goin' to run you in. Now you git, and git quick!"

He drew his pistol as he spoke and the Indians scattered before it, but Sycamore stood calm.

"This boy has told you a lie," he answered, dispassionately. "I was invited into that house by the Capitan here, as he will tell you, and I haven't made no trouble."

"Well, you git, anyhow!" commanded the ranger roughly. "You got no business here."

"That's all right," responded Sycamore quietly. "I've been an officer myself and I know you've got no authority to make me go—you got no warrant for me and I'm not disturbing the peace. So you might as well put up that gun. I just come out from Gun Sight, and I told Ruggles where I was goin', so you're not called in on this at all."

"Well, what about the woman?" demanded the ranger, quieting down a little at the news. "This boy says you're tryin' to steal a woman—did Lee tell you you could do that?"

"No, and I'm not tryin' to either." He turned suddenly upon the boy.

"Did you tell this ranger I was tryin' to steal a woman?" he scowled, and the Papago cringed and shook his head. "There, you see, do you? The kid was lyin' to you!"

"Uh!" grunted the ranger and stared about him hatefully. "What's all these people around here for then?" he enquired. "Hey, old man, what's the excitement?"

The Capitan frowned at the familiarity, but he saw his chance—and took it.

"This boy," he said in labored Spanish. "He want—marry my girl. This man"—pointing to Sycamore—"says 'No!' "

"*Sí*," responded the ranger eagerly. "I understand. This man"—pointing to Sycamore—"make trouble, no? You like him here? No? You want him to go? Yes? *Muy bien*! Mr. Brown, this Injun objects to yore presence here, and I'll have to ask you to go!"

Then in a moment Sycamore saw all his love dreams shattered; his castles tumbled in ruins—for he was up against the law. Slowly and reluctantly he slunk over and mounted his horse, while the Indians gloated and Lally looked on with a sneer. He ran his eye over the crowd and caught a flitting glimpse of the girl he had fought for—then he turned away, for fighting could not win her now. He was defeated, and his enemies made a mock of him—Sycamore Brown, the fighting fool, the man of many battles! With his chin on his breast he spurred rapidly down the trail, to get it over with, and then there was a great shout behind—a shout and a flash of blue, and Desert Willow came flying after him.

"I brought you your medicine," she panted, clutching pitifully at his stirrup, and held him up a bottle.

"Sure," said Sycamore and stooping down from his horse he caught her in his arms and swung her up before him. Then Round Valley leaped before the bite of the spurs and they went thundering out across the desert until San Ignacio was lost in the dust.

At the fork of the trail Sycamore gave her a rapturous kiss and set her astride of the saddle while he vaulted nimbly back behind.

"But I only brought your medicine, Sycamoro," she chided as he handed her the reins. "The medicine for your wounds."

"Sure," said Sycamore, "I understand." And then he kissed her again.

Center Point Large Print
600 Brooks Road / PO Box 1
Thorndike, ME 04986-0001 USA

(207) 568-3717

US & Canada:
1 800 929-9108
www.centerpointlargeprint.com